20 Weird Love Stories

The Cactus Critter

The ellie was faster than I expected.

It scrambled awkwardly over exposed rocks, flopped around a few saguaro, and just kept going, like it was running for its life.

Which it was.

I called to it. They generally respond to female voices. Not this time.

Lightning, my horse, was right behind it, matching it stride for stride, with me in the saddle, holding the reins and determined to keep the ellie in view.

We were even gaining on it. A little.

That critter from another planet carried at least 60 pounds of sweet prime meat that I was going to ship back east for fancy folks in fancy restaurants to eat. But first, I had to catch the damn thing.

The sun was beating down on me. Spring in Arizona. Not as hot as June or July, but hot enough that I knew Lightning wasn't going to last much longer. She was going to need rest and water. Soon. If we didn't catch that ellie pronto, it was going to get away for good.

The ellie went up a rocky hill, skittered over gravel, sending up sprays of dust and rocks, and made for a steep incline up a fair-sized mountain less than half a mile ahead. If it got that far, we were done for. Lightning couldn't go fast over rocks, and I wasn't going to catch the ellie on foot.

I dug my spurs in. Lightning surged forward, slowly. Kind of a slow motion surge. This was going to be her last gasp.

I doubled down on her, beating her hind end with my hat, trying to urge her on.

The ellie, loping along now, losing some of *its* energy to the heat and the arid surroundings, looked a little panicked, like it didn't know where to turn next.

I took my lasso off my saddle and swung it over my head, while Lightning, sensing an end to the chase, seemed to press on even harder.

We were gaining.

A few seconds later we were next to it, still going hell bent for leather.

I twirled my rope above my head for a few cycles, then launched it toward the ellie.

My lasso draped around the critter's neck. The ellie slowed, startled by its new necklace, then looked down, which was its mistake.

It tripped over some stones, fell forward on its shoulder, and skidded to a dusty stop on its back. It looked up at the sky and was blinded by the sun. It closed its eyes tight.

Lightning halted, panting for air. The ellie worked its six legs frantically, trying to undo the rope around it.

I pulled on the lasso, cinching it tighter around the ellie's neck, then slipped off Lightning and took a couple of steps toward the ellie and slapped it hard on its face.

It whimpered. They did that. Never much cared for it. Got my blood going though and I hit it again, just to knock the whimper out of it.

It stopped struggling. It looked at me. Its color changed from dull brown to the rainbow hues they seemed to adopt when they were scared. The ellie suddenly sported splotches of red and yellow, green and violet, all over its skin. And the splotches were growing.

I groaned. You never wanted your herd of ellies to look like a bunch of rainbows. That's when you knew they were going to be trouble, because all those colors meant they were stressed and stressed ellies, like stressed terrestrial animals, are not easy to handle. What you wanted was for them to look like they could blend into dirt.

I regretted slapping the ellie, but it had taken up a good chunk of my afternoon on a chase I didn't need or want and I was mad.

The other thing the rainbow colors did, if it lasted long, was make their meat taste sour. Basically made them useless for our business.

I went down on my knees and wrapped my arms around the wretched thing.

"Now calm down," I said. "No need for all that stress. You keep that color for much longer, I'm going to have to shoot you."

Don't think it understood. As far as anyone knows, none of them understand our language. Female voices, though, seemed to soothe them more than male. So, lucky I was female, I guess.

I didn't want to shoot it. But if it was going to ruin its meat, then I figured I had to. To cut my losses. Salvage what I could.

But better to keep it alive. This one was going to add a good 30 or 40 more pounds before it reached maturity.

I sang to it. A tune I learned from my mother. "Rock-a-bye Baby." Don't know where it came from, but there it was.

That seemed to do the trick. The colors started fading. I sang some more. Not as loud, but with heart. It was like I wanted to make the creature into a baby.

That was no good.

I shook my head.

Couldn't grow attached to it. I was going to slaughter it within the year.

It blinked at me. Its long snout of a nose was hanging off to its side. A clear fluid leaked out of its end. Tears, I guessed. The thing was crying. If they cried.

I stopped singing to it.

Its six legs fell to one side and it took in a deep breath, then let it out and I couldn't help putting my hand on its side. I felt its ribs through its skin.

It closed its golden eyes.

I swear, I thought I heard some angelic chorus behind me. Then I realized it was Lightning, panting for air. She snorted and I tied up the ellie by its legs, then hoisted it up and slung it over the saddle.

"Gotta be an easier way to make a living," I said to Lightning.

No answer from my equine pal.

I got on Lightning, and we began a more leisurely pace back to the ranch.

The ellie was completely subdued. Resigned to its fate, I suppose. It did not make a peep or a movement the whole way.

By the time we got back, the sun was just a fist width above the horizon.

I saw my ranch hands repairing the fence where the ellie had escaped.

"Hey, Ned," I called.

He looked up from his work securing barbed wire along the timbers that marked the perimeter of the pasture holding the ellies. Ned waved at me. "Mary," he said. "You got it back."

"Sure did," I said, as I dismounted Lightning.

Ned came over and took the trussed up ellie and called to Horace, another hand that worked for me. Horace came over and took Lightning away to the corral.

I followed Ned as he went to the pen and hung the ellie over the fence, undid the rope, and let it drop to the ground.

Much of the rest of the herd came to the ellie and rubbed up against it. The ellie, who had had a taste of freedom, however brief, was in no mood to respond to the homecoming welcome.

Ned and I watched them for a few minutes. The ellie I had retrieved would not budge from its spot on the ground. Just kept sighing and moaning.

"I'm worried about that one," said Ned.

"No need," I said. "It'll perk up."

"Maybe," said Ned.

"No maybe about it," I said. "I didn't push my horse to the breaking point and fly over ten miles of desert for it all to be worthless."

"Yes, ma'am," said Ned.

"What's Lynn got going for dinner?"

Ned shrugged. "Why don't you go ask her?"

I walked across to the house, brushing dust off my chaps with my gloved hands as I went.

Lynn met me on the porch, gave me a hug, and we kissed each other. Not in a lingering way. More in a way that indicated we had been together for a lot of years.

"What's for dinner?" I asked.

"Love you too," she said.

"I brought back the escaped ellie."

"Yee. Haw. My hero."

"Damn right.

"The sheriff was here today."

"What'd he want?"

"Said we might want to be careful. The federal government decided the ellies are smart. Or something. Didn't quite understand what was going on, but our business might be in trouble."

"Aw, Lynn," I said. "That can't be. We just started turning a profit. No ellie ever spelled a word or could tell you what one and one add up to."

"Don't whine at the messenger," she said. "Now go get yourself washed up. I don't want Arizona dust all over the dining table. And take those damn things off." She pointed at my chaps.

"Yes, Mom," I said.

As I washed my hands, I tried to figure why the feds would be bothering us about the ellies. Probably some easterner with a bleeding heart and a sympathetic congressman in his pocket got it into his head to mess with people like Lynn and me, just regular folks trying to make a living.

We used to live in Chicago where we found more than our fair share of meddlers. And people who didn't abide by our living arrangement. Ten years ago we decided to move out west where people kept to themselves and didn't give a damn what you did or who with, just as long as you were a decent neighbor and didn't make too much noise going about your business.

We took up the government's offer to homestead land. We tried running cattle for a while, but they needed more land than they're worth.

Then one night when Lynn and I were enjoying the night air of an evening, with the full moon lighting up the landscape all silvery and glowing, we saw a light streak across the sky. Much too bright for a meteor, and when it went over the horizon, we heard a crash like something breaking.

We rode over in that direction and found the strangest vessel. It was soft and round, like a giant puff ball maybe six feet across.

We heard moaning from the inside. Lynn and I, we didn't know what that might be, and we discussed maybe leaving it alone but neither of us was timid that way.

We plunged our knives into the thing and what should we uncover but four creatures that, to put it mildly, did not belong here.

They had six legs, a long snout, like an elephant, which is why we called them ellies, and golden eyes. Their eyes made us blink a few times. Really dazzling, like they held pieces of the sun.

Those ellies looked a little stunned. They were also in their rainbow phase, which, as I said, meant they were stressed, though we didn't know that then.

Lynn looked at me with deep puzzlement.

"What the hell are these things?"

"Don't know," I said. "But there's a dead one."

I pointed into the vessel. Lynn looked. Down in the folds of the vessel we saw an ellie that wasn't rainbow hued. Instead, it was all brown, just like the interior of the vessel and it was still.

The other ellies, seeming to notice it at the same time we did, turned on the dead thing and began eating it, which, to put it mildly, we both found more than a little disgusting.

The feeding ellies had these little nubs for teeth. Not much good for tearing up the dead ellie, but they had their legs for that. Each limb was capped with a short but sharp nail that they used for cutting up the dead ellie.

They all fell upon the carcass with gusto. Blood went everywhere.

A couple of drops landed on my face and I instinctively went to brush them away with my hand but then I stopped.

The most amazing aroma began wafting up from the dead ellie.

I looked at Lynn. "You smell that?" she asked.

"I do," she said dreamily. "What is it?"

"Gotta be this critter, whatever it is."

She bent down over the mass of ellies covered in blood and ellie guts, and breathed deeply.

"Yup," she said. "It's coming from there."

We grabbed up the living ellies and stuffed them all into a bag. They jostled around in there for a bit, then settled down.

We also grabbed up the remains of the dead ellie and took the whole shooting match back to the ranch.

"I'll take care of these things," I said to Lynn as I headed toward the barn.

"And I'll take care of this thing," she said as she took the dead ellie into the house.

I emptied the live ones into one of the horse stalls. They seemed to like it there. Began eating some of the straw we had lying around. I watched them with some interest. Wondered where they came from.

I'd heard about life on other planets and such. In Chicago there were people convinced we came from the stars or some equally looney nonsense. Who knows? And what did it matter? All I knew is these ellies ended up on our property, so they were ours.

As I watched, they seemed to settle down some. They gathered into a bunch, all of them huddled together in the center of the stall.

I left them there and went into the house.

Lynn already had a pot of water going on the stove and had chunks of the dead ellie's carcass cooking.

The meat was gold in color.

She held up a wooden spoon with some golden broth puddling in the center of it. I took the spoon into my mouth and—

—just about felt like heaven had decided to drape itself around me.

Never tasted anything like it, ever. It was sweet like apples, but there was a hint of earthiness to it, too. I tasted something close to sage and rosemary, but not quite. There was also a suggestion of vanilla there and to top it all off, a bit of spiciness, like it had been dragged through a field of hot peppers and soaked up that flavor.

It was all so subtle it was almost unnerving. I felt my whole body going electric, as though I was going to turn inside out.

"That is something," I said.

Lynn nodded. "Yup. I think we got a gold mine on our hands."

The next day we sold off all our cattle and got into the business of raising ellies.

We soon figured out we made the right decision. Ellies bred like crazy. They tasted good. Their meat kept. It was an easy call.

We made some contacts with businessmen from the east, and established markets for ellie meat.

The rest was just dogged work, expanding the business, building up our herd, and keeping to ourselves, like good westerners.

But now it looked like the feds were after us. Just go and try to make a success of yourself. See what happens then.

"Mary," called Lynn. "You die in there?"

"Coming," I said and left the bathroom and my trip down memory lane and came out.

"Well," she said. "Don't you look all purty and everything when you take a mind to it."

"I do," I said.

Our crew was already at the table. Ned and Horace on one side. Heather, who took care of the horses, on the other. She sat next to Mike, who more or less took care of the money aspects of our operation.

Lynn was at one end of the table. I sat across from her at the other.

A couple of roast chickens rested in the middle of the table. Platters of potatoes, vegetables, and greens surrounded it. No ellie meat, though. You don't eat into your own profit.

"Who wants to say grace?" asked Heather.

"You're not religious," I said to her.

She shrugged. "I don't think anyone here is religious, much, but that's what we do, isn't it?"

Mike nodded. "I'll say it," he said.

"Go ahead," said Lynn.

"To whom it may concern," he said. "Thanks for the food."

Everyone laughed.

"That's the best prayer ever," said Heather.

Ned and Horace grinned, like they had never heard it before.

We all dug in. I loaded up my plate, taking more than my fair share, but I had been the one who tired myself out today. I deserved it. If anyone noticed, no one said anything.

We all ate in silence for a while. Cutlery clicking against plates. Chewing noises. I drank some beer that Lynn had thoughtfully set out for me.

"This is good," I said.

"Thank you," said Lynn.

Murmurs of assent from everyone at the table.

More silence.

A lot of silence. The western way. If no one wanted to talk about anything, that meant there was something that had to be talked about.

"What the hell is going on?" I asked.

They all looked at me.

"No one's saying anything. It's like we're all at a funeral. Someone die I don't know about?"

"Everyone's afraid we're going to lose the business," said Lynn.

"We aren't going to lose the business."

"That's not what the sheriff said," said Mike.

"To hell with the sheriff," I said.

"Not that simple," said Mike.

"He told us the federal government doesn't like our operation," said Lynn. "It's illegal."

"How did it turn illegal all of a sudden?"

"There's this creature. In Washington DC. Strange creature."

"You talking about some congressman?"

My question didn't get a laugh. Which worried me.

"No," said Lynn. "Creatures. Green and skinny and with these long faces."

"Now you're just pulling my leg," I said.

"Nope," said Mike. He tossed me a magazine. *Harper's Weekly.* Issue of February 22, 1868.

"What the hell is this?" I said.

"Look at page seven."

I turned to the page. There I found a drawing of, well, an alien, I guess. The caption indicated the creature came in a space ship. What the hell was a space ship? And it went directly to the white house where it talked to president Grant. It told the commander in chief that it didn't want to meddle with earthly matters, but that it had somehow lost its collection of pets and thought maybe they had ended up on earth.

"What in the eternal damnation?" I asked the air.

"Keep reading," said Heather.

I did. The article went on to say that the creature was looking for five small animals. They had six legs each, a long snout, and liked to turn different colors when they were excited.

I dropped the magazine and I must have gone white because Lynn asked me if I should drink some more water.

"I don't believe this," I said. "Must be some kind of joke."

"No joke," said Heather.

Ned and Horace both shook their head. "No joke," they said in unison.

"The sheriff brought this over," said Mike.

"We've been breeding and slaughtering pets," said Lynn. "And the law of the universe just caught up with us."

The rest of the meal went by quickly. I had lost my appetite. I had half a mind to round up the entire herd and slaughter them right there on the spot and have a good old fashioned party. Invite the whole county. Invite all of Bisbee. It'd be a celebration for the ages.

But the other half of me knew that was not the answer here.

After everyone left to go back to their evening chores I asked Lynn what we should do.

"Can't fight the law," she said.

"Oh come on," I said. "If we listened to the law, we'd never have gotten together. We'd have stayed scared of each other in Chicago. We'd have been lynched. Or worse. We came out *here* to escape the law."

"This is different," she said. "In Chicago we had to worry about townsfolk. Here it's the government of the United States."

"Dammit," I said. "If we had statehood, we could do something. We could buy our own congresscritter."

"Stop dreaming," said Lynn.

"We're not the only ellie ranch," I said. "They going to shut them *all* down?" Once we got our herd going, we sold off some heads to other ranchers in the area. They saw the potential market just as well as we did, and they were willing to pay our asking price, which was pretty high.

"If that alien thing finds out what we're doing here it could be intergalactic war."

I stared at her like she was crazy.

She hesitated. "Whatever that is," she said. "The sheriff mentioned it."

"I'll tell you what it is," I said, "it's some pretty weak excuse for governing, that's what. People should be allowed to do what they want to do. We should be allowed to make a living."

"Mary," she said, "you're preaching to the choir, but we can't just ignore this thing. We have to do something."

I didn't disagree with her. The only thing is, neither of us knew exactly *what* to do.

That night, with Mary and me lying in bed, both of us feeling like our lives were going to change for the worse, sleep eluded us for a time.

"You ever think about what's out there?" asked Lynn.

"Out where?"

"You know," she said, waving her hand at the ceiling. "There. In the sky. The stars. The planets."

"Who cares?" I asked. "We got our own problems right here."

"I just wonder sometimes," she said. "The sky. It's so big. Maybe there's people out there. People like us."

"Maybe," I said. "And maybe those people like us are herded up into corrals and raised and slaughtered just like we do with the ellies."

Lynn made a noise, then shoved me. "You have a knack for exalted thought," she said.

"That's why you love me," I said.

"Who says I love you?"

"You did. When I came home today."

"That was just to massage your ego," she said.

"It worked! My ego is relaxed and ready to go to work."

She shoved me hard enough that I thought I was going to fall off the bed.

"Ah, Lynn," I said. "The way I see it, the universe or God, if there is such a gal, she gave us a gift. We have a pretty good life here."

"We work like dogs," she said.

"Well what else would we be doing? Work is not so bad."

"Ever think about taking a cruise?"

"When we retire."

"Our retirement might be coming a lot sooner than you think."

She had a point. "We're going to fight this," I said. "We have to."

"We're going to lose," said Lynn. "And you know it as well as I do."

The next morning was bright and sunny. Surprise! We were in the Sonoran dessert. *Every* morning is bright and sunny.

Lynn was already up. Probably getting some breakfast ready for us and the crew.

I got out of bed and dressed quickly. I went through the kitchen, gave Lynn a peck on the cheek—she responded with a sarcastic "Oh my." and a fluttery wave of her hand in front of her nose as she stood over a pan of bacon and eggs—and went out to the corral.

Which was empty.

I stood in the still air for a few seconds. The last wisps of coolness were just leaving. They would soon be replaced by the stifling heat of the day.

There were no ellies in the corral. I saw the gate hanging open. Ellie tracks—hundreds of them—indicated they were going south.

I trudged across to the bunkhouse, where my ranch hands all spent the night. Or so I had thought.

Empty as well.

I was putting one and one together and I didn't like the two that came up.

I went back to the house.

"Our crew stole our herd and ran off," I said.

Lynn dropped her wooden spoon and looked at me.

"Where'd they go?"

"Couldn't have gotten far," I said. "Not with 200 head of ellie."

"Why didn't we hear anything?"

"Ellie are quiet."

Lynn shook her head. "Never should have hired a single one of those hands."

"You got that right," I said.

"We going to go after them?"

"Damn right," I said.

We went to the horse stalls and got another surprise. None of our horses were there.

Now I was mad. I threw my hat on the ground and lifted my head high and cursed at the sky. I even cursed the stars, none of which were visible.

"They thought of everything," said Lynn. "Now we can't follow them. How far to the next ranch?"

"Olson's place is three miles away."

"You ready for a walk?"

"What's Olson going to do for us?"

"We could borrow two of his horses," I said.

"I'll get some food to take."

"I'll come help," I said.

We began walking back to the house when a motion on the horizon caught our eye. A lone horse approached. It was not a horse either of us recognized.

"I'll go grab the shotgun," said Lynn.

"Get mine, too," I said.

"Be right back," said Lynn. She went back to the house on her own. The horse was getting closer. It had a tall rider on it. I walked toward it, hoping the rider would see me and see that I wasn't afraid of him. Or her, as the case may be.

Don't know if the rider saw me or not, but the horse increased its speed some, sending a jolt of fear through me. Lynn and I did not need this right now. Everything was falling apart around us. And it all happened so quickly.

As the horse got closer I saw that the rider was skinnier than was reasonable for any human. I also soon saw that the rider was green.

Just like the *Harper's Weekly* article.

Lynn returned with two shotguns. She handed me one. I took it.

"Loaded?" I asked.

"Of course," she said, and raised her weapon high and held its aim on the approaching horse and rider, who did not break stride.

"The rider's green," said Lynn, wonder in her voice.

"Yup," I said.

I stepped away from Lynn a few paces and raised my shotgun as well. Two distinct sources of firepower was way more intimidating than if we were clustered close together.

"What if shotguns don't work on these alien critters?" asked Lynn.

"Then we might be slaughtered. Who knows what powers aliens have."

Lynn nodded. "Got that," she said.

"If things go bad," I said, "I want you to know I wouldn't have traded my time with you for anything."

"Likewise," said Lynn.

Then we turned our attention to the horse and rider. I felt the weight of the shotgun pulling my arms down, but reasserted myself and held the barrel fixed on the rider, who slowed down some and stopped a fair distance away.

It opened its mouth and sound came out.

Not exactly fair to call it a voice. More of a scratchy growl. Raspy. There were words there, though. English words.

"No harm," said the green thing.

"Does it mean it won't do us harm, or it doesn't want us to do *it* harm?" asked Lynn.

"Don't know," I said. "Maybe both."

The creature regarded us for a few seconds. We didn't lower our weapons.

Then it dismounted and stood beside its horse.

"I'm looking for my pets," it rasped. "Heard they were here. Crash site just over there." It indicated the general direction in which we had rode to retrieve the ellies. "I found craft remains, but none of my pets."

"How does that thing know English?" I said to Lynn in what I thought was real quiet, but not quiet enough to keep the green thing from hearing.

"Elementary language," it said. "I learned it in a day."

"There you go," said Lynn. "It's way superior to us."

"Not good," I said. "What kind of weapons you think it has."

"Sheriff said something about a ray gun. Possibly."

"What the hell is a ray gun?" I asked.

"Never mind," said Lynn to me. Then she addressed the alien. "We don't have your pets. We found them. But."

"Careful, Lynn," I said.

"But what?" asked the alien. It took a few steps toward us.

"Best to spill the whole story," whispered Lynn to me.

"Says who?" I whispered back.

"I have a feeling about this—creature."

"Fine," I said, not feeling fine about it at all.

"We didn't know they were your pets," said Lynn to the alien. "We found out they tasted good. Real good. So we've been raising them for people to eat. Your pets are long gone, I'm afraid, but they have lots of descendants."

The creature just stood there. For a long time. Staring at us. It had green eyes. Green skin. Green hair. Everything green. It was like a giant saguaro. All it needed was some thorns and it would fit the part perfectly.

"I don't like that stare," I said to Lynn.

"Easy, love of mine," she said. "Give it some time."

"I'm not lowering my shotgun."

"Wouldn't ask you to," said Lynn.

"Where are the descendants?" asked the alien.

"Well," said Lynn, "funny thing. They got taken away this morning. We've been robbed."

The alien stared at us for a few more seconds. It was good at that. Loved to stare. I didn't like it much. Made me nervous.

Finally it got back on its horse and went to turn away.

Lynn lowered her shotgun and started going after the alien.

"Lynn!" I said. "What are you doing?"

"Don't want to let it get away," she said.

"Why not?" I asked.

"Hey!" she said to the alien. "Hey! Cactus being! Wait up."

The alien stopped its horse and turned in its saddle and looked back at Lynn, who was already almost caught up to it.

I ran after her. Couldn't let her confront an interstellar visitor all on her own.

"Hey," said Lynn. "Where you going? We're sorry we—um—killed and ate your pets. Didn't know they had sentimental value."

We were now very close to the alien. It looked down at us. I swear I noticed some sadness in it. Not in the face. It didn't have much expression there. But in the way it held its body. Like it was suddenly fragile or something.

"Going to go find them," said the alien. That voice was still raspy and annoying.

"Take us with you," said Lynn. "We can track them."

The alien looked at the ground. "I can track, too," it said.

I believed it. It didn't take an expert to see where the tracks were headed. South. Towards Mexico.

"Okay," said Lynn, "but you don't know this country. We do. We want to find our herd. And the people that stole it."

"And Lightning," I said.

"And Lightning," said Lynn.

"You seek atmospheric phenomenon?"

"My horse," I said. "I miss my horse, Lightning."

The alien did some more staring. Quiet. It fit into the west, that's for sure. Not a lot of words from this one.

It stretched out a hand. A thin, kind of grotesque hand, I might add. It had a long green nail, and it was a little bit moist, and it was so skinny it felt like paper thin skin covering bone, but it had strength.

Lynn took the hand and the alien lifted her up onto the horse. Then me.

The three of us on that horse.

Good thing we were all small and the horse was big.

"Let's go find Lightning," said the alien.

"Yee. Haw," I whispered into Lynn's ear.

The alien could handle a horse. That put it high up in my book.

"Heard you visited president Grant," said Lynn after we had gone a few miles. The ellie tracks went almost directly due south.

"I did," said the alien.

"What's he like?" asked Lynn.

"Big breakfasts. With lots of meat from my pets."

That stopped the conversation for a while.

"So," I said after a while, "did you want to—oh, I don't know—destroy the human race for eating your pets?"

"Mary," said Lynn, "we don't want to give the aliens *ideas*."

"No wish to destroy anything," said the alien. "Only want some of my pets back. Will accept descendants. Without them I am—" here the alien struggled for a word. I figured whatever concept it was trying to unearth, there was no real English word for it.

"Lonely?" asked Lynn.

"Yup," said the alien. "Lonely."

"You don't want to live in the west if you're prone to loneliness," I said.

"I understand," the alien said.

"You travel a lot?" asked Lynn.

"Here and there," rasped the alien. "I take my pets with me. Sometimes they try to escape to other planets."

"Like ours," I said.

"Yup," said the alien. "Like yours. They get into the escape pods. It's very inconvenient."

"I like that you came after them," I said. "I chased down one of the ellies just yesterday."

"Ellies?" rasped the alien.

"That's what we call them," said Lynn.

"It's fine," said the alien.

"Don't mean to offend," I said.

No reply from the alien, so I couldn't tell if it was offended or just didn't care.

The alien stopped the horse.

"*Ellies*," it said, "are just on the other side."

We looked ahead to a fairly high hill. The tracks went up the hill, and, presumably, over the rise to the other side.

"We're still a long way from Mexico," I said.

"Mexico?" asked the alien.

"It's another country," said Lynn.

It nodded, then dismounted. Lynn and I did likewise and stood beside the alien.

"Should we make a deal, here?" I asked.

"Deal," said the alien. There wasn't the feel of a question in its voice. Just a repetition of my word.

"My partner here," said Lynn, "wants to know how this will play out. The ellies were raised by us, so we feel we have some claim to them. On the other hand, the original ellies were yours, so, you certainly have a claim as well."

"Your government says you can't raise them anymore."

"We heard that."

"So they are worthless to you."

"Maybe," I said.

"Maybe?" said the alien.

"Our hands might have had the right idea. Taking the herd to Mexico. Different laws there. We could still raise them."

"But the market is gone," said the alien. "You can't sell the meat. It was a goodwill gesture. I got it straight from your president. I think he's afraid of me."

"Well," said Lynn, "you are kind of scary looking. To easterners. Not so much to us. We're used to weird things."

"You think I'm a weird thing?"

"We all are," I said hastily. "Everyone's weird in their own way. Don't you think?"

The alien turned a darker shade of green. Didn't know what that meant.

"In any case," said Lynn. "We can get around the laws. That's what the west is all about. We make our own rules."

The alien was silent, again, for a long time. Living in the west, I had gotten used to the strong silent types. They're more common than weeds. But this cactus critter was a little unnerving the way it deployed it so casually.

"I'll take five of them for me," it said.

"Sounds more than fair," said Lynn.

"The rest I will help move back for you."

"Why would you do that?" I asked.

The alien looked me straight in the eye. Its green eyes did not blink. The sun beat down on them, illuminating them into strange jewel-like things that glowed and shimmered with a kind of trembling. The sight of them set the hairs on my arm standing straight up.

I wondered if it ate sunlight, like plants do. Like cactus. Was it here to drink up sunlight? Did it come looking for the ellies because it liked the desert?

"*Ellies* don't last long on our world," said the alien. "Here, they seem to live a long time."

"That's because we take *care* of them," I said.

"Damn right," said Lynn.

"I will tell your president Grant there is no reason to stop the trade in ellie meat."

Well, you couldn't have asked for a better outcome, I suppose. Our way of life was saved by an alien, by a creature from some other world. It felt fitting, in its way.

"So," said Lynn, "we going to take back our herd?"

"Yup," said the alien.

"Yup," I said.

The three of us, bending low, went over the rise and surveyed the scene on the other side.

The ellies were all there, tied up to each other by lengths of rope so that they couldn't get away without a miraculous feat of coordination, which they were absolutely not capable of. All of them, every single one, was rainbow colored.

I felt the alien's dark mood beside me.

"Shouldn't be colored," it said.

"When we have them," I said, "they're not. Just plain old brown."

Our ranch hands, all four of them, were on horses on the perimeter of the herd.

Mike was on Lightning. I didn't like that.

"Think they stopped for a rest?" asked Lynn.

"Must be," I said.

"Cactus critter," said Lynn, "you want to go first?"

The alien stood and began walking down the hill.

The ellies, all of them, as though responding to a call, turned and looked at the alien.

Our ranch hands, Ned, Horace, Heather, and Mike, all froze. The alien kept walking. All the ellies surged toward it and surrounded it. The alien looked somehow straighter and more full of himself. Don't how to describe it exactly, but the green it carried around, it seemed to fall into it, as though it was getting stained by the color, as though the color wanted to be a part of the alien.

The ellies, meanwhile, were losing their color. All of them were fading to brown.

Our good for nothing ranch hands stepped back from the herd and the alien.

Ned, who I could see was very agitated by the turn of events, reached to the side of his saddle and pulled out a rifle.

That's when Lynn and I, together, began running toward the traitorous bunch. We had our shotguns held high in the air and we were whopping and hollering and raising such a fuss, that Ned, the coward, dropped his rifle and turned his horse around and galloped off.

He was soon followed by Horace and Heather. Their horses left clouds of dust as they thundered across the desert.

I hated seeing them go. Those were our horses, for one thing. I wanted to capture all of them and teach them a lesson. Rustling is the biggest crime anyone can do around these parts. Anyone. And my entire crew was guilty.

Mike's face was a study in terror. I think he didn't know if he should be afraid of the aliens, or Lynn and me. Or neither. Or both. He dug his heels into Lightning's side.

Lynn and I kept running toward him.

Lighting saw me.

Now I'm not going to go all sentimental on you and say that Lightning knew me and didn't want to leave me. I'm not going to do that. Because, first, Lightning's a horse. And second, well, there is no second.

But I'll tell the truth here and say that Lightning was not responding to Mike's kicks.

Instead, she held her ground despite Mike starting to go a bit crazy and pulling on the reins and kicking for all he was worth.

Lynn and I just kept running.

Mike, finally seeing that Lightning was not going to do his bidding, climbed down off of her and began running away from us.

But we were too fast for him.

We caught up to him and tackled him. We went skidding to the ground, Mike rolling, me and Lynn tumbling after him. When we came to a stop, I was on top of Mike and he was cowering.

I slapped him a good hard one across the face.

He whimpered.

Worse than an ellie.

His face turned red.

I was ready to slap him again, and would have, if a bony green hand had not grabbed my wrist and held it fast.

Lynn, next to me, looked up at the sky behind me.

I fell back and looked at the green alien.

"No need for that," it said.

I was breathing hard. Arizona dust scratching my throat.

"Sorry, cactus thing," I said in a raspy voice to match his. "Won't happen again."

Mike confessed to the whole thing. How he and the other ranch hands aimed to take the herd to Mexico where they thought it would be easier to raise and sell ellie meat.

I asked him how he could do that to us.

He only shrugged, like it was no big deal he stole our herd out from under us.

"It's the wild west," he said.

"That's no answer," I said.

"It is for me."

The sheriff took him and hauled him off to jail. Good riddance.

That left us without a crew.

But it didn't matter.

Turns out the big green cactus thing liked living in the desert. Liked ranch life even more. And raising ellie's, well that just tickled it so much, it decided to hire on with us.

You come out to visit the ranch, you'll see it mending fences, feeding the ellies, and just plain fitting in.

It won't talk much. Strong silent type.

Then, of an evening, you might find the three of us, alien, Lynn, and me, sitting on the porch, eyes turned to the skies enjoying the view.

You might even get the alien to point out its home, up there in the star spangled blackness.

Driving Me Crazy

My husband Gabe, he liked to tell jokes. It was an obsession with him. I don't know if you can get addicted to telling jokes, but if you could, Gabe would have been an A number one first class junky.

"Maureen," he'd say all the time, "I have one. A joke."

Only they were never funny.

Ever.

Here's one.

"What kind of movies do the children of hens like to watch? Chick flicks."

Then I was supposed to laugh. Ha ha. And then he'd throw another one at me.

"Why did the dachshund turn on the air conditioner? Because he was a hot dog."

Ha ha again, only by the fifth or sixth such non-funny quip I was ready to slug him just to shut him up.

All that changed after he died, of course. Ah, bliss.

Sure I was sorry he was gone. We were married forty years. You don't live that long with someone without, you know, missing them a tiny bit once they're gone.

I say tiny bit.

Mostly, I wondered how I stood the guy all that time.

I was good at the funeral service. Kept my glee to myself, I'm pretty sure. Although I did see some puzzled faces amongst the mourners when they looked my way. Didn't get their sadness mirrored back to them, I guess. Not my fault. We feel what we feel. No shame.

Our friend Isabelle, she seemed the most puzzled. I always thought Gabe had a little crush on her so I wasn't too interested in making her feel okay about my grief.

"He was a wonderful man," she said to me.

"To be honest," I said, "I've seen better."

Well, you'd have thought I had advocated the overthrow of the government and mandated that all puppies starve to death, the way she looked at me for my perfectly reasonable and innocent comment. I told her love is complicated and grief is even more complicated and she nodded, like she knew what I was talking about. But she didn't.

All I knew was that I wouldn't have to listen to Gabe's jokes anymore.

Or so I thought.

Day after the funeral, there he was. In my head.

The jokes.

"How many psychiatrists does it take to change a light bulb? Only one, but the light bulb has to *want* to change."

I groaned. No. This couldn't be. I could not have a joke-telling ghost in my head.

But I did. I heard his jokes in my skull. Over and over again.

In my sleep I heard them, these terrible jokes.

While having breakfast.

"What do you call someone who shoots Captain Crunch, Count Chocula, and Snap Crackle and Pop? A serial killer."

I figured this couldn't last. It was all a part of the grieving process. I'd hear his jokes for a while, then I'd get over that and they'd stop filling my head.

Didn't happen.

Instead, I heard *more* jokes than when he was alive.

He'd be floating up above my head somewhere. Goofy grin. Big eyes. Always excited when he had a new one brewing. Then out with it.

"What did the glue say to the paper? Stick with me."

"Why can Mount Everest hear music? Because it has lots of mountain ears."

It got so I had to take to drink, just to shut him up. Once I had a couple of martinis in me, the awful jokes kind of went away. At least for a while.

Not a long term solution, I suppose, but chronic alcoholism seemed like a more agreeable fate than enduring the post-mortem would-be humorous obsessions of my dead husband.

Then he took over the car.

Our car. My car, actually. I used it most. A self-driving model. My husband thoughtfully bought me this car so I wouldn't have to drive it. This happened a year before he died. At first, I thought he was being a very considerate husband. Then I realized he was actually being passive aggressive. He didn't want me to drive because he thought I was a bad driver.

Me.

A couple of speeding tickets and all of a sudden it's a federal case that I am in possession of a driver's license. And all the while *he* was violating my sanity by his joke telling.

Thing is, I forgave him for the car thing. He thought I couldn't drive? Fine. I didn't have to drive. I had the self-driving car.

While Gabe was alive, whenever I got tired of his jokes, I'd hop in the car and tell it to take me—wherever. I didn't care. Told Gabe I had errands to do. Shopping. Something. What did it matter?

The car would talk to me as it took me around town.

Handsome voice, that car. And no jokes. Heaven.

Only here's the thing.

After Gabe died. The car. Well, how can I put this? The car got haunted. By Gabe.

When I told it to take me to the chocolate shop across town, I was expecting handsome voice to answer me.

Instead, Gabe's voice. There. In the car.

"What do you call a place where truffles drink? A chocolate bar."

I was so startled I grabbed the door handle.

"Where you going?" asked the car. In Gabe's voice. Like it was the most normal thing in the world.

"Gabe?" I asked.

"Yeah, Maureen. It's me. Want to hear a joke?"

"No, Gabe, I don't."

"Just one. Come on."

"Gabe," I said. "Listen to me. You know you're dead, right?"

Quiet. Just crickets for a while.

Then Gabe speaks up.

"This doctor tells a guy he's going to die. Guy asks for a second opinion. Doctor tells him he's ugly, too."

"Gabe," I said. "Stop it for a second. What are you doing in my car?"

"Don't know," he said. "Just ended up here."

"I can't take this," I said. "I don't believe in ghosts, Gabe."

"Neither do I."

"You can't believe in *anything*. You're dead."

"Yeah, well. Guess the universe has different ideas about that. Did you hear about the centipede with the broken leg? He went 99 thump, 99 thump, 99 thump."

I got out of the car and slammed the door shut. I stood in the garage, weeping, not knowing why. He wasn't really there. This was the grief, right? Had to be. I mean, I did have some grief. Didn't I? At least a little?

A teeny tiny smidgen?

I searched for it, the grief. Knew it was important to feel grief. Knew it was *human* to feel it. I was human. I was sure of that.

I put my hand back on the door handle.

I eased the door open.

Got back into the driver's seat.

"Gabe?" I whispered.

"You know how a porcupine makes love, don't you? Veeeeery carefully."

God help me, when I heard that last one, my heart melted and I fell in love with my stupid husband all over again.

Which was not, maybe, the best thing to have happened. Gabe lived in my car.

We'd take rides around town. It was nice. Then when we got back home, I'd tell him good night, he'd throw an awful joke at me, and we'd go our separate ways, me back to the house, Gabe stuck in the car.

I don't know what he saw in that car that made him want to live there, but I didn't complain.

A little joke now and then, while we were driving around town was fine. But I didn't need the constant barrage in the house, so it was a perfectly mutually beneficent arrangement.

Then one day I woke up and I'm missing Gabe, you know, like you do when the man you love isn't in bed next to you, and I got up and went into the garage to tell him hi, good morning, how you doing, and the car was gone.

I stood there in the door of the empty garage like I was on the shore of a dead ocean in a post-apocalyptic movie, the kind where all the trees stop producing oxygen because of a virus which makes the carbon dioxide concentration increase to lethal levels and then the greenhouse effect runs amok and all the oceans boil off and humanity is left with just a few bands of people huddling together while they wait for their food supplies to disappear and they look at each other with hunger and growling stomachs.

That kind of despair.

My Gabe was gone.

I shut the door of the garage and went back into the house. Tried calling the car. It had its own phone number, my car did. That was an extra Gabe sprung for.

Thoughtful guy.

As the phone rang, I remembered one of his jokes.

"How do you spot a tiger? You don't, because it's striped."

Ha ha.

Stupid joke.

I wanted to hear more of them. More of Gabe's stupid jokes.

"Hello?"

A woman's voice. Answering my car's phone. And it was someone I knew.

"Isabelle?" I asked.

"Who wants to know?"

"Who wants to know? Are you kidding me? It's Maureen."

"Oh," she said, then Gabe got on the line.

"Maureen, it's nothing. I can explain."

"Explain? What is there to explain? You're out with another woman. You think I can't see what's going on?"

"She likes my jokes," said Gabe.

"Impossible," I said. "No one likes your jokes, Gabe. Maybe I shouldn't be the one to tell you, but your jokes are awful. Every one of them. Stinkers. Not funny. Just plain dumb."

Like before, my comments were met with the sounds of crickets.

"Nothing to say?" I asked.

"Maureen, be reasonable."

"I'll show you reasonable," I said.

I tapped the connection closed, then pulled up the app for my car and punched in the coordinates for my house and ordered my car home, *my* car, the one Gabe bought for *me*, the one that was carrying Isabelle, who I now understood to be the worst kind of floozy, waiting for my husband to *die* before she made her move, waiting for me to let my guard drop so she could swoop in and—

What?

What was I afraid of?

Gabe couldn't *do* anything with her.

Could it really be the jokes?

My hand hovered over the phone. I was about to touch the key that would bring the car home to me, then I cancelled the app.

I phoned the car again.

Gabe answered.

"Maureen," he said. "Let's talk about this."

"Never mind," I said. "Put Isabelle on the line."

"Maureen?" Isabelle's voice.

"He's all yours," I said.

"What?"

"My good for nothing husband. You can have him. I'm done with him. And keep the car."

Then I hung up.

Felt good. Real good. Felt like I had finally broken the connection between me and Gabe.

That was needed. Grief had to have an expiration date, you know. You can't be grieving the rest of your life. It didn't work that way. Couldn't work that way.

That night I dreamed of Gabe.

He was telling a joke.

"What's a cat's favorite dessert? Mice cream."

I woke up groaning. Or thought I did. But then I saw what I was hearing was not my groans but the sound of the garage door opening.

I got out of bed and went to the door to the garage and saw my car pulling into its parking space.

It stood there, the engine purring, the lights on, like it was waiting for—something.

I folded my hands and tapped my foot.

The lights turned off. The engine turned off.

I heard the lock on the passenger door click and saw the door swing open.

I can recognize an invitation when I see one. Only I wasn't sure I wanted to accept.

I sniffed the air.

The car waited and waited.

I finally got in. Smelled some of her perfume. Isabelle. I didn't wear perfume. Never did. Never would. Wondered if Gabe liked that or if he didn't. Could he even tall? Decided it didn't matter.

"I'm sorry," he said.

"You should be."

"I just had this idea you didn't like my jokes. Never knew that."

"Gabe," I said, "how could you not know that? You ever hear me laugh at any of your jokes? Even one?"

"I thought you were exercising restraint."

The males of the species have their own peculiar brand of idiocy I have decided. Must be all the man hormones they carry around all the time. Obscures their reasoning power.

"You want to drive other women around," I said, "that's okay with me, but you gotta *tell* me. You don't just step out on your own like that."

"Okay," he said.

"So it's a deal?"

"Deal."

"Fine."

"You want to go for a ride now?"

"I'm tired, Gabe," I said.

"Oh, yeah. Sure."

We were quiet for a few seconds, maybe half a minute. It felt nice. Like we were sharing something. Feeling the love between us.

"You like being a ghost?" I asked.

"Not sure yet," he said.

"I miss you," I said.

He waited a beat. Maybe one second.

"Didn't know you were trying to hit me," he said.

Then he laughed.

For both of us.

Had to be that way, because laughter, at that moment, it was not coming to *me* with anything one would call great speed.

"Come on," he said. "That was a good one. Have to admit it."

I shook my head. No. It was not a good one.

Then I smiled and told my dead husband he was the funniest man I have ever heard in my entire life. Ever.

A Chair and Dirty Feet

Eric knew he smelled bad.

He had been working all day digging up roots for the harvest, which meant his skin was sweaty and grimy and his clothes were less than presentable, and his face and hands were stained with ground in dirt.

But he still wanted to spend the evening with Lynn.

So after he had dumped his last bag of roots into the big collection bin, he told his foreman he was done, and walked off the field, trudged the five miles back to town, taste of grit in his mouth, rough feel of pebbles under his soles, and stood in front of Lynn's door and smoothed back his rough hair, and knocked lightly with a seven rap melody to let her know he was there.

He waited patiently while the sun touched the horizon on the way to disappearing for the night. No answer from Lynn, so he rapped the door again, louder, but still with respect, and presently the door swung open.

Eric lifted his eyes to meet Lynn's gaze, hoping for joy in her face, or at least a smile. Instead she scrunched up her nose and looked down at his feet, which were covered in dirt and dust. Even his sandals were filthy.

"You have got to be kidding," said Lynn.

"Please," said Eric. "I've been working since dawn. I want to see you."

She shook her head. "Not until you clean those feet," she said. "You're not stepping in here with dirty feet like that."

Eric's heart felt broken. "Lynn," he said with more than a little pleading in his voice, "have some mercy. I'm tired and hungry."

"Everyone's tired and hungry. They still take time to clean themselves before they go to their girlfriend's house." Lynn closed the door slowly, moving her head with the edge, so that Eric saw her eyes blinking at him through the narrow gap until it closed to a thin line of light, then disappeared.

A chilly breeze seemed to descend from the trees around Eric. It raised goosebumps on his arms. He sighed and stepped back. His house was a long distance away. If we went home to clean up, he wouldn't get back here for probably another two hours at least. By that time Lynn would be ready for him to leave.

He turned to face the street. He knew some of the neighbors here. Across the way, there was Mrs. Boltin. He once cleaned the leaves out of her gutter. She would help him.

He walked up to her door and was about to knock when it swung open.

Mrs. Boltin was over eighty years old. She stuck her finger in the general direction of Eric's face.

"I saw you trying to get into Lynn's place," she said. "She put you in the dog house? What did you do?"

"Mrs. Boltin," said Eric, "I need to wash my feet. Can I use your bathroom?"

She took one step back and looked down at Eric's feet and made the same expression Lynn had made.

"You are too dirty to come into my house," she said.

"Please," he said, not particularly happy to be begging for the second time in less than two minutes.

Mrs. Boltin tapped her foot on the floor and folded her hands over her chest. Eric tilted his head and raised his eyebrows in a puppy-dog look.

"Wait here," she said and turned and walked away. Eric scratched his head and looked at the pink sky on the horizon.

Mrs. Boltin returned a short time later dragging a wooden chair behind her.

"Let me help you with that," said Eric.

"Not on your life," said Mrs. Boltin. "You stay out there."

Eric sighed and remained where he was. Mrs. Boltin got the chair right up to the door and pushed it through with a good firm oomph. She was stronger than she looked.

"Impressive," said Eric.

The chair was wooden. The struts were worn and the whole thing was rickety, as though it might fall apart if anyone sat in it. The arms bore upholstery in a faded blue cloth that had certainly seen better days. There were a few rips here and there and the tacks that held it in place were no longer shiny.

"You take this chair down to Morgan's house," she said. "This is my Brent's old chair—may he rest in peace—and I want it fixed up. Morgan will do it, but he won't come here to pick it up. You take it to him, then you can come back here and wash your feet. Got it?"

Eric searched his brain for an image of Morgan, trying to remember where he might live.

"Isn't he on the other side of town?" he said.

"Five blocks," said Mrs. Boltin. She told him the address. "Better get cracking if you want a shot at Lynn tonight." Then she smiled, pushed the chair out in front of Eric and closed the door.

Eric sighed and bent down and examined the chair a little closer. The thing must have been a hundred years old.

He hefted it, to test its weight. It wasn't too heavy. He lifted it off the stoop and held it up over his head so the seat rested on his skull. He wrapped his fists around its arms and began walking toward Morgan's house.

Thoughts of Lynn's home cooking and the taste of her sweet lips afterward filled his head and moved his feet with rapid steps.

It seemed like a long way to Morgan's house, but he managed the blocks in a few minutes and arrived at the address Mrs. Boltin had given him and dropped the chair on the grass in front of the door. He pushed the doorbell. Chimes rang out from somewhere.

In a few seconds Morgan opened the door wide and showed his teeth to Eric.

"Ah," he said. "You are the bringer of the chair."

"Can I come in?" asked Eric.

Morgan's eyes flicked down to Eric's feet then flicked back up. "I don't think so, my friend," he said. "Mrs. Boltin phoned me and said you had a deal."

Eric nodded. "I deliver the chair and she lets me wash my feet."

"She's a brave woman letting a dirty one like you into her house."

"I suppose," said Eric.

"I will take the chair," he said, "but then I need something from you."

Eric groaned. The vision of Lynn in his mind faded to a watery ghost and threatened to slide away into oblivion.

"What?" he asked.

"Wait here," said Morgan, and shuffled away on legs that seemed barely strong enough to hold him up.

"Of course," said Eric under his breath. "Of course I wait and wait and wait."

Morgan came back with a pie in his hands.

"Over on Thissom Street," said Morgan, "they are having a wake for Old Man Hentz. I can't make it. I am crippled. Take this pie to them with my blessings."

"That wasn't part of the deal," said Eric. "I was supposed to deliver this chair and then I could go back to Mrs. Boltin's place."

"You don't take this pie," said Morgan, "then I don't take the chair. Then you're stuck with the chair and having to explain to Mrs. Boltin why you didn't get it to me."

"But that's not fair," said Eric. "I'm here. Now. With the chair."

"My friend," said old Man Hentz, "has it really taken you this long to realize life isn't fair?"

Eric sighed and put out his hands, though he had no wish to take anything to anyone's wake.

Morgan dropped the pie onto his palms. "And I want the pie plate back," he said. "Tonight. Otherwise someone at the wake will take it home and I'll never see it again."

Morgan grabbed the chair and dragged it inside the house, then closed the door.

Eric knew where Old Man Hentz lived. He had a big family. His wife was still alive, two of his kids lived with him, along with their spouses and some of *their* children. Everyone always said Old Man Hentz would live forever because he loved life more than anyone else.

But he ate too much and they said it clogged up his heart and arteries. Eric didn't know if that was true. He just knew he had a pie to deliver.

He walked along the sidewalk and felt the night air getting colder around him. The pie smelled good, like fresh apples ripening in the sun. He thought he should just take the pie to Lynn's house and they could enjoy it together. After all, Old Man Hentz was dead. He would have loved the pie, but he wasn't going to taste any of it.

As he neared Old Man Hentz's house, he heard music, loud and bold, piano, guitar, and harmonica. The sound of all those instruments broke the still air as though a thousand choruses from heaven had decided to alight down here on Earth.

It seemed like everyone in town who knew how to play an instrument was there at the house and they didn't care if the whole world heard them.

Eric began humming along with the tune, imitating birds and the sounds of nature.

He heard other sounds, too, woven into the music, but could not tell what it was until he got right up to the door of the house and realized they were sobs. People crying.

He wasn't sure if he wanted to go into the house, not like this, not with everyone in grief over Old Man Hentz, but he knocked on the door anyway and stood shivering in the cold, hopping from foot to foot, the pie calling to him to take a piece.

He did not. He had too much respect for the mourners to steal their food.

No one answered the door. He knocked louder a few times, but when it did not swing open, he turned the knob himself and pushed it just enough to peek inside. No one was paying any attention to the door.

There were dozens of people. Some dancing, some standing and clapping along with the music. Other huddled together in small groups, with their arms around one another, crying. Still others sat by themselves in corners, as though they were in a quiet space all their own.

Were they all thinking of Old Man Hentz? Were they all feeling the pain of his loss, or were they in their own little worlds?

In the middle of the room a table bore the corpse of Old Man Hentz.

He was dressed all in black, with a bow tie around his neck and a flower in his lapel. His hair was gray and his face looked happy.

Eric found this more than a little disconcerting, to have a dead man in the middle of a celebration, but that's what a wake was, wasn't it?

Off to the side Eric saw a table laden with food. His mouth salivated at the sight of it all. He pushed the door open further and stepped inside and walked across the room and put the pie on the table, next to a platter of pork chops, which, itself, was nestled against a bowl of apple sauce beside another bowl of bean salad, next to a steaming pan of lasagna, and so on and so on. So much food.

Eric noticed a clock on the wall over the table. He had been at Lynn's half an hour ago. It would take another half an hour to get back to Mrs. Boltin's, then ten minutes to clean up, then across the street to Lynn's. That wasn't so bad, he thought.

He turned around and began walking toward the door when he stopped and slapped his face. Morgan wanted his plate back. Eric would have to find something to put the pie on.

He went into the kitchen, pushing his way past mourners and revelers to look for a big plate. He elbowed a couple of people out of the way, gently, and opened cupboard drawers.

Nothing like what he wanted presented itself.

"You looking for something?" a female voice, behind him, dripping with indignation.

Eric turned around. "I need a plate to put the pie on," he said as he turned around to see Jan Hentz, Old Man Hentz's granddaughter. She glared at him, and Eric realized he had been very rude not to tell anyone in the house that he was there.

"Feel free to look around," she said. "We'll try to stay out of your way."

Eric felt his face flush. He looked down at his feet, suddenly realizing, again, how dirty he was.

"I'm sorry," he said. "I was delivering this pie, and—"

"What pie?" said Jan.

"It's on the table."

"Then why do you need a plate?"

"It's complicated," said Eric.

"You're the guy who digs up the roots, aren't you?" she said.

Eric thought to bow to Jan, to try to lighten the mood, which had become frosty and a little bit intimidating.

Behind her, two big guys stepped closer so they were on either side of Jan and looking at him with a certain menace in their demeanor, as though they would gladly break him in two.

"A picker," said one of them. "A dirty one, too. What are you doing here, at this wake, bringing your filth into our house?"

Eric made sure his next words were modulated and low in volume. "I was just explaining," he said, "that I was bringing—with respect—a pie for the wake. From Morgan."

They all three studied him with an expression of disbelief on their faces. "Morgan sent *you*?" said Jan.

"It's complicated," said Eric.

"You said that already," she said.

Eric felt his face get even hotter.

"Wait here," said Jan, and ducked back between the two men and ran into the living room.

Eric's mouth went dry and his legs felt weak as he looked at the two men who folded their arms over their chests and glared at Eric, making it clear they were not about to let him out of their sight.

"You know," said Eric, "Old Man Hentz really liked the roots I picked. People talked about it. I should have brought some here tonight. You know, out of respect. Everyone could have eaten some and kind of—well— remembered him. Cherished the memories, like. I should have done that."

They said nothing. Just let him keep talking.

Jan returned, hair flying, stepping high, full of liveliness, as though she were a bird. No, a gazelle. Eric shook his head. He told himself to focus.

Jan held a box in her hands. Not a very big one. It was made of cardboard and looked like it was more than a few years old.

"This is for Morgan," she said. "From my grandfather. You'll take it to him."

Eric ran his tongue over his lips and put out his hands, embarrassed that they were shaking. "Of course," he managed to say.

"I know Morgan could have come over. He says he's crippled, but he isn't, not really. He's just old and doesn't want to go places anymore. He's afraid of people."

Eric nodded.

"Make sure he gets this," she said.

"Okay," said Eric.

"I'll get your stupid pie plate."

"Thanks," said Eric.

She went to the cupboard next to the fridge and retrieved a big plate and took it into the living room and returned a few seconds later with Morgan's pie plate. She rinsed it under the faucet and dried it off with a towel and handed it to Eric, who took it with both hands and gripped it tightly. The box Jan had given him earlier was nestled inside the crook of his elbow.

"Now get out of here," said Jan.

The two burly guys hustled him outside the house. The air was even colder than before, which, combined with the possibility that he might get to see Lynn in a short time, hurried his pace considerably.

He arrived at Morgan's house and rang the doorbell. Morgan did not come to the door, even though Eric rang the bell several times. He stepped back to take a look up at the face of the house, trying to see a window with a light.

None presented itself. Eric took deep breaths while trying to decide what to do. He left the plate and the box in front of the door and went around to the back of the house. The grass was damp, and there was no light at all. He kept one hand on the side of the house to guide him.

When he got to the corner, he followed the wall to the back door. He didn't see a door bell, so he knocked on the door. He was getting impatient, and the knocks were strong and insistent. Where was Morgan?

He turned the knob and put his mouth to the door frame.

"Hey," he said. "Morgan? Where are you? I have your stupid plate and a present from a dead guy. Morgan?"

He stepped into a kitchen teetering on all surfaces with piles of dirty dishes and old newspapers. A small bare light bulb overhead illuminated, as best it could, a landscape of severe clutter, with trash on the floors and dirt on the walls.

Eric stepped through the mess and came to the top of a flight of stairs that led to a very slightly illuminated basement.

"Morgan?" he shouted.

Morgan's face appeared at the bottom. "Yeah?"

"I have your plate," said Eric.

"I have Mrs. Boltin's chair," said Morgan.

"What? Already."

"Come fetch it and you can take it back to her."

Eric descended the stairs, expecting to find a wasteland of trash and grime at the bottom, but instead he was presented with a neatly appointed workroom, everything in its place, clean and inviting. The workbench was without a scratch, the tools were shiny and stowed on a board against the wall. Cupboards of impeccable workmanship were arrayed over the workbench. A neat trash can stood next to the workbench. Eric saw that remnants of upholstery had been tossed into it.

The chair, Mrs. Boltin's chair, rested on the floor in front of the workbench. It had new upholstery on its arms and seat, and all its parts were tightened and smoothed out. The tacks were black and shiny. The chair looked splendid.

"You want to try it out?" asked Morgan.

"I gotta get going," said Eric. "Your stuff is on the front porch."

"Don't worry about that," said Morgan. "Sit in the chair."

Eric glanced up the stairs. Lynn was waiting for him. At least, he hoped she was. Maybe she was getting bored of waiting, which meant he shouldn't spend a lot of time here at Morgan's house.

"Sit, for chrissakes," said Morgan, now more than a little irritated.

Eric sat in the chair. It felt comfortable and he told Morgan so.

"Of course it's comfortable," said Morgan. "It's an old chair. All old chairs are comfortable, otherwise they wouldn't be old. People would throw them out."

Eric nodded. He felt the tension in his legs dissipate. He felt his chest cave in slightly from the relief of sitting down, of not having to dig in the earth or walk all over town helping people he didn't want to help.

"Brent and I were good friends for a while," said Morgan. "But then me and Mrs. Boltin, we had a little hanky-panky once. Only once, a long time ago, but Brent never forgot it. He hated me."

"Um," said Eric. "Okay."

"So now she likes me to do things for her. I ask her over, but she never comes. Guilt. It's a terrible thing. Don't ever let it take over your life, Eric."

"No sir," said Eric.

"So that's it."

"It?"

"The advice to the younger generation from the older generation. Have to have that, you know."

"Oh," said Eric. "Right."

"Now you take this chair back to her."

"I will."

"Tell her I love her still," said Morgan.

"What?"

"*Tell* her."

"Yes sir."

"Don't forget."

"I won't."

"Now git."

Eric rose out of the chair and carried it up the stairs and through the kitchen, but not to the back door. He went through the living room, which was as cluttered and unkempt as the kitchen and put the chair down near the front door and opened it.

The box was still there, right on top of the pie plate, where he had left them. He bent down and picked them up and handed them to Morgan, who was standing close to him.

Morgan put the pie plate on top of a pile of newspapers next to him. "What's the box?" he asked Eric.

"Jan said Old Man Hentz wanted you to have it."

Morgan laughed. "Old man Hentz wanted me to have something. Well isn't that rich?"

Eric wanted to leave, had his hand on the door knob and was ready to turn it, then lift the chair over his head and walk to Mrs. Boltin's house, but he also wanted to see what he had delivered to Morgan.

"You going to open it?" he asked.

"You want me to?"

Eric nodded.

Morgan smiled. His face seemed to register an expression Eric couldn't quite identify. Was it pain? Sadness?

Morgan slipped a finger under the flap of the box and pulled it open, stretching the tape that held it down to the breaking point. Eric had one hand on the doorknob, but he didn't open the door.

Morgan peered into the box, then closed it tight.

"What?" said Eric. "What was it?"

"Never mind," said Morgan. "It's none of your business. Take that chair to Mrs. Boltin."

He opened the door and pushed the chair out and Eric followed.

Eric said bye to Morgan and lifted the chair over his head and set out for Mrs. Boltin's place, still wondering what could have been in the box.

About halfway to his destination, Eric heard a sound he didn't want to hear. At first it was far off, but even so, it was loud enough and sinister enough to make the pit of his stomach fall and his heart rate to increase.

The barking of dogs always did that to him. He couldn't help himself. As the barking got louder, he realized the dogs were getting closer and he quickened his pace, stepping as fast as he could, panic gripping him so solidly that he wanted to drop the chair right in the street and run as fast as he could, Lynn be damned.

No, that wasn't right. Lynn was not at fault here. He could have said no to the deal. Right from the beginning, he could have told Lynn she was right, he was filthy and not fit for companionship tonight and gone home to his own bed and then he wouldn't have been in this mess right now.

The dogs were closer, but it didn't seem like they were intent on Eric. At least not yet.

His senses were all on high alert, as though he was a super tuned receiver. The smells of the night: dead leaves, wet grass, his own sweat, all snaked up into his consciousness and they were all leavened by fear.

He was afraid the dogs would smell *him* and find a way to inflict wounds with their teeth on his legs and feet.

Eric found he was breathing hard, in gasps, and his legs were getting shaky and weak. His arms and neck were sore from the weight of the stupid chair on his head.

He rounded a corner in the street and saw Mrs. Boltin's house, a single light bulb illuminating the front porch. A quick glance to the side confirmed a light in Lynn's house, which was a good sign. She was still awake.

He pressed on, but then saw that three snarling dogs had decided to put themselves between Eric and Mrs. Boltin's front door. They stood in a triangle formation, each of them with tongues hanging out and looking in Eric's direction.

Eric put the chair down on the ground and instinctively eased himself to the other side of it so that the chair was between him and the dogs. He knew it would be scant protection, but it was all he had.

He looked across the street. A quick sprint to Lynn's door could save him, but the dogs, he knew, ran faster than he could.

That was also true of all the other houses in the area. They all were too far away for Eric to outrun the dogs.

As he considered his options, few as they were, the dogs decided that Eric was of interest. They turned towards him and began walking in his direction.

Eric's blood rose with alarming intensity. His legs wanted to run as fast as they could, but Eric quelled them. He knew that would spell his doom. Much better to stand his ground and face down the animals.

He stepped around the front of the chair. He stood up as straight as he could. He felt the top of his head touch the clouds, high above him. He lifted his hands high, making himself as big as he could.

The dogs hesitated. The growled, their tails were down. Eric didn't know the breed of these animals, maybe something like a terrorist breed.

They belonged to no one. They roamed the town for a time, then moved on, but always came back.

There had been talk of killing them, with guns or poison, but no one had the heart to do it. Too many dog lovers, even of nuisance dogs like these.

They were thin, Eric could see that. Which meant they were hungry. Hungry enough to make a meal of him.

He stepped toward the animals. They held their ground. His hands were still high above his head, but he dropped them to unzip his jacket and spread the flaps open, to present an even bigger profile.

The dogs silenced themselves, studying him.

Eric felt a weight in one of his pockets.

He dropped his jacket long enough to reach into his pocket and find bits of the roots he had been digging up. He pulled them out of the pocket, and without giving the matter much more than a fleeting thought, hurled the pieces across the street, away from himself, Mrs. Boltin's house, and Lynn's house.

The dogs, sensing nourishment, broke into a fast run after the root pieces. They flashed by Eric, not more than five feet away, but no longer interested in him in the least.

Eric took the opportunity to grab the chair and run as fast as possible to Mrs. Boltin's door.

He banged on the door, loudly, with no respect whatsoever, and did not stop until Mrs. Boltin opened the door.

"What's this racket?" he said with more than a little irritation in her voice. "You got something against being civil?"

"I have your chair," said Eric. "Let me in."

She stepped back and Eric pushed the chair into the house and stepped inside himself and closed the door behind him.

"What the hell's wrong with you?" she asked him.

"Dogs," said Eric. "They almost attacked me."

She blew air through her lips so it sounded like a fart. "Those dogs?" she said. "You afraid of them?"

Eric nodded.

Mrs. Boltin shook her head. "How do you expect to keep a girlfriend if you're so afraid of a few pups?"

Eric had no wish to debate the lethality of the neighborhood stray dogs. "Can I use your bathroom, Mrs. Boltin? We had a deal, remember?"

She looked at him blankly. "Deal?" she said. "What's a bathroom?" She looked around the room with a dazed expression. Then she looked up at him with eyes blinking rapidly. "Who are you?"

"Very funny, Mrs. Boltin," he said. "But Lynn's waiting for me."

She slapped him on the shoulder. "You wish," she said. She pulled the door open wide. "Come on in," she said. "Bring the chair."

"Thank you," he said and picked up the chair from the porch and stepped inside. He was about to put the chair down, but he was shocked into stillness by what he saw: a living room crammed to the ceiling with piles of junk, just like Morgan's house.

"Well, put it down," she said.

Eric looked around. There wasn't a lot of room, but she had trails going through the stuff, and a clear space around the door. He put the chair down and saw there was a big basin of soapy water there at his feet.

"Now sit," said Mrs. Boltin.

Eric sat. She pushed the basin next to him.

"Take off your sandals," she said.

Eric undid the straps on his sandals and slipped them off and kicked them to the side. He put his feet into the basin without asking.

"That's the way," said Mrs. Boltin.

The water was warm and so soothing that Eric sighed.

"Now scrub them clean. You want to make Lynn happy, don't you."

Eric nodded.

"Or is that you want her to make *you* happy, hmmm?"

Eric's face turned hot. Mrs. Boltin chuckled. "I know what goes on between you and her," she said.

Eric couldn't help grinning. Mrs. Boltin pointed at him. "I'm right, aren't I?"

"Thank you for letting me wash my feet," said Eric.

"Think nothing of it," said Mrs. Boltin. "You got my Brent's chair back to me in no time. You're a good kid."

She handed him a wash cloth. Eric dipped it into the water and used it to scrub his feet, taking great care with the toes, which had dirt ground into them. And the heels, which had caked dirt ringing the back and bottom.

The water in the basin turned distinctly brown, almost black.

All the while, Mrs. Boltin examined the chair.

"Morgan did a good job," she said. "I knew he would." She put her hand on the back. "See how he sanded it here. He hardly had it for half an hour, but he used the half hour well."

Just as Eric was finishing his clean up, she got a towel from somewhere in the mess that was her living room and handed it to him. "You might want to wash those sandals, too," she said.

Eric dried his feet with the towel, then dipped his sandals in the basin water, and the mud and dirt on them washed away. He pulled them out of the water, and they looked new as the day he had first put them on.

He dried them off with the towel Mrs. Boltin had given him and put them on.

"Thank you," he said, and then an awkward moment presented itself to both of them. He wanted to get up, but they had created a moment there in her living room and he didn't want to break the spell.

"Do you know what Old Man Hentz gave Morgan?" she asked Eric.

"A box," said Eric. "How did you know?"

"Morgan called me, yes a box, but what was in the box?"

Eric shrugged. "I wanted to know, but he wouldn't tell me and I wanted to get your chair back to you."

"It was a letter from Old Man Hentz."

"In a box," said Eric.

She slapped him on the back of the head, not hard, but enough for him to know she wasn't kidding.

"Yes, in a box," she said. "So what? Old man Hentz was friends with my Brent. Did you know that?"

Eric shook his head.

"They palled around. Drank together. Who knows what else. They were best friends when Morgan and I—well, we had our little fling. Then things got ugly."

"I think I heard something about that," said Eric. He glanced at the door, trying not to be obvious about it. It would be a miracle if Lynn was still awake and willing to let him through her door.

"The letter said to Morgan that he should come over to my house."

Eric looked up at Mrs. Boltin. He was suddenly very aware that she was elderly, standing over him, and he was sitting. He got up and stepped away from the chair and said she should sit in it.

She shook her head.

"Morgan and I," she said, "we don't have a lot of time left. We're old, if you haven't noticed."

"People are only as young as they feel," said Eric. "At least, that's what I've heard."

"That's bullshit," she said.

"Right," said Eric.

"He's coming over," she said.

"Tonight?"

She nodded. "I think that's him now."

Eric heard taps on the porch, the sound of canes touching wood. Then a pause, and a knock on the door, three short raps.

"We won't answer right away," said Mrs. Boltin. "Don't want to look too eager."

"Right," said Eric.

More knocks. They were so close that they sounded harsh in Eric's ear.

"We'll let him knock one more time," she said.

The next series of three were just as sharp and well-modulated as the first. Eric heard no hint of impatience. He looked at Mrs. Boltin and tilted his head toward the door.

She looked flushed and expectant, taller than she was, more regal, somehow, as though she was about to meet greatness.

"Go ahead," she said. "Open the door."

Eric swung the door open. Morgan stood there with a slight smile on his face. The teeth were hidden, this time, and he had a hat over his heart.

"Is Olivia home?" he asked.

"She is," said Eric. He stepped aside to let Morgan enter the house. He stepped through the doorway, which gave Eric a chance to slip out.

The door closed behind him.

The dogs were gone from the street.

Eric walked down the sidewalk to the street. Without looking either way, he walked across the street and up the walk to Lynn's door. His feet felt clean and fresh, like new clothes.

He paused on the front steps, took a big breath, let it out slowly, and tapped a seven note melody with his knuckles on Lynn's door.

Broken Hearts

Rush hour. Rainy October evening in Portland, Oregon. Chain of white headlights and red tail lights stopped on every street. Incessant wiper beat on windshields: thunk-thunk, thunk-thunk.

Drivers impatient at intersections, as if poised for a starter's gun to fire.

Jeff Garner, public defender, over-worked and over-stressed after losing a tough trial. Stopped at a red light downtown on Burnside Avenue. Ready to be home. A bit less observant than usual. A little more impatient. Didn't wait for the intersection to clear before he jumped the green light.

A truck on Broadway, the cross street, bore down. That driver figured he had plenty of time before traffic started up the other way, even though the light was yellow and he had a distance to go. Didn't want to wait for another light cycle. Leaned on the gas pedal.

Ran the red light.

Never made it through the intersection.

The truck hit Jeff Garner's sub-compact above the wheel in the front fender and sent him spinning like a windmill over the slick pavement. Jeff threw his right hand to the side, instinctively trying to protect Dominik, who wasn't there. Where was she? He didn't want to die alone. They had a deal. He would go first. But that didn't mean he would go alone.

Did it?

Adrenaline pumped into his bloodstream as white and red streaked past his windshield in a blur. A traffic light post stopped him cold, shattered his windows, and bent his car so it looked skewed and *wrong* even from the inside. It also threw his head against the door where the broken glass opened a gushing wound above his eye.

The adrenaline kick-started his heart into overdrive. But that didn't last. His vision clouded over. He put his fist on his sternum.

Something heavy there.

Where did that come from?

A warm creek of blood pulsed down his face over his cheek to his chin, then turned cold as it dripped onto his shirt.

He felt his system sputter. It tried to start up again, but sputtered a few times more, then rattled to a stop.

Jeff slipped out of himself with his hand clutched to his chest. His seat belt ripped through his torso and bisected his heart. He fell through the car and hit the pavement.

There was still—*something*— on his chest. He wanted that elephant *off* him. Needed some *air*. He made a motion to push the damn thing away.

So he could *breathe*.

Then realized: there was nothing *to* breathe.

At the same instant, in an office tower on Alder Street, four blocks away and five stories up, Dominik Garner's heart skipped a beat.

She looked up from her computer, where she had been digitally airbrushing a magazine ad for toothpaste, and felt a twist in the universe.

Like something had been turned inside out.

She looked around at the other desks. Her graphic design colleagues, all under deadline pressure, concentrated on their computer screens as if nothing had happened.

Dominik couldn't shake the cold feeling in her gut. She called her husband's cell phone number. It rang and rang. No answer. That wasn't like him. Dominik began to worry.

Nothing to breathe. Weird.

He thought of Dominik. This was going to ruin her day. Maybe her life.

No, she was stronger than that. She would get through it.

Jeff thought he heard something in the distance. The far distance. A few notes of Bach drifted up from somewhere a million miles away.

A call coming in. He moved his hand from his chest and reached for the phone in his pocket.

Old habits.

He never got close to the phone. His heart communicated pain to him in a straightforward and insistent manner.

Jeff took notice. He grimaced and put his hand back to his chest. He expected to encounter resistance. Instead, his hand penetrated his skin, sailed on through his sternum, slipped past squishy viscera, and nudged itself against his heart.

Jeff wrapped his hand around his own heart.

Which had stopped beating.

Not good. Not good.

He felt the muscle, dead in his hand. Where was that familiar lub-dub? Where did it go?

He wanted to feel the blood, his blood, pour through his valves and flow into his arteries.

He massaged his heart. Worked the muscle.

Nothing happened.

He felt a chill weaken him further.

His heart was dead?

His heart?

It appeared so.

Then why did it hurt so much?

Dominik called home, just to be sure, but Jeff was not due home for a half hour at least. Unless he got out of work early, but he would have called her and told her. The home phone picked up after four rings. Dominik hung up without leaving a message.

Now she was even more worried. Something happened. Something wasn't right.

Her hands shook. She tried to still them by holding her palms one against the other, but that didn't help. Her chest felt like it had been hollowed out and scraped clean. She put her hands, still clasped like a double fist, up to her sternum.

The woman at the next computer glanced over and saw Dominik doubled over, rocking in her chair.

She went to her and put her hand on Dominik's back and leaned down.

"Dom," she said. "Are you okay? What's wrong?"

Jeff stopped breathing.

There was no point, so why bother.

And his heart had stopped.

This puzzled him. Not the stopping, but the knowledge. He had figured out he was most likely dead. He got that. Also, he understood that certain biological activities were worthless in the afterlife.

So why was he still aware?

He had to ponder that one.

He noticed he was drifting down. This raised his eyebrows. He expected to go *up*. Apparently, that's not how the universe worked. He looked around and saw he was under his car. The dirty brown pipes and tanks sat inches from his face.

The impact with the post shook him loose from his body and sent him down through his car seat and the floor to the street surface underneath his car.

The pavement intersected his back and buttocks. He felt gravel there; a layer of it sat beneath the pavement and now his layers commingled with it. Odd sensation. Vaguely ticklish. Strange to have gravel invade your body with a minimum of fuss.

Dust to dust. Ashes to ashes.

All those funerals had it right. You really did go back to the earth.

It was a hell of a thing to discover.

He wanted to see the sky. Damn his car for obscuring his view. He was never going to see the sky again.

Never going to see Dominik, either.

He pulled his hand away from his heart and pushed it through the muffler of his car and up through the carpet where the fibers raked his flesh. He kept pushing.

Reaching.

For something. Some contact.

Then: activity around him at his eye level. He saw feet on the pavement. People bustling around the car. A stretcher unfolded. Its wheels touched the wet street. Water dripped off of them.

Must be taking out my body, he thought.

He wouldn't see it. He was too far down. And his car was in the way.

Just as well. He didn't need to see himself dead.

No one needed that.

"There's something wrong with Jeff," said Dominik to her colleague. "I know it."

Others in the office gathered around.

"Should we call someone?" "Are you all right?" "What's wrong?"

"I feel him reaching for me." Dominik held out hand, palm up, with the fingers spread wide. It had turned white, and trembled in the air.

Her desk phone rang.

She straightened up and seized it before it could ring a second time.

"Hello?"

"Dominik Garner?"

"Yes. This is Dominik. Who is this?"

A brief silence that no one else in the world would have noticed, but which to Dominik was as final as a life sentence. She heard the remainder of the conversation in unconnected phrases.

"—regret to inform—" "—my sympathies—" "—organ donor—" "—Providence Hospital—" "—need you to sign—"

She dropped the phone. It clattered on the desk, the only sound in the office. Everyone else had stopped working and looked in her direction.

Dominik felt their stares.

She heard her own heart beat. So loud. So strong. Where did that strength come from, now that Jeff was gone?

She rose unsteadily from her chair and stood with her hands on the edge of her desk.

"I have to go," she announced to the room.

They wanted his heart. It was that simple.

He died and now it was up to her to sign over his heart.

Someone wanted it.

Someone needed Jeff's heart.

She fumbled for her own car keys and ran to the elevator.

They rolled the car away.

Uncovered the overcast sky. Rain still fell.

And Jeff still descended. That vaguely uncomfortable feeling of gravel invading his body got much more uncomfortable in a hurry. It felt like mice crawling around in his back. Little feet everywhere in his spine and coming up through his kidneys and bowels. Nasty feeling.

And where was the white light? He expected a white light. Didn't everyone say there would be a white light?

All he saw was dismal Oregon fall light, darkened by rain. Who needed that in the afterlife?

Jeff began to have thoughts of haunting something. Anything.

He should have grabbed onto the muffler of his car when he had the chance. Sure. Better than gravel. Better than the cold dark earth. Clutch the muffler and crawl up into it. Fold himself into the nocks and crannies of the muffler.

Then when they parted out the wreck, he'd be there, transplanted into a new vehicle. Maybe give someone a scare every time they started up the car.

That would be fun.

This sinking into the ground wasn't fun.

Didn't Dominik say they would never be apart? Didn't they have a deal like that?

Something. He remembered something about what they would do *if*. They were going to try to contact each other. Wasn't that it? Communicate from the dead?

Something.

Only it wasn't coming back to him. The memory. It was like a lot of that stuff, the stuff of life before the wreck, it had all slipped away.

Well, why wouldn't it?

What was he now, anyway? A bit of energy, maybe. Or not even that. Maybe he was nothing but a memory.

That was disconcerting. Made his heart twitch.

Whoa.

His heart twitched.

He put his hand back in his chest, just to check. He squeezed his heart, to try to get it going.

Nothing.

He sighed.

He wanted this over, whatever it was. Couldn't they just take him?

Please.

Dominik drove the couple of miles to Providence hospital and went directly to the emergency room.

Awful place. Bright fluorescent lights. Sick people stacked up in the waiting area like kindling about to be fed into a fire. She shuddered.

This wasn't the way they had planned it.

A doctor found her and explained the situation.

"The police saw the red heart on his license," said the doctor. She had a low voice, trying to be soothing and understanding, but it didn't sound real. To Dominik it was like she was *trying* to be compassionate. Trying too hard.

"He's an organ donor," said Dominik. She remembered when Jeff got his license in the mail. That red heart up in the corner seemed a little ominous to her. Jeff kind of liked it. Said it made him feel good.

Dominik thought it was tempting the fates, but she didn't say anything to him. He wanted to be a good citizen. It didn't mean anything. Not really.

"I'm very sorry for your loss," said the doctor. "As his spouse, we need you to authorize the harvesting—" She stopped, suddenly aware that her words were a little cold and clinical.

"Can I see him?" said Dominik.

"This way," said the doctor and walked with Dominik down a corridor to an operating room. An operating room? Already? They didn't have her permission yet.

Someone put a mask on her. It felt foreign, like something trying to smother her.

"There's a girl in Seattle," said the doctor. "She's waiting. We have a helicopter ready."

Dominik got it. Speed was of the essence.

Three people in white coats stood around him. She only saw their eyes over their masks. They looked blank. No one wanted to meet her eyes.

She approached Jeff.

They had cut away his shirt. Had already marked a line on his chest. So efficient. That girl was waiting, after all.

They'd cleaned up some of his blood. Jeff's blood. A cut on his eyebrow. It looked bad, but also dead. White. It made her shudder.

None of this seemed real yet. They had a deal. She was going to go first. She told him that. He could not die before her. She didn't want to bear the loss, work through the grief, gather up her life and start again. She never wanted that.

Someone had a clipboard in his hand, ready to put it in her hand.

She ignored the man and the clipboard.

She didn't need a pen in her hand, didn't need to hold a hard surface.

Instead, Dominik stepped forward, lifted Jeff's hand, and held it in hers.

The gravel felt like, given a chance, it would grind him into a puddle.

He tried to fight it.

He jerked himself from side to side. He moved, not much, but enough to get some tiny traction.

He stretched out his arms, to try to keep himself afloat on the wet pavement. The water lapped at his skin, and leaked into his body, filling him with a dampness. It felt so cold. Rain spattered through him. He felt the trail of the drops like bullet holes tunneling through him.

His arms did not slow the descent.

The ground awaited him. It seemed more than eager to swallow him whole.

Jeff scrambled for some kind of purchase. He kicked his legs, hoping the motion would propel him forward.

But it was not like swimming. He couldn't push the earth aside. Couldn't make the gravel do anything.

Although.

Now that he noticed it, a pleasant warmth seemed to wrap itself around his hand.

There was something familiar about that warmth.

He had felt it before.

Many times.

He wracked his rapidly failing memory, trying to place the sensation.

There was not only the pleasant temperature involved, either. A definite yielding also played a part. Like something accommodating itself to his own hand. Another hand?

Where did it come from?

Dominik wanted tears, but they didn't come. Why didn't they? She wanted to ask someone, but none of the white coats could know. They didn't care, either.

"You shit," she said. "You weren't going to go first. You promised."

Someone behind her cleared her throat. "He can't hear you, Ma'am. He's gone."

Doctors. They always thought they were so smart. Thought they knew everything and you didn't know anything.

She leaned close to Jeff's ear. "Did you hear me?" she said. "I want you back. Now."

She yanked on his arm. Gave it a good strong pull, because she knew she wouldn't get another chance. They wouldn't let her.

The arm felt limp, like a plastic bag, floating on the air like it didn't weigh a thing.

Someone grabbed her from behind. Someone else wrested Jeff's hand out of hers.

She hoped what she did was enough.

Jeff's eyes, only an inch or so above the pavement and about to be sucked under to what darkness he could only imagine, opened wide.

He felt a violent pull at his arm. Someone had grabbed hold of him.

The arm stretched out.

It snaked through the air. He saw the hand, miles away, against the overcast sky, with the long thread of his arm undulating down to his shoulder like a kite string.

He wanted to follow that arm.

Needed to.

He let himself slip out of his own skin.

It was easy. Nothing to it, once he made a bargain with the universe and agreed to the procedure. His flesh slid out of his skin. He left it behind like a cocoon husk, and followed the arc of his hand. It rose to the sky and angled over the river and started coming down a couple of miles away.

Jeff, fascinated, went along for the ride. He arched up over the city. The tops of the buildings looked like kids wooden blocks. They looked like they could support all of creation. They had strength beyond his imagining.

His hand increased its acceleration and started coming down. It aimed for one of those building blocks. A helicopter perched there. The hand sailed through it.

Jeff followed. Machinery parts flashed by his eyes.

He went through the roof of the building and burst through into impossibly white halls. Bright lights. More floors. Pipes and insulation.

And finally, at the end of it, his own bare-chested self, lying stretched out on an operating table.

The hand rejoined its original substance and flowed into the body.

The rest of Jeff followed.

Got swallowed up.

Nothing ever felt better.

He wiggled around, settling himself back into his true self. His organs realigned themselves. His ghost heart, the one that wouldn't work, meshed with his other heart, and he heard the familiar lub-dub lub-dub.

And then his eyes fluttered open.

"Dominik?" he said, so quietly he himself had difficulty understanding the syllables.

They wouldn't let her bring him back, was all she could think about.

They pulled her out of the surgery room and pushed the clipboard into her hand.

"Please sign," they said. "The little girl is waiting."

Well, yes, she could see that. A little girl. Innocent, no doubt, needed her husband's two or three pounds of flesh. That was important. Yes.

But she, and Jeff, and the universe had a deal.

It didn't include an innocent child. Not yet.

Behind her, she heard a door swing open.

A small voice, awed by something big. "Doctor," he said. "I think you need to come see this."

The doctor dropped the clip board, turned, and went back.

Dominik followed.

Went through the open doors.

Swept past the masked ones in white gowns.

Saw Jeff's fluttering eyelids.

Went to him slowly, as in a dream, reaching for life. She hesitated for a second. Whispered a prayer to the wind and hoped it found someone, anyone who needed help.

Then let it go. This was the answer to her prayer. This life before her. Jeff's life.

And hers.

The City of Golden Light

Driving south to Bandon from Portland, on Oregon's coastal Highway 101, David saw the city of golden light. It shimmered before him and he studied it intensely, looking for details he had not seen before.

He pumped the windshield wipers a couple of times to clear the view and pointed at the image. "Look," he said.

"Ah yes," said his wife Betty, beside him in the passenger seat. "David's famous mirage."

David grunted. They always saw it at night on this stretch of road. It was a grouping of yellowish lights, a fat line in the distance that glowed and seemed to hover above the road, miles away. As he watched closely it resolved into many separate blotches of light, flames that combined to form a larger fire.

"Heat waves," said Betty. "That's all it is, just heat waves,"

"I think it's a city," said David.

"Oh brother. Here we go again."

"No, really. Don't you have any poetry in your soul? Look at the way it hangs there, tantalizing us with its magic. I think it's the image of some lost city. Maybe a city of the future, who knows?"

Betty looked out the window, away from him. David knew she wanted to be home in Bandon, where she grew up, and from where she seldom ventured.

"I know what I have in me," she said to the window.

"Hmmm?"

"It isn't poetry, David. It's a creature. A slimy, energy sucking *thing* lives in me, and I'm trying to get rid of it. So please, no talk about magical cities. I swear, you talk about it so much, I'm beginning to see it in my dreams."

"Really?" he said excitedly. "Do you really dream about it? That must be great."

"No," she said. "It's not. It's getting tiresome and I wish it would stop."

When they were first married—David had met her soon after moving to town and the wedding was soon after that—he was attracted to her no-nonsense, matter-of-fact attitude toward life. He thought it would effectively balance his love of fantasy, of things unreal and shadowy. Then he realized her joylessness was a symptom of an illness. He noticed that no matter how much Betty ate, she could not gain weight. She had no energy, was constantly depressed, and would sometimes have attacks of acute anxiety. She complained of a feeling that she was being invaded from within and this frightened her.

They consulted doctors, but none could find an answer. Many spouted the medical profession's party line of the "hysterical female in need of control," and prescribed downers. Finally a referral from a friend sent them to a homeopath in Portland named Dr. Hill who diagnosed her problem almost immediately.

She had candida. A massive yeast infection had invaded Betty's body and was threatening her health. It was a serious condition, requiring serious care, but it troubled David to hear Betty talk about it as though it was a creature, some monster.

"Do you think it's a good idea to personify it in that way?" he said. "It's not really a creature, you know. It's more like an infection."[H]

She turned from the window and looked at him in the darkness. He tried to read her face, but the shadows only made him think of the darkness outside.

"I'm just being poetic," she said.

He winced, and decided he deserved that one. He fixed his attention on the glowing city in the distance until it was eclipsed by a curve in the road.

Isabella, a good friend, dropped in on David at the Bandon Historical Society Museum, where he worked.

"How did it go in Portland?" she asked. "Betty getting any better?"

David looked up from a grant proposal he was working on. He was trying to get some money to set up a small press using an old Linotype and letterpress that had been donated to the museum.

"It's hard to say," he said. "I *think* she is. At least, she says things are better. Hill still says we should move away. Coastal humidity just makes those little beasties grow."

"Betty would never move," said Isabella.

"She was born here, why should she? We *both* love it here."

"What's Hill got her on?"

"A yeast killing drug, nystatin. Some homeopaths. Strict diet." He shrugged. "It's a tough thing to control."

Isabella nodded. "She ought to try meditation."

"She does meditate."

"And herbs. Herbs really help."

"Uh huh. We know."

"And reflexology, have you tried that? Acupuncture too."

David smiled at her. Everyone had their own idea of how Betty should handle her Candida.

"We'll look into it," he said evenly.

"I know someone," said Isabella, "who couldn't take nystatins I mean,

she was allergic to it. She would get nauseous and Jumpy, and, oh God, I can't tell you."

"Never mind," said David. He hated If-you-think-that's-bad-let-me-tell-you-about-my-disease stories.

She looked him square in the face. David had always considered her a good judge of character, shrewd and experienced. She used to work at the museum, before she went freelance as a story and fortune teller. Now she did not spend much time in Bandon, she was always on the road doing shows and readings.

"Okay," she said. "You want me to mind my own business."

"It's just that we can't lose confidence in the treatment or else—"

She cut him off with a wave of her hand. "You need say nothing more," she said and bowed full from her waist.

He laughed.

"I am very nosy," she said, "and I should not be." He watched as she walked around the room, touching a corner of the wall here, running her fingers along framed pictures of old shipwreck photos and before and afters of the great fires of 1914 and 1936. "You're right about the confidence thing. It is important to keep a good mental attitude. I myself have been kind of confused lately, and it's disturbing."

This was news to David. "Really?" he said.

Isabella nodded. "I threw the I Ching the other day and found out my Tarot cards are all worn out and I'll have to get a new deck."

"That's too bad," said David.

She looked at him out of the corner of her eye.

He stared back blankly.

"My *God* you're in a foul mood," she said. "What's the problem?"

"It's nothing," he said.

"Bull. Tell me."

"Well, it's that city I see on 101."

She spread her hands and looked up at the ceiling as though looking for guidance from above.

"Are you *still* on that?"

"I can't get it out of my mind."

"For once I think Betty's right. It's nothing, just a mirage or something."

"Half the time I think that's right."

"But the other half?"

"I don't know. There's *some*thing there. It feels like more than an illusion. I mean, sometimes I really do think that I'm looking at another world."

Isabella was still walking around the room. She reminded David of an animal in a cage sometimes, as though she yearned to break free of some invisible bonds.

"You're a practiced dabbler in the occult," he said. "What do you think of it?"

"Not everything out of the ordinary needs to have a paranormal explanation, David. This is one of those things. Let it rest."

"I know. Still." He looked at her. "You know, Betty's been dreaming about it."

She shook a finger at him. "That's because she listens to you talk about it all day. She's trying to clear her mind of it, and you should help her by dropping the subject."

"Okay, okay," he said, holding up his hand. "It has been on my mind a lot lately. Ever since . . ." He pulled out a drawer and rummaged around in some papers. "Ah! Ever since I got this."

He brought out a weathered and wrinkled brown booklet. It was dusty and mottled with gray mold spots. The string along the spine was yellowed and brittle.

He handed it to Isabella. She opened it just enough to look inside and tilted her head to read the writing there.

"It's a diary," said David. "I haven't had a chance to read it all yet; the writing is starting to fade and I haven't had the time to study it. But what I *have* read is very interesting. It's from 1937. Over 80 years ago. The author was part of a group that was trying to create deliberate out of body experiences. These people were serious occultists, I think. They really believed." He paused. "Not like you."

She raised her eyes to look at him without moving her head.

"Your stuff is a put on, Isabella. A show. That's not true of this group. They were serious. Why don't you read it and tell me what you think?"

"Where did you find it?" she asked.

"An old house, out of town. The owner had just died, and willed all the contents to the museum. Most of it was junk, but this—" he pointed to the diary, now closed and resting delicately on Isabella's open hand "—is a genuine find. She was the daughter of the author, I think."

"It was written the year after the second fire," said Isabella in a far off, dreamy kind of voice.

"That's right," said David. "That makes it one of the oldest surviving records in Bandon."

"Here's hoping it survives the next fire," she said cheerfully.

David shifted uneasily in his chair. There was a legend that Bandon had been cursed to burn three times. It had already been destroyed twice by devastating fires, but, so far, had managed to avoid a third destruction. Sometimes David felt that the whole town was waiting for that third time, and it gave him an eerie feeling. It was like they wanted it to happen, wanted to get it over with,

"You shouldn't tempt the fates," he said as she laughed and walked out the door.

As he approached his house he saw that the lights were out. Odd. Usually Betty had the living room light on. He walked up the step and turned the knob on the front door. It was locked. That was odd, too. Betty never locked the door. She refused to be a victim of fear, she had said many times.

David fumbled in his pocket for his keys, finally extracting them from the jumble of coins and paper scraps there. He unlocked the door and swung it open.

"Betty," he called. "I'm home, Babe."

He found her sitting in the kitchen chair. She turned her head and her face was as white as the moon. She spoke in a horrible, quiet monotone, like a person in a trance.

"I tried to call you," she said.

He could barely hear her, but the words penetrated.

"I was on the phone all day. What's wrong?" He walked toward her. Her face was stock still. Her lips were pressed tightly together and her hands, spread on the table in front of her, were trembling very slightly.

"I think there's something very wrong with me," she said even more quietly. She looked up at him. Her face was twisted into an expression David took to be fear. Her eyes were blank, open wide. He reached for her, intending to stroke her back.

"I love you," she said.

He was going to answer her automatically "I love you too," but he was startled into shocked silence by a long, loud scream. She held her hands up to her face and began clawing at her cheeks. She screamed and screamed. "Oh my God, David, it's in me, it's invaded."

He grabbed for her hands. She shook him away and began pacing the room. Her voice was a steady stream, low and insistent. "It's in me, David, it is, get rid of it, get rid of it. Oh my God I can feel it, I love you, David, help me help me get rid of it oh my God get rid of it I love you what's happening to me I love you get rid of it."

She pulled at her clothes and her whole body seemed twisted into a grotesque shape, almost like she was trying to rid herself of some cloying slime, rub her skin off of her body.

He reached for her again.

She jumped away and pressed her back against the kitchen counter.

"No," she screamed. "No. Stay away or it'll hurt you, too."

He felt an ominous tingling in his stomach, a lightness as adrenaline flooded his body. He lunged toward her and caught her in a bear hug as she twisted around in an attempt to escape him. He clasped his hands below her sternum and simply held her in place, whispering into her ear.

"I love you I love you, don't be afraid, it's only me, everything's all right, I love you Babe, I love you."

He stroked her hair and felt her relax in his grip. She started sobbing after a while and her whole body relaxed. He let her slip to the floor and knelt down beside her, still stroking her hair, still murmuring soft words.

"I tried to control it," she said haltingly, her words distorted by her crying. "I tried."

"Shhh, don't worry about it. It's over now."

Her body was convulsed with jerking sobs. "Call the doctor, David. I need help."

He held her for a while longer, then walked her to the couch and put a blanket over her. He got a fire going in the fireplace then sat beside her. They both stared at the flames for a time and felt the comfortable heat on their faces.

"It's very cozy," said Betty. "The fire." She took David's hand and squeezed it in her own. "It feels like a great cleansing, a wonderful warmth. It goes right to my bones. I think if I could disappear into that fire I would be okay. I would be happy." She leaned back and smiled, then took a deep breath and let it out.

He stood up. "I'll make that call now," he said.

She reached for him.

"Don't leave me. I'm afraid I'11 . . . lose myself again."

He patted her hand. "Don't worry," he said. "You're fine now. I just want to talk to Hill for a minute or two. I'll be right back."

He went to the phone and dialed Dr. Hill's number in Portland. When he answered, David explained, quickly and in gasps, what had happened.

"I don't know what I can do for her from here," he said. "Do you still have those tranquilizers left over from before?"

"What?" said David in a hiss.

"The tranquilizers."

He clenched his teeth, tried to remain calm. "She doesn't want to take those. Don't you understand? That's why we came to you."

"Just take it easy, David. I only meant for tonight, as an emergency measure, to help her relax."

"She is relaxed. Now. I want to know what's going on." David heard a long sigh at the other end of the line. "Look, bring her in tomorrow. Probably her homeopaths need to be changed. It sounds like she's had a reaction to a chemical or something. If she has another attack, get her to a hospital."

David heard a click and held the phone in his hand for a few seconds. Betty called from the couch. He went to her and stroked her until she fell asleep.

The drive to Portland took five hours. They left early in the morning and Hill was finished with Betty by two. He could find nothing different about her condition. He wrote out a prescription for tranquilizers and handed it to Betty without looking her in the eye. She took it from him with a limp hand, and turned to David with a blank and lost look on her face. David stared at Hill.

"You should move away," said Hill quietly. "Move somewhere dry and hot. It kills the Candida."

David felt an almost tangible hatred growing within him. They had trusted him and now he was letting them down.

Outside, in the cool November air, he felt a little better and suggested they make a day of it, have dinner, see a show, maybe even stay the night.

"No," said Betty. Her voice sounded weak, resigned, as though she had come to the end of a fight, and had lost. "I have to get back to Bandon. I need to be home."

Neither of them said much on the way home. He looked for the city of golden light but did not point it out to Betty when it appeared in the distance over the highway.

They were almost to the place where it usually vanished when Betty snapped up in her seat and pointed through the windshield. "There it is," she said brightly. "There's your city, David. Isn't it lovely?"

He hesitated. She had never shown the slightest interest in the city of golden light before. "Yes," he said. "It's very pretty." He glanced at her to see if she was teasing him, but she seemed truly interested. She smiled and looked at the image until it disappeared.

Isabella swept into David's office and placed the diary on his desk. "I stayed up all night reading it," she said.

David was collecting papers, files, and notes into a pile on his desk. He barely looked up to acknowledge Isabella. "I gave it to you a week ago," he said absently.

"I read every word. It's fascinating."

"I really don't have time now," he said. "I just came over to get some work. I'm way behind, and Betty's having trouble, I have to stay home with her."

Isabella hooded her eyes. "What sort of trouble?"

"She keeps dreaming about that damned city. Or mirage, or whatever it is. I'm telling you, she's obsessed, and I don't know what to do about it."

"Sound like anyone we know?"

David shook his head. "I haven't even *mentioned* it for days. It's all her now, and I don't like it. Mostly she Just sits by the fireplace and stares into the flames." He turned his eyes to an empty spot in front of him.

"Just give me five minutes to tell you about the diary," said Isabella. "It'll do you good to think about something else."

He looked at the booklet lying on his desk. He glanced up at Isabella. She looked like she was about to burst from restrained excitement. "I don't want to leave her alone."

"What can happen in five minutes?"

He looked at his watch, bit his lower lip. "Okay," he said, falling back into his chair. "Shoot."

She began pacing the room. "You were right. There were four of them and they were attempting an out of body experience, but whose?"

David shrugged. "I assumed one of themselves."

She shook her head. "Wrong."

"*All* of themselves?"

She laughed. "No. *Bandon*. They were trying to astrally project Bandon."

"What?"

She laughed again and brought her hands in tight fists under her chin. "Isn't it marvelous? They wanted to make Bandon fly."

David leaned back in his chair and searched Isabella's face. "You're kidding, right?"

"No. Listen." She took the diary from the desk and opened it and began reading. "'Tonight we try again. Yesterday we felt the town shake, we felt the soul of Bandon tremble a little, begin to move to the other plane of existence. I feel we are very close and only a slightly stronger push is necessary now. One of our group thinks that we need one more to succeed. But I believe we have enough mental energy with only the four of us. However, I did get more candles, to make a bigger light for us to focus on. We will save Bandon. We must. Tonight is the night.'"

She closed the volume carefully. David heard the covers creak and the paper crinkle.

"That was the last entry," said Isabella.

"But why?" asked David after a silence had passed.

"Simple," said Isabella. "He talks about it in here. They were trying to save Bandon from the third fire. They had just been through the second destruction, and were rebuilding the town. You can imagine how that curse was probably weighing very heavy on their minds. They didn't want the third fire to happen. All their rebuilding would have been wasted. So their plan was to pull out the soul of Bandon, send it adrift in some other dimension, and set fire to it, thereby fulfilling the prophecy in a harmless manner. Neat."

David pondered this for a moment.

"So that means," he said slowly, "that there is an image of Bandon in some other dimension, and it is . . .*burning*?"

Isabella nodded.

"What—" David cleared his throat. A realization was slowly dawning on him. "What do you think it would look like?"

"I don't know," she said, "Why? Does it matter?"

David felt as though he were swimming in a thick fog. Betty, home alone, staring into the fireplace, thinking of the city of golden light, thinking about Bandon, about her home. A hot feeling of desperation invaded his body. He stood up, hitting the edge of his desk and sending shooting pains through his thigh.

"David? What is it?"

He brushed past her and ran out the door. He took the stairs two at a time, nearly falling twice. At the exit the wind from a gathering storm hit him square in the face with a spray of droplets. Cold and wet, cold and wet. Betty hated this weather. It was killing her. He heard Isabella's footsteps banging down the stairs behind him as he bolted from the door to the car. He got in the driver's seat and started the engine.

Isabella was pounding on the passenger's window. He leaned across and opened the door for her. She jumped inside as the oar lurched away from the curb.

"David, what's wrong?" she said.

He glanced at her. Her face was wet, her eyes were screwed up with concern.

"Betty's been talking about the mirage for days. She dreams about it like it was a place, like it was a place she wanted to go to."

"So? You've always talked about it like it was a place, a magical city."

"She calls it 'home.'"

He took a hand from the steering wheel and wiped his face.

"But she was born here," said Isabella. "She's always called Bandon her only home."

"Only now we know there's another Bandon."

Isabella looked at him. "You don't mean the diary?"

"That's exactly what I mean."

"But you don't believe any of that, do you?"

"I have to believe it. I've seen it. I've seen the burning soul of Bandon."

David pulled into the driveway and they both got out of the car before it stopped completely. He ran up the walk, with Isabella close behind him, and burst through the doorway."

"Betty!" he called. "Betty!"

No answer.

He ran to the living room. She was lying on her side, in front of the fireplace, as though she had been sitting and then fell over. The fire had died out. There were only a couple of glowing orange embers remaining.

He knelt down beside her. "Betty?" He brushed a strand of hair away from her face. Her cheek felt hot, almost too hot to touch.

"I have to go home," said Betty in a barely audible whisper. "Where it's dry . . . and hot . . . where I can be—happy."

He lifted her and held her as she slipped away into what seemed a deep sleep. He shook her by the shoulders.

Isabella leaned over him. "She's contacted the soul of Bandon," she said. "David, she thinks she's found her salvation, but I'm afraid—"

David held Betty, rocking her in his arms. She was so hot. It seemed to come up from deep inside her, the heat, as though the fireplace had transferred its flames to her body.

"Help me get her to the shower," he said to Isabella. "We have to cool her down."

David felt his own heart race as they each took an end of Betty, Isabella her arms, David her legs, and half carried, half dragged her into the bathtub. They sat her up and David aimed the shower head at her and turned on the water.

Betty seemed completely oblivious to what was happening. She sat with her head tilted to one side and pressed against the tiles of the bathroom wall. Her hair stuck to her head and water streamed over her body.

David put a hand on her forehead and felt her arms and cheeks.

"She's still hot," he said. "It's like she is burning."

"I'll go call a doctor," said Isabella.

"No," said David. "Go into the kitchen and bring back a glass."

"But—"

"We have to help her. Go, now."

Isabella stared at him for a beat, then bolted down the hall. David turned off the water and held Betty's hand. He was trembling with cold and panic. Isabella returned, breathless, with a drinking glass in her hand.

"How did they do it?" he said. "How did they make Bandon fly?"

"David, I—"

"She's gone," said David simply. "Betty's gone to the burning image of Bandon. We have to get her back."

Isabella wrung her hands and wiped tears from her eyes. Betty was slumped beside them.

David filled the glass with tap water and set it carefully on the floor. Isabella watched him dumbly.

"How, Isabella? There was something about candles. Tell me."

Her eyes were wide, her mouth slightly open. "They got in a circle," she said. "Held hands. Then they stared at the candle flames and they concentrated on Bandon's soul. They visualized the soul until they had a clear picture of—David, this is insane, this can't work."

He pressed gently on her shoulder, guiding her to a kneeling position on the floor. He put Betty's hand in Isabella's and then took Betty's other hand in his.

"Stare at the glass," he said to Isabella. "Concentrate on Betty. This is the real thing. No more games, no more tricks. We have to get her back."

Isabella's hands tensed. David gripped Betty's hand tighter.

"Even if it really did work," said Isabella, "there were four of them. And they were trying to save their town."

"I'm trying to save my wife," said David quietly.

Isabella seemed surprised. She glanced at Betty, then back at David. She nodded and looked down at the glass of water.

David stared at the rippling surface where the ceiling light was reflected on each wave like a tiny flame.

He listened to water drip from the shower head, but presently he seemed to be alone with the liquid in the glass. There was no other sound, no other motion anywhere in his existence. He felt absorbed by it, engulfed in its welcome softness.

The fog that had encumbered him at the museum cleared away completely and his mind knew only the awful warmth in Betty's hand and the wonderful comfort of the water.

Now he seemed to be inside the glass and it had grown to an enormous size, filling the universe around him. He looked around himself and saw buildings, painted in iridescent orange and red and yellow, some of them falling, crashing in on themselves.

The light filtering through the water hurt his eyes with its intensity and it was everywhere, all around him, engulfing him in some great destructive force. He closed his eyes, but the light still penetrated. He released Betty's hand and put his own to his face.

Betty. She was gone. He had lost the sense of her. The light and the heat seared his eyes. He felt that his flesh was coming off his bones in great globs, his hair felt as though it were frazzling away.

The water was useless in its glass. He had to use it to douse these flames. He looked around wildly but could not see it.

He lifted his eyes and tried to make out some detail. He saw her. He saw Betty trapped in a falling building. She had her hands to the sides of her face and she was screaming. A gray string of slime emerged from her open mouth like a tentacle.

David felt a rush of horror and revulsion wash over him. The tentacle snaked out and was immediately vaporized by the flame. Another slimy tentacle followed the first, and another after that, each one seemed larger than the one before, and more grotesque, with stringy bits of slime hanging from them like lengths of entrails and mucus.

Betty was ridding her body of her energy-sucking monster. As each section of the monster emerged, it was eaten by the flames.

Finally Betty closed her mouth and looked across the streets of flame to David. He called to her. She did not seem to hear him. There was a blank look on her face, then an expression of pain and pleading. Her eyes grew wide. David called her name again and looked around wildly. What was she frightened of?

Then he saw the flame at her feet. The fire had finished with the monster and was now moving on to the host. David's mind became confused. He knew he had to get to Betty to save her from the fire, but he could not move, as much as he tried, his legs simply ran in place. He needed some help. A distant level of his mind seemed to remember that he was still in the bathroom at home.

He reached out his hand.

"Here." Isabella's voice from somewhere he could not imagine.

He grasped, and held a drinking glass in his hand. With all the power he could summon up from his soul, he hurled the water it contained in Betty's direction.

At first nothing happened. Betty's eyes were still wide. A flame was still crawling up her leg. David felt despair.

Then a raindrop landed on his nose.

He looked up. The sky, through the orange iridescence, was opening up and pouring out a bounty of water, cool quenching rain. In a few seconds the flames were doused. The ruins of Bandon were around him, black, steaming, dead. He stretched out his hand. Magically, Betty was there to grasp it. The rain came down very hard. It streamed over his body, down Betty's face. He thought the rain would never end.

"I don't understand it," said Dr. Hill. "The Candida. It's completely gone."

They were in his office in Portland. Betty seemed bright, radiant, happier than David had seen her in years. Isabella sat beside her and grinned foolishly.

"We knew it would be," said David.

"But how?" said Hill

"We moved," said Betty. "Temporarily."

They all three burst out laughing. Hill looked puzzled.

"Aside from that nasty burn on your foot, there isn't a thing the matter with you, and that'll heal nicely within a few weeks." He stood up and extended his hand to Betty. "Congratulations," he said. "It's the most complete recovery I've ever seen."

Betty, David and Isabella left Hill's office and piled into David's car.

"I'm glad I was here," said Isabella. "Just to see the expression on his face was worth the trip."

David nodded. "If he only knew how we did it, it would revolutionize medicine, wouldn't it?"

Later, on the way home, they all strained their eyes looking for the city of golden light, but none of them could find it in the distance where it usually sat silently waiting.

"What happened?" said Betty. "Is it gone?"

David drove on for a few miles. Then he had a thought. He stopped the car at the side of the road and turned off the engine. They all got out and David put a finger to his lips. "Shhh." he said. "Listen."

From the direction of the city of golden light they heard the unmistakable sound of a soothing, steady rain.

Comfort Food

Even mermaids and mermen like a good basket of fries now and then.

Which is why the first thing I did when I swam out of the Pacific Ocean and up onto the beach at Lincoln City, Oregon, was to pick off the strings of kelp from my hair, shake the water off my scales until they turned into legs, and walk in the direction of The Clam Grotto.

I was pretty sure I was going to find LeeAnne there. And if I didn't, I was pretty sure I was going to find someone who knew where she was.

If you don't know The Clam Grotto you're missing an experience. The place sits on the bay at the south end of town. You don't see it from the highway, you have to get off the main drag and head to the water. When you can't go any further without getting sopping wet, you've found the Grotto. The crowds of diners, who often can't fit in the thirty or so tables they've got strung out along the picture windows with an awesome view of the ocean, tells you you've found a place everyone wants to be at.

I came from the other direction, of course, but the Grotto is just as famous in my world. Only thing is, my people show up only after the Grotto closes to the regular customers: the tourists and the locals.

LeeAnne and me, we got married I don't know how many centuries ago. We've had our ups and downs just like any couple. But we're merfolk, know what I mean?

Half fish, half human. That leads to conflict. Like this latest thing where LeeAnne made it clear she thought I didn't understand her because I wasn't spending much time with her, what with all my swimming around collecting old sea shells.

It's a hobby of mine. What's the big deal? So I clicked at her that of course I didn't understand her, she was a mermaid, which meant *no one* could understand her and she clicked right back that she understood me perfectly even though I was a merman. At which point I clicked back to her that if she didn't like me the way I am then why didn't she leave and she clicked okay, I'll leave.

So she did.

Three days ago.

The first day, I thought: fine. Good riddance. Who needs her?

The second day, I kind of missed the salmon smell of her and the way her tail drew curves in the water in the most graceful and beautiful way, like she was an artist painting in water.

The third day, I was mentally slapping myself, wondering what kind of a jerk could kick out the only woman he ever loved.

Me, that's what kind.

So I waited until the sun dropped into the blue and headed over to Lincoln City.

Lincoln City mostly shuts down about 9 p.m. That's our time. Along about two or three hours later, if you're down on the beach, you might see us, the merfolk and the selkies, come up through the surf and head for a good meal at the Clam Grotto.

There are lots of clam chowder joints on the coast. You can't take three steps in this town, or any town within a hundred miles, without stepping on the shells that these eateries discard on an hourly basis. Tourists come to the ocean and expect to find clam chowder so places like the Grotto give it to them. And clam chowder is amazingly good.

Especially the way the Clam Grotto does it.

I've gotta say, even though I was missing my true love, and sick that she ran off because of me, my mouth was watering thinking of that clam chowder.

There was a heavy red moon that night. It turned the beach into a rough sculpture of glowing silver. The peaks of the sand looked like frozen waves. It went with the way my heart felt: cold and heavy.

But I kept going.

LeeAnne and I sometimes went to the Grotto together. The regular staff at the Grotto, the ones you see when you go there during the day, I'm sure they're friendly and polite and everything, but the night crew. Well. If you want to see friendly, walk in my flippers some night.

You step into the Clam Grotto and first thing that hits you is all the blue. It's like they took the ocean and plastered it up on the walls. You think blue is a sad color? Not at the Grotto. Everything about the Grotto is happy. From the smiling waitresses who slap you on the back as you come in, to the pictures behind the counter of merpeople smiling and laughing while sitting at a table at the Grotto.

I step into the restaurant, all dim, but with enough light that I see merpeople sitting on clunky wooden benches at round tables. I look down to the far end and I see LeeAnne.

She's got her curly red hair slinking down her back, and her legs are crossed under her bench and she's got a fry halfway up to her mouth and she's giggling.

I'm ready to call her name and sit next to her and giggle right along with her, so I start walking in her direction, but then I see she's not alone at her table.

There's a—how shall I put this?—*muscular* merman on the bench next to her. He's got this crown of curly blond hair and his skin is the color of copper, and he's leaning pretty close to LeeAnne. I mean, close enough that he probably knows what kind of shell she's got tattooed at the base of her neck. (It's mussel. I put the ink there.)

I was ready, right there, to turn around, wade into the ocean until my legs turned back into flippers, and be done with the both of them.

But I was at the Grotto. Things always turned out okay at the Grotto.

I hoped.

I walked up to copper man and put my hand on his shoulder.

He and LeeAnne stopped giggling.

LeeAnne looked up at me with a "what the—" kind of look and me, just as casual as can be, I reached across her friend's ample chest and dipped my finger into his bowl of clam chowder and brought it up to my mouth and licked my finger real loud. Enough for everyone in the place to hear it.

Things got deep sea quiet in a hurry. Dozens of eyes were looking at me.

Copper man's hue turned a definite shade of red, like something you'd expect to see in a boiled lobster.

LeeAnne hit my arm.

I didn't look at her. All my attention was on copper man.

Except, I have to say, I liked the taste of that clam chowder. Something about the creaminess of it, the way it filled my mouth. Made me think this was going to be a good night. It settled me right down.

The thing about really good clam chowder, I mean world class first rate clam chowder, is that you get the earthiness from the cream, the farm goodness, like you'd been hanging out with the cows, working the land. Then at the same time you get these bits of clam and you're plunged right into the sea. You got land and sea in the same mouthful. You got the contradictions of the planet in harmony on your tongue. That's the joy of clam chowder. That's what people come back for again and again.

When I got just about all I could get of the chowder off my finger, I made like I was looking around for a napkin, patting my chest and my sides and staring blankly at nothing. Then I held my finger up in the air and then I put it down on copper man's hair and just kind of rolled it around in his curls until it was good and dry.

LeeAnne gasped. I couldn't tell if she was shocked or pleased. I didn't have time to ask her, because as soon as I cleaned my finger in his hair, copper man stood up and kicked his bench to one side and turned around and put his face right up to mine.

He had to bend down a little to do it.

"You got a problem, *friend*," he said.

"No problem," I said.

Well, actually it was more like: "N-n-no pr-pr-prob. Lem." Which didn't help convey the image I wanted to give, that I was a tough guy. I knew I wasn't a tough guy. Everyone in the Grotto knew it too. I was just a shlub who wanted his beautiful wife back and if he couldn't get her back then he didn't mind dying in the attempt.

Well, maybe I minded a little.

Copper man couldn't pummel me right there in front of LeeAnne. That would make him look bad, even though I could tell it was what he wanted to do with every waterlogged bone in his body.

I didn't blame him. I *wanted* him to think that. In the long run, it made me look better in LeeAnne's eyes.

So copper man takes one step back and puts his chin in his hand and looks me over. Studies me.

I'm still not looking at LeeAnne. I *can't*, much as I want to. I can't break my concentration.

Then copper man laughs at me. He sticks out his finger, points at my chest and laughs.

Not just a polite laugh, either, but a real belly roller, like he just heard the funniest joke ever spoken or clicked anywhere.

So I lean over and bite his finger. Nearly take the tip of it clean off. It tasted like rotten fish. Seriously. The kind you leave under a rock for a long time and don't remember is there and then when you roll over the rock the stench of it gags you and you have to aerate the sea around it for days just to get rid of the taste of it in the water. That kind of rotten.

There was blood.

Not a lot. Barely a trickle, really, but I broke some skin and the salt of it slid onto my tongue and it was just about then, I suspect, that he saw red.

He pulled his finger back. The nail scraped against my teeth. The finger joined his other fingers and curled into a fist, which pulled back, way back, until it looked like it was a mile away, and then it came straight at me.

I was ready to live with a broken nose, face, cheekbone, eye socket, and teeth for the rest of my life.

Only LeeAnne, my sweet LeeAnne, came to my rescue.

While copper man was about to smash me, LeeAnne stood up from her bench and pushed me to one side.

She saved me. More or less. I fell over and ended up sprawled on the floor, with sand and dirt imprinting itself on my palms.

I wanted to get up. I moved to get up, but it was like I was still in the ocean. I moved slower than an outgoing tide.

I pushed myself up and just about then the rest of the restaurant, all the sea creatures that had come to the Clam Grotto for a night of fine dining, they all descended on copper man.

Now I don't delude myself into thinking they had any sympathy for me. That would be asking for quite a lot, since I had pretty much started the altercation, but I'm darned sure they were concerned for LeeAnne. They ran over from their tables and surrounded her in a protective hub, keeping her safe from copper man's fist. Not that he *wanted* to hit her, but he could have hit her by accident and hardly even know it.

That's how *brutish* the guy was. Really. Off the scale.

So anyway, they hustle LeeAnne away, down the row of tables next to the picture window, and past the pile of yellow shell buckets they put out on tables for people to throw their shells into, out the front door, down the wooden steps, across the beach sand, and back into the water.

So fast I hardly had time to see who they all were. They moved like they were fish in water, even before they *got* to the water.

I scrambled up and was ready to go after them.

Something grabbed my hair.

Or, rather, some*one*.

"Where do you think you're going?" said copper man. "We have a score to settle."

"Nothing to settle," I said. "You win." I grabbed his hand, which had a hold of my hair and tried to yank it off. It wasn't yanking. It wasn't moving. The dude was *strong*.

"Not yet I haven't," he said. He turned me around. I was on the tips of my toes. He held me like I was a puppet and my hair was the strings.

"Can't we just forget the whole thing? A misunderstanding, don't you think?"

"You scared off my date."

"She's my wife."

"Not my problem. Tonight she was *my* date."

"Yeah, but even when she was your date, she was still my wife."

I was trying to buy time. Trying to get him to see things my way. And if he didn't, I had a plan. Not a big plan, but a plan. Maybe it would be enough.

"If she's so into you," he said, "what was she doing with me? She told me you're a piece of slimy seaweed. Nothing more."

Hard for me to believe LeeAnne would say that about me, but okay.

"That may be," I said, "but I'm *her* slimy piece of seaweed. We have a history."

All this time he was pulling up on my hair, making me extend my legs, which I'm not that used to. I only have legs when I'm on land and I don't get up on land all that much.

One of the things we don't have in the ocean is knees. So that means I don't always know how to use them. Sometimes, when I have my land legs, I forget how to walk.

But I think by that time of the evening I had pretty much gained sufficient mastery of them to be able to do what I needed to do.

"You make me sick," he said.

"Not as sick as this will," I said, and planted one foot on the floor as firmly as possible, then lifted my other foot as fast as I possibly could up and toward him so that my knee connected in the most strategic spot on a male's body.

The man released my hair. His eyes bulged out and his hands went straight down to his crotch and he doubled over.

I ended up on both feet, standing over him.

I had a good mind to knee him in the face, but kept my cool. No reason to hit him while he was down.

And he went down. Hard.

He keeled over like a waterlogged vessel and ended up curled like a shrimp on the floor, with his hands still cradling his manhood.

I'd like to report that I stayed to make sure he was okay. But I didn't. I'd even like to tell you that I got him some ice for his injury, but I didn't do that either. I figured he got what he deserved.

I turned and ran to the exit and down on the beach. I followed the tracks of LeeAnne's protective shell and headed into the water.

The ocean took me in like she missed me. I followed the scent of LeeAnne.

Salmon smell, didn't I say? No one else smells like her. I smell that gorgeous fish odor and I'm alive again. I want nothing more than to bury myself in in. Plunge my flippers into it. Push my nose into it. Fill my lungs with it.

I swam and swam.

Where was she? I could smell her, she had to be around.

I clicked her name, broadcasting on a far range frequency. I turned up my receptors. I strained to hear something.

No answer. Nothing.

Dammit dammit dammit. Where did they take her?

I swam in wild circles, then I picked up something else. Nothing big, but definitely different.

Oily smell. Kind of meaty in a strange way, but not quite.

I knew that smell.

I swam toward it. I smelled that same smell every time we went to the Clam Grotto because every time we went to the Clam Grotto LeeAnne always ordered a basket of fries.

Always.

I heard my name clicked at me.

I turned around.

"What took you so long?" LeeAnne clicked.

The rich and comforting odor of french fries trailed away from her mouth and came snaking into my nose. I took it in with a kind of gratitude I didn't know I had in me.

She floated behind a stand of kelp, looking out at me through the floating fronds.

"I had some business to take care of," I clicked.

"You mean that waiter?" she clicked.

"Copper man is a waiter?"

She nodded. "You didn't hurt him too bad, did you?"

"Um," I clicked.

"Should we go back and check on him?"

"He can take care of himself," I clicked.

She swam over next to me. There was that salmon smell again. I shivered and my scales rustled.

"I expect you're right," she said.

Getting it Right

"My father died," I told my grief group. "He taught me about cars. Even though I didn't care about cars."

There were nine of us in the basement of the church. We all displayed haunted looks on our faces. We sat in chairs in a circle. The floor was tiled with alternating black and white squares, like an infinite checkerboard. Alice, whose baby died, sat across from me and was clearly impatient with my story. I could see it as soon as I opened my mouth.

The ceiling above us was tiled with white squares, each one speckled with varying sizes of holes and stained brown in one corner where it looked like water had once leaked from the floor above where services were held on Sunday mornings and Wednesday nights. To get to this basement room we all had to descend some dark steps from the sidewalk outside and pull back a heavy gray door, like we were entering a bomb shelter. Maybe it was a bomb shelter. Or had been. Did churches have bomb shelters? It seemed plausible.

"Parents are supposed to die before you," said Alice. "What are you even doing here, Gary? You don't have grief. My baby died when she was four months old. Four months. *That's* grief."

The group was run by a retired psychologist. She did this because—well, I guess because she wanted to keep her nose in other people's business. Or so it seemed to me.

"Alice," she said, "Gary has the floor. We need to let him finish. We owe him the courtesy of listening to the details of his grief."

No one said anything. Not me. Not Alice. No one.

I cleared my throat. Alice was far more compelling than I was. She had silenced the room with her story of grief, and then again with her comment about my story. I wasn't able to do that. While I tried saying something about my father, people fidgeted and bounced their legs up and down. Nervousness permeated the group like a fog.

"Sorry," said Alice, but she didn't mean it. I could tell. Everyone could.

I got up.

"Gary?" said the retired psychologist.

"I don't want to be here anymore," I said.

"Please," she said. "We all want to listen."

No, they didn't.

I fled the room. Ran up the stairs. The evening was dark and cold. A west wind was coming in off the Pacific. It blew across the dunes on the Oregon coast, howled up and over the coast range, and descended into the streets of Portland where it snaked past my collar and chilled my chest and my arms. I pulled my jacket tighter around my throat.

I stood next to the stone walls of the church. Heard the door open at the bottom of the steps.

The psychologist's voice. "Gary? Are you there?"

I ran from the words.

My grief was not earned, was it? Alice was right. Parents died. That was the way the world worked.

I had not even wanted to go to a grief group. But people recommended it. Linda, my ex-wife, said it would do me good. She went to one after we divorced.

"I wasn't dead," I said.

"Doesn't matter," she said. "Something died. We didn't. But *something* did. Our marriage. Our bond. Our life. Something. I felt grief. It was good to share it with someone. You must have felt it too."

She told me this at my father's memorial. I liked that she came. I thought it was a lovely gesture. Made me want to love her again. Or so I thought. Then I realized I had never really stopped loving her. Which made the memorial seem even harder. I should have been feeling sad, but I was feeling love. I didn't know if that was normal or not.

"I always liked your father," said Linda. "He was funny."

"That's what you used to say about me."

"I'm pretty sure you got it from him," she said. "Then it went away."

Old issues. We didn't need to chew on those again. And we didn't. After the memorial I asked Linda if she would come have coffee with me.

She said she couldn't. What she meant was she shouldn't. Or didn't want to. No reason to make things seem normal when they weren't.

My mother, who had remarried and moved across the country, came to the memorial too.

We didn't have much of a relationship. I talked to her occasionally. I think she thought I was too much like my father to spend much time with me, even though I was her son. This bothered me for a while, then it felt like the way the world was.

At the memorial we hugged. I wept in her arms, but it didn't help. Didn't mend anything.

"You want to come back with me for a few days?" she asked.

I shook my head. "No."

"Well, I can't stay here," she said. "I have a job and a family. A life in Boston. I'm happy. You should visit."

I said I would, but we both knew I wouldn't.

My father killed a man. It was on purpose. I'm not saying he was a killer. Even though he killed.

It's complicated. I wanted to tell the grief group how complicated it was. But all I told them was that I missed the times when I was a kid. A teen. That's when he would tell me about cars. How they worked. What the pistons did. How the fuel injector got the combustion going. How the brakes needed maintenance. How to change the spark plugs and oil in a car. He loved doing anything with cars. Anything.

He owned a car repair place. I went to it a few times. He wanted me to work there. Learn the business. Eventually take it over. That wasn't for me. I didn't care about cars. Never did.

He kept the business. Loved his cars more than his family, I think. I left home. Got married. Grew older. My father and mother split. He spent even more time at the garage.

I would visit him now and then. After Linda and I divorced I spent a lot of time with him. Two divorced guys lamenting the deal life had given us. But then that petered out and we had our separate lives again.

He was working late one night when a guy broke into the shop. No one knows what he was trying to steal. Money? There wasn't much there. Parts? Easier ways to get those. Could be he was just a stupid thief. Definitely not a professional, my father told me later. Didn't know what he was doing.

He carried an aluminum bat. He threatened my father, who would have none of it. My father picked up a heavy wrench and advanced on the guy. Told him to get out. But the guy didn't. He lunged at my father. My father struck him on the head. Hard. He told me later he wanted to kill the guy. Then he regretted hitting him as hard as he did. He didn't have to. He just wanted to. That troubled him a lot. Made him question who he was.

The guy went down. Dead before he hit the floor, was how the district attorney put it during the trial.

My father was protecting himself and his business, but he used too much force. Was too zealous. He ended up getting convicted for manslaughter.

Got seven years in prison. I went to see him a few times. He killed himself halfway through the second year of his sentence.

I never got to that part at the grief group, the fact that my father killed himself. Just said he died. I wondered what people thought. I don't know what Alice thought. Maybe that he died of some illness. Or an accident. But suicide is different. I should have said that. Should have told them right up front. "My father killed himself." But it seemed like cheating. Like I had a fake ace up my sleeve. If I threw it out there, it would trump everything. A parent that kills himself. That's got to be big, right? Especially a parent that had also killed a guy himself. That's even bigger, isn't it? Having a convicted killer in your family that then kills himself?

I didn't know. Other people in the grief group, they talked before me. Michael's wife died in a house fire. That was pretty bad. Alice, I've already said. Baby died of SIDS. Ghastly. Another woman, Rose, her daughter was killed by her son-in-law. She cried as she told us that she had her suspicions about him. Before her daughter married, she knew something was wrong with the guy. Knew something bad was going to happen.

Even the retired psychologist didn't have much to say about that. What was there to say? Rose told us she wished she had killed the guy before he ever married her daughter. She would gladly have gone to prison for life for her daughter. Gladly.

So then I spoke. "My father died," I said. "He used to teach me about cars."

Even as I said it, it felt somehow small. I knew I could have made it bigger. Knew I could have upped the ante.

But I didn't.

After I ran away, unwilling to hear anything more from Alice, or the psychologist, I called Linda. Standing there in the streets of downtown Portland, the air getting colder, the wind starting to carry drops of rain like the sky was spitting on me, I tapped her number into the phone and waited while it rang.

"Hello?"

"It's Gary."

"Gary," she said. "What's wrong?"

"Everything," I said. "Why did we split? Do you ever wonder?"

"I can't talk about this anymore," she said. "I'm going to hang up."

"My father killed himself," I said.

"I know that, Gary. I was at the memorial, remember? Why are you calling?"

"It's cold."

"I'm really going to hang up now."

"I went to the grief group."

Silence.

"Linda?"

"And?"

"It didn't go so well. I ran out of there. They said I shouldn't be there."

"Gary," she said. "That's hard to believe. What happened?"

I told her. I could talk to her. Even on the phone, with me shivering, the city taking on splats of rain, me unsure what to say, I could still talk to Linda.

My father picked a particularly odd way to die. I suppose there aren't a lot of options in prison. Ingenuity was the order of the day. His cell was narrow, with a concrete floor. According to the investigating detective, my father took the bedding off his cot and set it aside. Then he upended the bare metal frame of the cot and leaned it against the wall. He stood next to the cot so the metal bar that curved up to form a kind of headboard was against his neck.

How long did he stand there like that? It was impossible to tell. Maybe a second. Maybe an hour. Was he ready to die? Or did he have to talk himself into it, remind himself of the misery his life was and what he had done to the guy who broke into his garage? He felt bad about that. He told me that more than once.

Eventually, or instantly, he made his decision. He pulled the cot close to his body and let himself fall back in a swift arc onto the concrete floor. His head struck the floor hard enough to crack his skull. He lost consciousness.

The metal bar of the cot followed a split second later and put enough pressure on his windpipe to collapse it.

He stopped breathing soon after that. Prison officials found his body the next morning.

My father was good with mechanical things. He knew the vulnerability of machinery and of human skulls. He always told me, with cars, never guess. Always troubleshoot. Figure out what needs doing and do it right the first time.

Like he did with the intruder. One blow was all it took. Well aimed.

A few days after I ran out of the grief group, I got a call from an unknown number. Going against my usual instinct, I didn't let it go to message and instead tapped on the screen.

"This is Gary," I said.

A female voice spoke. "You the son of the guy who killed himself in prison?"

I hesitated. "Who is this?"

"I'm the sister of the guy your father killed. I just want you to know I'm glad your father is dead. Couldn't have happened to a nicer guy. You have a good day, now."

Then she hung up.

I held the phone for a long time. My hand was shaking. I felt a pressure in my skull, like the contents wanted to escape and couldn't. My ears were hot. My face felt like it was blood red.

I called the number back, but there was no answer and no voice mail. I learned later it was a burner phone. The woman must have bought it just to tell me what she had to tell me.

I have to admit, I kind of admired that. The effort it took to do such a thing. The need to let me know what she thought. It felt very healthy. She knew how to handle her grief. I wished I had that kind of instinct.

Of course I had dreams of my father. Of course I did. He was covered in grease. Or blood. Sometimes both. Sometimes I couldn't tell which.

I had waking dreams too. I'd see him, the back of him, going around a corner. I knew he wasn't there. It was a trick of my mind. Some motion made me think of him. Or made me imagine him. That's how ghosts were made, after all. The grief of loss turns the brain into an innovator.

I followed the apparition down the hall of my house to the window at the end, which was closed up tight. I stood at the window and looked down to the grass. I half expected to see footprints there, but I didn't. Also expected, or hoped, to see drops of blood. That would have meant he *had* been there.

But nothing of that sort appeared. It was just a normal window with normal grass on the ground on the other side of it. It wasn't a portal to anything. Was not a way for me to get back my feeling of things being okay. Things being normal.

Would the unsettling sensation in my stomach ever go away? Should it?

My mother called. She begged me to come to Boston. "Just for a few days, Gary. You need to have someone around you who loves you. You shouldn't be alone."

"Mom," I said, "I don't want to. I don't want to go to Boston."

"It's something new, Gary. I'll come out to Portland. We can fly back together. What do you say?"

All I could think of was my father. That he was in my house. I needed to stay where I was. Needed to be there if he showed up.

"I love you Mom," I said.

"That's not enough, Gary," she told me. "You need to be close to me. That's what counts. For real. If not me, then someone else."

I knew she was right, but, somehow, it felt like it didn't matter.

I went back to the grief group. Alice was still there. She acknowledged me as I sat down. It was just a slight raising of her eyebrows, as much surprise as greeting, but at least it was something.

The retired psychologist expressed her admiration for me deciding to return.

"You won't regret it," she said. "We've made a lot of progress in the weeks you've been gone. We would like you to be part of it."

Michael was gone. Rose was still there. I wondered if she still felt the need to kill her son-in-law. Should I ask? I wanted to. I wanted to tell her that it might actually be easier for her. She had a target she could fantasize about dispatching. I didn't. The guy who killed my father was my father.

"Let's let Gary start," said Alice.

"I don't know," I said. "I've been out of it for a while."

"You came back," said the psychologist.

"Yes," I said.

"There must be a reason."

I licked my lips. They remained dry. I hadn't got it right the first time. I thought about what I was going to say. Then I told them.

"My father killed a guy," I said. "Then he killed himself."

The room went silent.

Then I kept talking.

Giant Office Supplies

After my husband Jeff died, I went through the requisite grieving process. I put my life back together, reconnected with lost friends, developed new interests, *grew* as a person, etcetera etcetera, yadda yadda yadda.

I don't mean to diminish the tragedy, but it was my tragedy. Jeff had gone through a red light and been hit by a truck coming through the intersection. Stupid thing. But there it was. One mistake and his life was instantly over. No pain, no fuss.

Left me high and dry, though. I hated him for that mistake for a long time. But I got past it. Had to, for my own sanity.

I found a job at a graphic design firm in Seattle. I moved out of our house, too big for little old me, and found an apartment close to work in a good neighborhood. After a while I grew sick of people expressing their sympathy to me. Jeff was dead. It was sad. That had been established long ago. Okay. Let's move on from that, shall we?

Only Jeff, my dear sweet Jeff, he had other ideas. About three years after his untimely demise, he began to appear in my dreams on a regular basis. Three or four times a week. In each one, he piloted a sailboat in Puget Sound, wind in his hair and his hand on the tiller as the sails rippled with that *snap-snap* sound he loved so much. All that was fine. Jeff loved to sail and I loved going with him. We had some of our best times on the sound when the two of us sailed aimlessly through the San Juan Islands on lazy summer afternoons and the spray doused me with sea water and the hull slapped the waves.

I think I could have had those dreams for the rest of my life and been deliriously happy.

Except they changed.

Along about the third month of those great dreams, Jeff stood up from the tiller, turned towards me, grabbed his left arm, and clutched at his chest. He looked puzzled, then scared and pained. The sailboat rocked from starboard to port. I tried to get up, but I couldn't. He fell to his knees, clawed at his chest, looked at me with this incredible agony on his face, and then he slid off the deck and into the water. I screamed. I tried to get to him, but I couldn't move. The sails dropped from their masts and covered me. I couldn't breathe. I fought for air. Gasped for it.

The nightmare woke me up and I found myself wrapped in a sheet, sweat pooled on my skin, and seized by a vertiginous sensation like I was about to slide off the edge of the bed into the ocean of my carpet. My heart beat like crazy. I *heard* it.

That first time, I thought it was a passing thing. Everyone had nightmares at one time or another. No big deal. I didn't go back to bed that night, though. Didn't dare.

Instead, I thought about Jeff's death. His *real* death, not the one in my dream. I wondered why he was on a sailboat in my dream. Did he want to die in the water? Was that better than getting crushed in a car? And why was he showing heart attack? There was never anything wrong with Jeff's heart. He had been as healthy as any man his age. Probably more than most.

At work the next day I dragged my ass around like I was a short timer. One night of almost no sleep wiped me out. I tried to put the dream out of my mind.

Only the next night it came back. Exact same scenario: Jeff felled by a heart attack, slipped into the ocean while I tried to move to help him but could not.

It woke me up, just like the first time. Another night of no sleep. Things went on like that for a couple of weeks. That's when Linda, my friend at work, told me about Ziggy. "He's a therapist and his name is Sigmund," she said. "If you can believe that. I just call him Ziggy. He's got some—slightly *peculiar*—methods. But they work."

I made an appointment and went to Ziggy's building and rode the elevator up to his floor, which harbored a maze of hallways. I felt like a mouse looking for that elusive bit of cheese as I navigated the numerous and confusing turns and corners. When I got to his lair, he greeted me at the door. He stood over six feet tall, and he took up his space. Filled it. It seemed like there was no way even a tiny ray of light could fit between him and the door frame. "Miss Jenkins, is it?"

I nodded, too intimidated to say anything. He bowed and stepped aside and I slipped by him into a room that looked way too small for him. Ziggy needed an expansive arena, and this wasn't it. The ceiling was too low and the walls, lined with bookshelves, looked like they might cave in on us.

Sigmund in Seattle.

He did have a nice view of Puget Sound from his lofty window. I noticed the outsized office supplies immediately.

He had a giant paper clip on his wall. Two feet long. What good is a paper clip that big? Who has paper so large that they would need a paper clip of such gargantuan proportions to keep the pages together? No one. Not even, I guessed, Ziggy. So it must have been some kind of odd art piece.

Except he also had big pencils. Ziggy owned several six foot long pencils. I saw them propped up in a corner of his office, like wizard wands waiting to be taken out for a stretch of spellcraft. I imagined Ziggy standing on a mountain and waving one of those giant pencils over an invading army and thundering them back to where they came from with some heavy duty mojo blasted from the sharpened lead: rainbow-colored lightning bolts simultaneously aimed at each would-be invading soldier.

He gave me confidence, is what I'm saying. Right away.

"You treating a giant or something?" I said, indicating the eraser, big as a brick, on one corner of his desk.

Ziggy smiled and took my coat and hung it up on a rack with a delicate motion, like he was tucking a child into bed. I think I fell in love with him on the spot.

Then he showed me to a comfortable chair, and sat across from me.

"Tell me what's troubling you," he said.

I immediately felt free and at ease. His mere presence did that for me. He seemed so interested in *me*. Like maybe it was *me* who had the answers to everything. So I talked. I told him about Jeff. Our happy marriage. How he died. And the nightmares. Oh, the nightmares, which had robbed me of my rest and was about to take away my sanity. I talked for a long time. He listened to every word. His interest never wavered. His eyelids never trembled. Then I got tired of talking and stopped.

"Forgive me for saying so," he said, "but it appears to me as though you are suffering from a haunting."

"A haunting?"

"Yes indeed. You have a ghost presence in your life who wants something from you."

"I thought I had some nightmares."

"Ghosts can manifest in many ways. Tell me, have you ever entered into therapy before?"

"No," I said. "I never needed to before."

"And may I ask, the apartment you moved into, is it large?"

"No," I said, mystified by his question. "Just a normal sized one."

"Does it have big walls?"

"What are you getting at? What does my apartment have to do with anything?"

"It is my firm belief that most people's problems are small problems. They tend to make them bigger than they really are."

I glanced at the six foot pencils in the corner. Okay, doc, I thought.

"I have something for you to do," he said. "I said you are an artist, yes?"

"I do commercial art. For print ads. It pays the bills."

"I want you to find the biggest wall in your apartment. Then I want you draw on it. Draw the biggest portrait of your husband Jeff that you can. Fill the space. Will you do that for me?"

"On my walls?" It was not the kind of advice I had expected.

"If you're worried about the walls," said Ziggy, "use washable paint. But my advice is not to concern yourself with the walls. They aren't important. Remember to work big, always big."

Work big.

Most of my art ended up in newspaper and magazine ads. Small. But I decided it wouldn't hurt to try Ziggy's suggestion. I stopped by a hardware store and got some spray paints. Yellows and light browns for Jeff's blonde hair. Then some black for his eyes, and a few assorted pastel shades for his skin. As I pulled them off the shelf, I felt a strain at my heart, like it wanted to pull me down. A peculiar sensation I had not experienced before.

At the counter the guy who rang up the cans lifted his eyebrows slightly and studied me carefully. "Going to do some tagging, are we?" he said.

I wanted to tell him yes, I was a tagger. But I didn't. I shrugged instead and he let it go.

At home I chose the living room wall behind the tv. I pushed the stereo to one side, and a couple of big chairs. I took the tv off the wall and dumped it on the couch. I cleared away my plants and moved the phone onto the couch as well. Then I put an old sheet over everything. I stood in front of the wall and took a deep breath. I shook one of the spray cans. The ball bearing inside rattled louder than an earthquake.

I wasn't sure I had it in me to do this. A big portrait of Jeff on my wall?

I raised the spray can with my finger on the nozzle. My hand trembled.

I pressed down. The phsssssssst sound startled me. I let go of the nozzle.

The first spurt left a round spot in front of me and dripped wet pigment down the wall. I had forgotten to move the can.

I took a breath, caught the whiff of hydrocarbons, and moved the can quickly over the wall as I pressed the nozzle again. Phsssssssst! Not so startling the second time. In fact, I liked the sound. The line I put down pleased me. It had a nice curve to it. And it matched the curve of Jeff's hairline.

Okay. I could work with that.

I picked up another can of paint and made an outline of his face. I stood on my tip toes to get closer to the ceiling, but I was too short to reach. I brought in a stool from the kitchen and stood up on it so I could get some paint all the way to the top of the wall.

I swooped my hand in big arcs and gushed paint with each swoosh.

The sensation was all freedom. The *big*ness of the picture gave it a power it wouldn't have had otherwise. By the time I finished, I felt like Jeff had moved in and looked down on me.

That night I slept on the living room floor.

I had no nightmares.

I went back to Ziggy the first chance I got.

He seemed glad to see me that second time. Ziggy oozed politeness the way a layer cake, in hot weather, sometimes leaks liquid sugar down the sides. He greeted me with a smart tilt of his head, accompanied by a "How are we today, Miss Jenkins?"

That was his way of greeting me. Concerned, in a mannerly and respectful way. Pleasant. Accommodating. I thought I could get used to it.

"Much better," I said.

"I'm glad to hear it. Tell me what happened."

That's the way it was with Ziggy. He was always interested in *me*. I suppose that's what you want from a therapist, but it was all new to me.

I told him about the picture and how I didn't have the nightmare.

"Excellent," he said. "Now I want you to imagine setting fire to your apartment."

I did not expect him to say something like that.

"You're not serious," I said.

"I am. Make it a big fire. A conflagration of immense proportions."

Despite my misgivings, I went along with the fantasy. I closed my eyes while he directed me to douse the portrait with gasoline and then set a lit match to it. I did all this in my mind's eye.

"Are you seeing his portrait burning up?" said Ziggy.

"Yes," I said.

"Good. Not let the flames build. I want them to fill the apartment, the building, the city."

I balked at that. Why would I want to imagine Seattle burning to the ground? What good would it do?

"Are you resisting?" said Ziggy.

"I feel like I'm doing something wrong," I said.

"You husband needs to be purged from your dreams. This is the way to do it. Burn his image away. That will bring him rest."

But what would it do for me? "He doesn't need rest," I said. "*I* need rest."

"Keep your eyes closed," said Ziggy. "Do you see the flames?"

I did see the flames. They rose above my head. They rose to the ceiling, began crawling along the top of the apartment, and then dropped to the other side where they began consuming my furniture, the carpeting. Thick smoke filled the room and began pouring out of the window. I had a vivid imagination. I turned my attention, my mind's eye, back to the wall, to Jeff's portrait. I knew the wall was safe and secure back in my real life apartment, but the one here, in my head, in Ziggy's office, it didn't have that luxury. It was melting. Jeff was melting. I wanted to stop the process, but something about it, something about Ziggy's insistence on the value of the exercise kept me going. I wasn't sure how a wall would actually behave in a fire situation, but in my mind's eye, as the fire spread through my apartment, it melted the portrait. Jeff became rivers of color flowing down off the wall to pool in hot puddles on the floor. I walked over to the puddles and jumped in them, as though I was a child jumping in rain puddles just to make them splash. The paint rose from my soles in waves that splashed onto the furniture, now wrapped in the gauze of smoke and flame. The colors of Jeff's portrait mixed into a kaleidoscope of swirling liquid, as though I had taken a snapshot of the interior of a marble. Or the inner workings of a rainbow. A memory of Jeff on a sailboat came to me. A rainbow behind him, like a parent overseeing him. Now where did that come from? It was like the rainbow had decided it need to look after Jeff. I made a noise. A pathetic mewling sound. I was aware of Ziggy in the room. His presence seemed to evoke from me a kind of dependency that I was unused to. I kept my eyes closed. I didn't want to see Ziggy, not then. Maybe not ever. I wanted Jeff. I wanted to see him. Wanted to hold him. I reached for him. He didn't notice me at first, then caught my eye and smiled at me. As I watched, he started melting, in imitation of the picture on the wall. His skin and flesh liquified and ran down his bones to puddle at his feet.

This did not startle or alarm me. It felt completely normal. Necessary. Once that process was completed, and the liquid flowed off the deck into the water, his bones started crumbling. His femur, his thigh bones, his pelvis, his chest. Then his arms and skull. All gone into dust, which the wind caught and blew into the air.

I was aware that my vision, my imaginary scenario, bore some resemblance to my nightmares, but the correspondence was not exact. There was no pained expression from Jeff, for example, which made the scene much more bearable. And I was in Ziggy's office. I can't convey how much difference that made.

I stepped to the spot where Jeff had been and bent down and picked up an object. I was unsure what it was at first. It had a crack in it that separated it, slightly, into two lobes, held together by the merest hint of material. At first I didn't want to know what it was, but, gradually, my awareness of the object could not prevent my faculties from understanding its identity: a heart.

Jeff's heart. The heat of the fire had cracked it.

I clutched at my own chest.

I remembered what Ziggy said. A big portrait. Big. Always think big.

I took that crack from Jeff's heart and superimposed it on the sky. It broke the blue dome in two. The smoke and fire from my apartment, from my city, rose up through the air and entered the crack in the sky.

"What are you feeling?" said Ziggy.

I opened my eyes. Ziggy sat back in his chair and looked at me with soft eyes and a softer expression. The giant paper clip behind him made me think of Jeff's heart. It was the same color: bright red. It had lines and empty spaces in it. Like Jeff's heart.

I looked down at my hands. Red dust covered them. I blinked and the dust disappeared.

I looked up at Ziggy.

"I'm not afraid anymore," I said.

"That's good," he said. He stood up. "The session is over," he said.

"It can't be. I've only been here a few minutes."

He pointed to a clock, a giant clock on the wall opposite the window. It showed that I had been there for almost an hour. I shook my head. "How can that be?"

"You were in a different sate," said Ziggy. "I'm glad you aren't afraid anymore. The fear may come back, but you know how to deal with it now. Invoke the flames. They will cleanse everything."

I thanked Ziggy. He extended his hand, which seemed oversized for his body, bigger than it had any right to be. I put my hand in his. He wrapped my palm and fingers up. I thought I was going to lose myself.

"You're bigger than you think," he said. "If you have any problems again, come see me. My door will always be open for you Miss Jenkins."

I left Ziggy's office and stepped out into downtown Seattle. The sky had opened up a little. The clouds parted and let in a little sun. Not enough to make me think I wasn't living in the Northwest, but enough to illuminate my world.

I got back to my apartment and sat on the couch opposite the portrait of Jeff. I didn't see the picture as a picture anymore. Instead, it looked like a collection of giant doodles. Disconnected painted loops and curves. They filled the wall, that was for sure, but they didn't coalesce into anything. I could not step back far enough to make them blend. I wondered how the portrait could look so different now. When I had painted it, it sure looked like a coherent picture. Not anymore.

I stepped closer to the wall. I put my hand on the marks I had made with the spray cans. There was an unexpected grit to it, like find sandpaper. I ran my fingers over the grit. My heart, which had been beating like crazy, calmed itself. I placed my palm on the wall. The wall, in its turn, pushed back. It was a big wall. It had all these dots on it. Big dots. I knew what those dots signified, I had painted them. Every one. But I didn't *see* it.

I put my face right up to the wall. I pressed my nose on the wall. My eyes were so close, my eyelashes brushed against the portrait. I felt my breath coming back to me, as though the wall itself breathed. It was a big breath, a big sound, like immense sighing.

The Masks

"Here, try this one," said D'arcy, and handed Linda a paper maché mask from the trunk. It was painted bright blue. The beak was yellow and purple feathers were glued on the sides and front so that they dropped over the eye holes.

Linda took the mask and put it on. It rested on her shoulders, covering her entire head like a helmet. It tended to droop down a little in the front so that she had to to tilt her head back to see clearly. She felt awkward and foolish.

"How do I look?" she said.

D'arcy smacked his lips and held his hand up with the fingertips pressed together. "Magnificent. With the blue lace wrap and the blue gloves, you'll be the hit of the dance."

"I don't know," she said. "It keeps falling off my nose."

"That's because you don't know how to wear it properly. Here, let me." He stepped forward and adjusted the mask higher on her face. Linda liked the scratching sound of his hands on the shell of the mask. The inside of the mask smelled warm and faintly dusty. Her field of vision was cut to two small holes that didn't mesh properly, and she had a comfortable wall only inches from her head. It was a pleasant little world of her own.

D'arcy stepped away. "That's better," he said. "How do you feel now?"

"Better," she admitted, then laughed.

D'arcy grinned. "What?"

"You sound funny under here. You sound like you're far away."

He bent over the trunk and rummaged around in it for a moment. He stood up after some seconds and displayed a set of vampire teeth. Linda giggled. D'arcy put them in his mouth so that they clamped onto his upper teeth and hung over his lower lip.

Linda tilted her head back to get a better look. "Are you sure that's enough?" she said.

He shrugged. "With a little makeup and a cape, it'll be fine."

She smiled. "This is so much fun. I've never been to a costume ball before."

D'arcy swung the top of the trunk down so that it closed with a loud bang. Linda jumped, startled by the noise. "What was that?" she said.

"Just the trunk," said D'arcy and pointed to the closed lid.

Linda put a hand to her chest. Her heart was beating wildly and a tingly sensation of fear settled down and through and out of her body like a burning liquid. She put her palms on the sides of the mask and lifted it up and over her head. She placed it on the bed.

D'arcy looked at the mask and she felt like he was avoiding her eyes. She stared at him, but he refused to look at her and something inside her grew cold and empty.

"It scared me," she said. "It sounded like something evil."

D'arcy glanced at her, and she could see him forcing himself to hold his gaze.

"And you said you didn't have any imagination," he said. "*I* certainly never thought this trunk was a vessel of evil."

She closed her eyes and took a deep breath and let it out. How could he know? He wasn't there when the accident happened. He didn't hear the explosion, the terrible sound that insulted her life, made her face into a grotesque image.

"Don't play with me," she said quietly. "I was really scared. It was like something went right through me, like it ripped at my insides."

D'arcy's grin turned stiff on his face. Linda could see he was losing his humor, becoming impatient with her. "Come on," he said and turned away from her. "We have to get ready."

Linda put the mask on again and watched him walk out of the bedroom toward the kitchen, where he had set out the makeup earlier. The coziness under the mask was comforting, not like the world outside. Here she could be whatever she wanted to be, and no one would know her. She decided she would not remove the mask for the rest of the evening.

Smoke rose up through the air, making dancing clouds appear around the lights. The band was playing a merry Dixieland jazz number, and there were a few couples on the dance floor, most of them awkward and hesitating, unsure how to dance to this music. Linda looked around from her seat at the end of a long table. D'arcy had stepped into the lobby for some drinks.

"Great costume, Linda," someone said from behind her. She whipped around, only to dislodge her mask slightly and throw her little world out of kilter. When she adjusted the mask again, she looked into a sea of masks and anonymous faces and had no idea who had paid her the compliment.

She sighed and turned her attention back to the dancers. She wished the band would play some rock and roll. That at least was easy to dance to. Just get up and move around however you wanted to.

"Here we are," said D'arcy, thumping down a couple of glasses of beer and settling into the seat next to her. He smiled at her and took a long slow drink from his glass.

Linda put her hand around her glass, but didn't raise it from the table.

"Want to dance?" asked D'arcy.

"Not right now," said Linda.

He nodded and looked away. She sensed he was not enjoying himself because she was not enjoying herself. She felt like a bit of a stick in the mud, but this was his idea from the beginning, and she had to be talked into it. She had become self-conscious after her accident, thinking people were always staring at her. Even after the surgery on her face, she felt different, somehow permanently sullied and tarnished by her appearance, so different now from what it had once been. She had never thought herself a striking beauty, but she had at least been presentably human. Now her face was a crisscross of healing suture lines, and they were settling into someone different. She had seen it in the mirror: her new face was not her old face. D'arcy had noticed it too.

He turned to her. "Aren't you going to drink your beer?"

She tightened her hand around the glass, felt the cool wetness there. "I'll just hold it for a while," she said. "It feels nice."

He nodded. "I can get you a straw," he said. "If you don't want to take off your mask."

Did he know how cruel he could be, how his words could cut through her to the bone, like ice water?

"That's okay," she said.

He grunted and turned away again, giving his attention to the band for a while.

Linda lifted her mask just enough to put her hand underneath and wiped away a layer of perspiration on her forehead. The beer would feel good right now, but she couldn't bring herself to remove the coziness of her new home. D'arcy said the mask would make her feel like a new person, but she didn't feel any different at all. She felt like the same person as she was without the mask, only she was safe, covered. She liked the feeling very much. Lately, even being herself had become difficult with D'arcy's moodiness and his refusal to admit that things had changed between them. No, she would simply sit back tonight, listen to the music, feel her own warmth, and just be herself.

She leaned against the back of the chair and shifted her mask until the eye holes allowed her to see forward. The band was certainly lively, if a little different, and the dancers were beginning to warm up to the music. Beer and wine working their effect, she supposed.

"I'm going to get another beer," said D'arcy and stood up.

Linda watched him walk away through the smoke and the noise, and a great sadness seemed to sweep over her. Did she love him? She thought so, but she couldn't tell anymore. He was so distant from her. She could feel it in his touch—when he did touch her, which was seldom now—a hesitancy and stiffness, a need to pull away quickly. Gone were the lingering caresses she remembered with longing. She traced her finger along the length of the glass still sitting in front of her. A ring of water had formed around the base, and the beer had gone flat and uninviting.

She felt a hand on her shoulder. "I'm going to dance with Esther," said D'arcy.

Linda turned around and said, automatically, "Of course." Esther worked at the plant with D'arcy. She watched as D'arcy the vampire and Esther the clown edged their way through the people standing in little groups. They weren't holding hands, but they were very close.

"Bastard."

Linda jumped in her chair and turned around. "What?"

"He's a bastard."

She didn't see who was talking. There was no one within ten feet of her and the voice was very close, practically right next to her.

"Why do you let him get away with treating you like that?"

Linda looked around again. "Who said that?"

Someone in a surgeon's mask and gown turned and stared at her, then walked away toward the dance floor.

A low chuckle came from the same place as the voice. She put her hands to the sides of the mask and looked up at the inside, only to see out-of-focus lines of gray newspaper print. "Don't you know?" said the voice.

She felt a chill stiffen the back of her neck. She became conscious only of the moist warmth of her own breath against the wall of the mask and on her upper lip.

"Wake up," said the voice. "Wake up and see what's happening around you."

She shook her head. "No," she said loudly. The mask rotated around her head until it was sitting sideways. The chuckle came back, low and ugly, like a demon's laugh. "Stop it," said Linda, and now a hand reached out and patted her back. Someone pulled off the mask and laid it down on the table. Linda looked wildly around. A woman was crouched down in front of her. Her face was kind and soft.

"Are you all right?" she said.

Linda looked up at the ceiling. The smoke was just a dirty fog now, all the patterns had disappeared. She felt a rush of coolness as a draft of air blew across her sweat-filmed face.

"I'm fine," she said and tried to smile. "I was getting a little too warm, I guess."

The woman patted her hand. "Maybe you should drink something," she said.

"Yes," said Linda, without looking the woman in the eye. She turned and reached for her beer. She didn't want anyone to see her face. She wanted the coziness of the mask around her again. She stood up abruptly and walked out to the lobby where she paced around in front of the exit door.

D'arcy came out after a while. "What is it?" he asked.

She turned to him and felt an urge to press herself against him, hug him close, but his body was a fortress, arms folded on his chest, mouth in a scowl.

"Let's go home," she said.

"Linda, we just got here. What's the problem?"

"Please? I can't stay here anymore. They saw me."

His mouth twitched. He threw up his hands and let his arms fall to his sides with an audible thump. "Is it Esther?" he said. "Are you jealous of her?"

The bartender was trying not to stare at them. "D'arcy, please," she said. "I just want to go home."

He let a heavy breath escape his lungs. "All right," he said and went back to the dance hall.

Linda watched him return with his jacket over his shoulder and the mask tucked under his arm like a bag of groceries.

In the the darkness she felt the smoothness of his chest, the curve of his body, and wondered at the resilience of his flesh. It was soft and yielding and warm, yet it had a shape, it was a recognizable form. D'arcy moved under her and she heard the sheets rustle. She remained still with her palms on his chest and her legs straddling his pelvis.

"What's wrong," came his soft voice.

"Nothing," she said.

"You stopped . . .

No, she wanted say, it was you. You stopped.

"The light," she said quietly. "You turned out the light."

Now he became still and they were no longer together. She felt his hands on her thighs like rocks, hard and heavy where a moment before they had been soft and caressing. Abruptly he shifted awkwardly beneath her and she understood the motion to be his signal. I have had enough, he was saying, I wish to be alone now. She hesitated a split second, then rolled off and lay beside him. The coldness in the air made her want to cry.

"Am I really that different, D'arcy? Have I changed so much?"

The room was filled with the sound of his breathing. She turned to him. His face was lost in the darkness, she could see no features, but she sensed motion there and she could imagine his flaring nostrils and his corrugated forehead.

"Do you love me?" she said.

A sharp intake of breath. The sound of his hair rolling on the pillow, a familiar scratching noise that seemed to clutch at her heart.

"Of course I love you," he said and a rush of warm air escaped his mouth and hit her face like the blow of an open palm.

"My face is just a mask," she said. "Underneath I am exactly the same person I always was."

"I know."

She took his hand and placed it on her cheek. She felt pressure on the ridges of scar tissue still healing. The doctor had done a wonderful job. He had rebuilt her face to a recognizably human form and D'arcy would not touch it, would barely even look at it. She squeezed his hand tighter in her own, and pressed it harder against her cheek. She squeezed his hand so tightly that she felt the bones of his knuckles rub against each other. He would not touch her. He tolerated her holding his hand to her skin, but it was like holding a dead thing. After a few seconds he tugged very gently, and she released his hand.

He rolled away from her in the darkness.

D'arcy got up with the alarm while Linda pretended to be asleep. She listened as he shaved and showered, then went into the kitchen and made his breakfast. After she heard the front door slam she jumped out of bed and opened the curtains to let in the sun. Its warmth splashed across her face and she stretched her body like a cat, letting the rays drench her.

She went into the kitchen and tried to read the morning paper, but it was just a jumble to her. She couldn't sit still. She rose from the chair and began doing unnecessary household chores. She vacuumed the carpet, even though D'arcy had done it only a couple of days ago. She did the dishes, though there were only a couple of plates and a pan. She had an excess of nervous energy, and she did not know ho to rid herself of it. She turned on the television, but found the programs either stupid or boring or both.

She decided she would write letters and went into the bedroom where she kept her stationery. She pulled open a drawer and took out the ruled pad of airmail paper. She she turned to leave, the trunk, still resting in the same place it had been the night before, caught her eye. She stared at the trunk for some time. All of her energy seemed to dissipate into the air and she felt very relaxed. She suddenly knew what she had been avoiding all morning. D'arcy had placed the mask back into the trunk when they came home from the dance last night.

She moistened her lips with her tongue and trapped her lower lip between her teeth. She felt a hotness invade her neck and head. Her hands were light and laced with tiny pinpricks.

She went to the trunk, kneeled in front of it, and lifted the cover open. The mask lay on top, with the eye holes staring at her blankly. She picked it up by the pointed beak, and placed it over her head.

The cozy world she remembered came rushing back and with it a sense of wonderment and happiness. She was hidden from the world. No one could see her. She giggled and stood up. The mask felt better on her head today, like it belonged there. Not like yesterday, when it was more of an encumbrance.

She sat down at the kitchen table again, pushed away the newspaper and set the pad in front of her. She had not had a good long bout of letter writing for months. She remembered how she used to fill pages and pages and write for hours and hours, catching up with her friends and letting them know how she was getting on in the world.

She began writing. Before long the table was littered with curled sheets of blue onionskin torn from the pad as she finished each page. She stopped for a moment, thinking about her next line, and absentmindedly reached across the table to turn on the radio.

"Don't do that," said the voice. "I like the quiet."

Linda's hand stopped just inches from the dial. The voice was clear and coherent. There was no way to blame it on a fogged head or believe that it was a stray remark from someone else.

"Just take your hand back," said the voice.

Linda slowly moved her hand to a resting position on the table.

"There you go," said the voice. "Isn't that much better? Isn't it lovely to have this quiet?"

Linda swallowed hard.

"Who are you?" she said to the empty room.

"Honey, if you don't know yet, we're going to have a tough time getting along with each other."

Linda's mouth moved in small chewing motions. She wanted to answer the voice, but she didn't know what to say. She tapped the side of the mask with her index finger and heard the cozy scratching noise again. Her throat was dry. She felt tense and fluttery in every part of her body. "You're in the mask?"

Silence. Then a chuckle.

Linda looked around the room to be sure she had not been transported to some spirit world. Everything seemed just as it had always been. The same sharp edges to the world were still there, the same colors, the same smells. She looked at the sea of blue paper wavelets, frozen in place on the kitchen table. Everything was exactly as it should be except for one thing.

"Why can I hear you?" she demanded.

"Because," said the voice, "you need a friend."

A half hour before D'arcy was supposed to come home, Linda took off the mask. Immediately she felt a rush of fear wash over her. Her own face was exposed to the world. D'arcy would see her and she would have to endure his sour expression. She had a wild thought that she should just leave the mask on, but that didn't seem right. He would probably think it peculiar, and even if he did not, how could she talk to the mask with him in the house? No, it would never do. This was going to be her secret.

She carried the mask to the bedroom and lifted the trunk lid carefully and placed the mask inside, then gently closed the trunk with a soft click of the lid. When D'arcy came in she gave him a hug and a kiss on the cheek. He acknowledged her with a vague gesture of his hand and a barely mumbled "hi." Linda didn't care. She had someone to talk to know. Someone real, who understood her and knew everything about her. Someone who would forgive her for anything that she had ever done, or ever would do. Above all, she had someone who would accept her, completely and without question, exactly as she was. She had a friend.

In the days that followed, Linda lived for the hours when D'arcy was out of the house at work. She would wait until the car was down the street, then rush to the trunk and take out the mask and put it on. The paper maché smell and the snug fit were always welcome sensations to her, and before long the voice from the mask came forth with a friendly greeting, or a playful tease. She would wear the mask all day, and the two of them would chatter the hours away while watching television or doing household chores. She was always careful to take off the mask before D'arcy returned, and each time the voice went away as the mask came off. The house without the mask seemed endless and horrible to her, lifeless and dull.

"I like you," said Linda to the voice one day as they were playing solitaire.

"Black nine on red ten," said the voice. "I like you too."

Linda placed the card and began humming to herself.

"I've been thinking," she said. "Maybe it's time for me to go outside."

"Why would you want to go outside?" said the voice.

"All I do all day is stay here, in the house. I'm missing the whole world, it's going right by me."

The voice didn't say anything for a while. Linda counted off three cards, turned them over, and placed them on the table.

"Don't you want to be with me anymore?" said the voice.

"Of course I do," said Linda. "It's just that I need a little more."

"Like D'arcy?"

Linda felt stung. "No," she said quietly.

"Then why? Why would you want to leave your only friend?"

Linda sighed heavily. "I just want to get outside for an hour or two. Go to a restaurant, maybe. Or take a walk in the park. Anything."

"There are people outside," said the voice. "They'll see you. They'll see your face."

"That's the *point*," said Linda. "I want to be seen. I don't want to be a prisoner in this house. I don't want to be trapped here."

Now the voice laughed at her, and it was a cruel laugh, mocking. "Go ahead," it said. "Go outside, see what the great big world is like. But you'll come back. You won't stay out there for long because no one else will be your friend. I'm the only friend you have."

"I wish I could take you with me," said Linda. "Really, I do." She looked around the room blankly, turning her head this way and that, searching for acknowledgement from the voice. None came. She methodically picked up the cards and arranged them in a neat deck. She riffled them, shuffled them a few times, turned them over in her hand. She took a gasping, fluttery breath. She felt her eyes well up with tears, but blinked them away. Time to be grown up, she told herself. Time to do something for myself.

She put down the cards and placed her palms on the sides of the mask. With a quick motion she pulled it off and shook her head out from under. She put the mask on the table and felt a welcome sensation of freedom as her hair fell to her shoulder, free of paper maché walls.

She put her hands to her face and wiped away the dampness there. Her face felt strange, and she had to fight an urge to slap the mask back on. She ran her hand along the curve of the mask and twined her fingers around one of the feathers. There would be time for the mask when she returned. It would not leave her.

Eyes.

There were eyes everywhere. They were all set in perfect faces and they all seemed to be watching her. Linda stepped quickly along the sidewalk conscious of a crush of people around her. This was without question the worst part of her outing. Getting into the car and driving into town was easy; no one saw here. She felt protected in the car, safe and secure behind solid steel and glass. She had a thought that she might simply drive around for a while and then come home and tell the voice she had been out and done many things, talked to numerous people, been *seen*, but something inside told her that would not do. It would be cheating, somehow, and she couldn't do that.

Instead she parked the car in a curbside parking place and stepped hesitantly onto the sidewalk. She didn't raise her eyes to the level of the faces around her, but instead stared at the ground and occasionally glanced up to be certain she was not about to run into anything. She ducked into a movie house, paid her money, and almost ran into the darkened theater, where she sat through a mildly amusing comedy in the comfort and security of total anonymity. No one could see her face and that knowledge made her relax, brought her breathing to a normal, steady pace, and quietened her heart.

When the light came up as the credits rolled, she pulled herself out of her chair with slow, deliberate motions, and stepped out into the late afternoon sun. She had every intention of getting back into her car and driving home, but through a quirk of memory, she had completely forgotten on which street she had parked. Panic rose within her immediately, but she quelled it and sat on a bench to think through the situation. She retraced the drive into town, remembered the trouble she had finding a parking spot, and how she had driven around and around, looking for an empty space. She became conscious of her face as she sat, and it seemed to her that it was not a part of her body. Her face, a conglomeration of skin grafts and sutures, seemed to hang on the front of her head like a picture hanging on a wall. Or like a mask.

She moistened her lips and looked up and down the street. She was pretty sure the car was east of her. She rose and began walking.

She felt the faintest hint of the voice, somewhere deep within her, and she willed it to come forth, she yearned for it to talk to her again, prove to her that she was not alone, but the hint remained no more than the merest whisper. It floated up, like a trail of smoke through her body, only to be scattered by her own breath as she inhaled deeply.

She quickened her pace to a run. Her face was very heavy now, and she could almost imagine it falling off as it pulled at her head with each jarring impact of foot against concrete. She stood on a corner and remembered where her car was. Yes. She turned to one side. This way. She made her feet move and began to smell a burning odor in the air. The smell clicked with her memory of the accident, the smell of burning gasoline and plastic, hot metal, seared flesh…

She stopped. The car was down the street, waiting for her. Black smoke billowed out of a building a block farther from her car. The smoke seemed to be propelled from the depths of the earth with an almost demonic force. It went straight up into the air, with some spilling over into the street. People ran here and there, bent over and coughing into their hands or covering their faces with handkerchiefs and coats. The air was cloudy and dark. There was the sense of an eerie kind of twilight.

Her car. She had to get to her car and escape this conflagration. She started walking again and felt the heels of her shoes like jackhammers against he concrete sidewalk. An explosion from inside the burning building blew glass into the street, and caused her whole body to shudder. That sound. That explosion. Her heart seemed to thump against her chest, trying to escape her body as the smoke was escaping the building. The smoke covered her like a blanket. People ran toward her, shouting. Someone grabbed her shoulder as he passed by. Linda jerked around for a second, then straightened and kept walking. The fire, the building, the consuming fire. It was like her accident, like the time she was burned and her face had been destroyed.

Her eyes began to hurt from the heat. Cinders pecked at her face and she slapped at them like they were mosquitoes.

The car. She had to reach the car.

It had been a mistake to leave the house. She wanted to be home again, put on the mask and be with the voice, with her friend. She wasn't ready to come out here. This fire was a warning to stay away, and she didn't need to be warned twice.

She finally reached the car. The door handle was almost too hot to touch, and she thought for a moment that the car's gas tank might explode from the heat, but she didn't care. She had to leave here. She had to drive away and find her voice again.

She opened the door and climbed inside. Sweat began forming on her body instantly and she had to wipe it off her forehead in a sliding wet motion.

She closed her eyes and started the engine. It caught and she practically jumped out of her seat. She put the car in gear and drove through the black smoke towards the brilliant light in the distance.

D'arcy's car was parked in the driveway. She didn't care. All that mattered was the voice. Let D'arcy see her put on the mask and talk to the air. She didn't care.

She burst through the front door. D'arcy stood in front of her with a suitcase in each hand. He looked u at her. Linda's hands trembled. She swallowed hard.

He looked down at the floor.

"I'm leaving," he said. "I'm moving out."

"Then go," she said. "I don't want you here."

Her voice was shaky, not at all as defiant as she wanted it to be. Inside she hurt, and she didn't really know why.

"Try to understand," said D'arcy. "This is hard for me to face."

The sound of the word "face" brought a force from the depths of her and she felt her eyes widen, felt her mouth quiver, and rage sweep through her like a lethal hotness.

He still did not look at her.

"Go!" she screamed. "Get out of here."

A silence followed as the ringing in the walls died away. D'arcy took a step forward and Linda ran past him. He looked up, for an instant, as she went by, but he was only a blur himself in her peripheral vision.

The mask. The voice.

She ran into the kitchen and froze in her tracks. She brought a hand to her mouth. The mask was not where she had left it on the table.

She looked frantically around the room.

"D'arcy!"

She went back to the living room. D'arcy stood in the doorway, with one hand on the doorknob. He turned to her and forced himself to look at her.

"Where's the mask?" she asked. "What did you do with the mask?" Her hands were wrapped around themselves. Her body trembled with fear and anticipation.

"Oh," said D'arcy. "The bird mask. I was in here earlier getting some things, and I saw it here on the table, and I remembered how much Esther said she liked it at the dance. I gave it to her."

Linda's mouth dropped open. She felt her knees growing weak. Esther had her voice? *Esther?*

"Well it is mine," said D'arcy. "I mean, I've had it for years. I *made* it, for God's sake, so you shouldn't look so hurt."

He stood for a few moments in the doorway, then turned around, and walked outside. The door swung shut behind him.

Linda slumped to a kneeling position on the floor, then bent forward until her face touched the dust and grit there. She remained motionless for some time, alone, feeling the weight of her own body against the floor.

She didn't quite hear it at first. She sensed something in the darkness, though, and snapped her head up and looked around, alert to anything that could bring some spark of hope to her loneliness.

"Linda," said the voice. It was soft, almost a whisper, but she could her it, there was no mistaking it. The voice. It was still there.

"Have you learned your lesson? Will you stay here now, with me, where I can protect you and be your friend?"

Linda looked up at the ceiling and brought her hands to her face, to the mask where the voice lived.She opened her mouth to scream. No sound came out, but a soft chuckle, sprinkled like salt grains, fell upon her and she knew she would never be alone again.

Giving Voice

The cemetery overlooking the Columbia River rested just a couple of miles from Silverdale, a small town surrounded by flat wheat fields and watched over by two monumental mountains, like sentries overlooking the land. The cemetery reminded Chris of a pond where lily pads poked up and floated on the murky surface. It was a typically wet and mossy early December. Here and there a few patches of ground hugged the surface like seaweed clinging to life. He stepped across the entrance and walked through the grass.

"So these are all unmarked graves?" he said.

Linda walked with him. "People can't always afford to buy monuments, so they bury their loved ones and no one can see where they are. You have to go to the cemetery office and look on a chart."

"It feels weird to know there are people buried here and no stones to mark the graves."

"I know. When there are stones, you feel a connection to the buried person. It's like you can talk to them."

"I don't even see white crosses. They even have those at the sides of roads."

"Most cemeteries don't want them," said Linda. "Makes it look—I don't know—kind of chintzy, I guess."

Chris stopped in front of a modest stretch of bare ground.

"This is where a child was buried," said Linda. "That's why it's so small."

Chris removed his hat and held it to his chest. "I had no idea."

"It's an issue all over the country. Lots of people want stones but can't afford them."

They held a sliver of silence between them, letting it expand into a few seconds.

"We don't even know who this is, and we feel the power of her loss," said Linda.

Chris was there to be convinced by Linda. Linda did not have to do much more than take him to the cemetery and state the facts.

Thousands of families are unable to mark the graves of their deceased, usually because of financial constraints. A piece of marble is not an inexpensive item, and the dictates of polite society have conspired to make the thrifty purchase of anything associated with death into a hopelessly kitschy exercise.

Chris and Linda decided to produce good, small, low-cost grave markers that they would then offer by mail order. Their profit margin would be small, but if they got enough orders they could make a good living on marking the no longer living. They set up a website and placed classified ads in rural newspapers and magazines. They located a wholesale source of marble that could deliver small stones which they would then carve and mail. Then they waited.

While they waited, Chris set up a studio in the garage. He practiced his carving technique on random rocks he found by roadsides. He employed a mixture of fine sand and compressed air on the rocks to produce lettering and pictorial designs. Chris practiced angels quite a bit, anticipating that many people would want angels on the markers they were going to buy. The wings, especially were tricky. Getting the feathering right, the subtlety of them, the sweep and the lightness, yet showing them strong enough to lift. It got to be so Chris saw himself as an angel of sorts, lifting the spirits of those who had anonymously buried people they loved.

It was a tendency Linda saw immediately and quashed as fast as she could.

"It's a business," she said. "Don't make it anything bigger."

"Everything is business," said Chris, "but some business is more important than others. Some business is a calling."

"That may be so," said Linda, "but it is best not to get too emotionally involved with rocks."

"It's not me," said Chris. "The rocks, when they get words and pictures on them, it's like they're talking. They get a voice."

Linda was not sure how to respond to that. She patted Chris on the shoulder and he went back to carving.

Along about the third week after they placed their first ads, they started getting orders. A man in Wyoming ordered eight headstones. All of them a foot wide, a foot and a half tall, and two inches thick. All of them were white marble and easily mailed. They were to mark the graves of his grandparents, parents, and some uncles and aunts who had been buried on the family property for years, but had never had proper headstones.

A woman in Idaho was fed up with the hard sell tactics of the local monument store that tried to sell her an overly elaborate stone for her recently deceased welder husband. She turned to Chris and Linda for help. They were happy to oblige her with a cheap stone decorated with an angel holding a welding torch. This was the woman's suggestion, not Chris's.

A family in Alaska had kept a distant relative's existence a secret because her grave was unmarked and they were shamed by this fact. They ordered a marker by mail order from Linda and Chris. After they received it and installed it at the head of the plot, they wrote back to Linda to tell her how much better their lives were now. They felt able to hold their heads up in town. They felt as though they had a right to be happy and to live as free beings. They said they were able to speak to the relative and they felt the relative was able to speak to them.

They didn't use quite that language, but Linda read between the lines and reported their high spirits to Chris.

"We are doing important work with this," said Chris. "This is like a ministry."

Linda told Chris again to not get too excited. It was simply a money transaction. The people who bought the stone got a fair product for their cash. That was all. But she had to admit she felt some of the pain they had endured. It came through in the letters. She found she almost had to agree with Chris, but retained her business smarts.

"We could exhaust the market in no time," she said. "Don't get too attached to this model. We might have to leave it and move on to something else."

Chris nodded. He knew it. But he had faith it was not going to be so. He pulled his safety goggles down from the top of his head and over his eyes, then turned on the air compressor and guided the nozzle over another monument rock.

Linda was wrong about the market. They had found a vast untapped need. She got a big map of the country and put it on the board behind her desk. She put a plastic thumb tack on the map for every monument they shipped. In just a few months they map was thick with thumb tacks. She bought them in packs of fifty each and was soon on her 20th pack. Most of the tacks were clustered in the northwest and California, but there were a few as far east as Ohio, and quite a few in Arizona, New Mexico and Texas. A couple hovered like birds over Florida.

It was about then that the peculiar man came to the office. Linda had been careful to leave her exact location out of any advertising. She operated the business out of a PO Box and had no signage at their house to indicate what they did there. She had also learned to keep the letters from customers away from Chris. He was prone to sentimentality anyway, and some of the letters were unbearably sad and poignant. They would move her to tears and she was not prepared to see what they would do to Chris.

She was in fact opening the mail and noting with satisfaction that it was a day of six orders, not bad at all. Each accompanied by a check. Even better. When the doorbell rang.

Chris was in the garage, carving rock, filling orders. She went to the front door and opened it.

A man stood in front of her. He looked like he wanted to sell her something.

"We're not interested," she said.

The man held up his hand. She noticed then a certain quality in his face. Not earnestness or slickness. A sadness in the drawn features, but also an urgency in the way his head was thrust slightly forward. He wanted something, but it was not to sell Linda anything.

"I won't take more than a minute of your time," said the man. "My name is Harry Tisdale. I want to employ you in redoing my mother's memorial."

"How did you find out about us?" said Linda.

"Ma'am, a lot of people know about you. A lot of people know you do good conscientious work. I'd like to hire you to do a job for me."

She invited him inside. "We don't usually do business this way."

"Yes, Ma'am, I know that," said Harry. "But I don't live far away and lately I've been having this odd feeling that something is wrong. My mother died a long time ago. I'm sixty years old and I was only fourteen when she passed. I've thought about her probably every day of my life since then. I go to her grave most weeks. But lately, something has been wrong. Lately, my mother needs to rest."

Linda began to regret offering her hospitality to this man. "Before you continue," she said. "Let me get my husband in here."

Harry smiled. "Of course."

He sat at the couch. Linda went to the garage. Chris saw her and turned off the compressor.

"There's a man here. I think we should talk to him," said Linda.

Chris pulled off his goggles and dusted off his hair and removed his apron and hung it up on a hook.

"You looked scared," he said.

"I'm not scared. Just kind of—wary."

They went back to the living room. Harry rose and offered his hand. Chris shook it cautiously.

"What can I do for you?" said Chris.

"Well, I'll get right to the point. I had a dream a few nights ago. It was about my mother. Nothing odd there, I dream about her all the time. Only thing is, she asked me to do something for her in this dream. She told me she wants her headstone blanked out."

Chris looked at Linda. Linda shrugged.

Harry cleared his throat. "The words on her headstone. My father had them put on when she died all that time ago. 'Beloved wife and mother.' And then her dates. She wants all that erased. See, what she said is that those words, on the stone, they let other words in. It's like her ears and she doesn't want to hear anything anymore. She wants the words gone so she can have some peace and quiet."

Linda glanced at Chris.

Chris scratched his head. "It's not like a pencil line," he said. "It can't be 'erased.'"

"Are you sure you want to pursue this?" said Linda. "I mean, a dream, you know. It's not really your mother talking, it's you, kind of, talking to yourself."

Harry tilted his head and smiled. "Yeah, I thought about that. You're probably right. But it does feel real to me. It feels like that's what she wants." He turned to Chris. "And I understand about how it can't be erased. I'm not asking you to fill in the words. What I had in mind was blasting out the rock all around the words so it looks like a flat window pane. You can do that, can't you?"

Chris considered this. "Sure. I could do it. But I still don't really understand why."

Here Harry rose from the couch and stood with his hands on his hips. It was a stance Chris recognized from some of the memorials that people wanted for their graves. Not the hands on the hips part, but the looking up part, the way Harry lifted his jaw, as though he was gazing at something *above* the horizon in the extreme distance.

Linda made a motion to rise with Harry, the stance had that kind of power, but Chris put a hand, gently, on her shoulder. Instantly she understood something that her often business-like nature did not allow: Harry was creating a moment, and it would perhaps be best to allow the moment to come to fruition.

"I have come to see that my mother has said her peace," said Harry. "She is tired of the world, and she has asked me to ease her into her silence, her solitude. We all need a rest at the end of a hard day. My mother wants this rest."

He lowered his gaze down to Chris and Linda. They looked down at the floor in the manner of people embarrassed by something genuine in their midst that they do not understand.

Finally Chris spoke. "We have spent the last few months *giving* voice to those that had none. This is the complete opposite."

"Yes," said Linda. "Also, we can't do it here. We would have to move our equipment to the grave site. That's not really part of our operation. We're not portable. The sand blaster is big." She tried to smile, tried to be kind, but ended up simply feigning politeness.

"I have to agree with my wife," said Chris. "We do understand what you're trying to do, but we aren't really in that business. We truly believe it is better to have words on a headstone than not."

There are awkward silences that are embarrassing for everyone involved. Such an interlude descended on the three of them until Harry saw the futility of going on and let his hands drop to his sides. He nodded first at Linda, then at Chris. "I'm sorry to have wasted your time," he said. Then he turned and walked out the door.

"That was odd," said Chris.

"He kind of gave me the creeps," said Linda. "There must be something wrong with a person who wants to censor the dead."

"Censor the dead," said Chris. Then he laughed. "That is a good one."

Three months later the mail order monument business was doing very well for Linda and Chris. They had completely forgotten about the visit from Harry. They were doing so well, in fact, that they were planning a vacation. They spent many hours poring over brochures for holidays to foreign lands. Linda wanted very much to visit the British Isles. "So much history," she said. "So much to see. I just want to go there and absorb it all. I've never been anywhere. I want to see part of the world before I die."

Chris was partial to Egypt. "The pyramids," he said. "Don't you want to see the pyramids, Linda?"

"Well, sure, I suppose so, but after the pyramids, what is there? Sand and a big polluted river? Think of England, Ireland, Scotland. Stonehenge, London, the moors, we could go on and on for weeks, months. Just walking around the countryside."

"The pyramids are so ancient," said Chris. "They are the most incredible things ever built. Of stone!"

And so they went back and forth like this for some time. Until a knock on the door. Linda and Chris never had visitors, or very rarely. The knock reminded them immediately of their visitor from twelve weeks ago. They glanced at each other.

"I hope it's not that guy again," said Linda.

"Harry," said Chris, walking to the door.

"Yes. Harry."

Chris swung the door open. A police officer stood before him.

"I'm looking for Chris and Linda Jones," said the cop.

"You've got us," said Chris. Linda came up and stood beside him.

"What's this about?" she said.

"We found this among the effects of Mr. Harry Tisdale." He presented them with an envelope. Linda took it. It had their address on it. "There was a note that we should give it to you."

"What happened?" said Chris.

"Mr. Tisdale killed himself last week. He left a note and some addressed envelopes. This one is yours." The office tipped his hat, then stepped away, got into his car and drove off.

Linda and Chris felt sick at heart. How could this have happened? He must have been thinking about suicide that day he was here. He was doing that thing that suicidal people often do: clean up loose ends. Take care of affairs. Keep his mother from knowing. Erasing her so she wouldn't see how depressed he was, and never know he killed himself.

Chris could hardly move. Linda guided him to the chair.

"Did we do this?" said Chris.

"No," said Linda. "He did it to himself."

"But could we—"

"Stop it," said Linda. "Don't let yourself think those things."

She opened the envelope. There was money inside. Enough for a monument. Linda's hands were shaking. A short note.

"I chiseled away the words myself," it began. "It wasn't so hard. Took some time, is all. My mother always understood and she always wanted to help, but there was nothing for her to do anymore. This is enough to cover a monument for me. Make it small. Make it say: Harold Tisdale, beloved son. Tired, needed to rest. I'm sorry to trouble you, but you seem like nice people. I know it was wrong to silence her. She needed her voice, like anyone else, but I just couldn't let her know the truth. Not about me. Not like this."

She passed the note to her husband. "Here's a job," she said. "Prepaid. Cash. Isn't that great?"

Chris took the paper. It rattled in has hand, like bones of a skeleton at a

Halloween party where everyone pretends to have a good time and no one understand what they are doing there.

Martians Come From Everywhere

The year they discovered fossils on Mars was the same year Seagull Cove had a visitor from an unknown origin.

He strode out of the sea one morning between Pawn Rock and Lincoln Rock. It was low tide and he came up on the beach and made his way to the cliffs next to Tide Street, which was a good 80 or 90 feet above the sand.

He was a little disoriented. After all, up to then, for at least thirty years or so, a far as he knew, he had been living in the ocean.

But things were getting strange in the deep waters way off the coast of Oregon. Big hunks of plastic were everywhere, and the sun could not penetrate down as far as it used to, which meant living in the ocean was living in darkness, and that wasn't to Fred's taste at all.

So he thought he'd try landlubbing for a while.

The first person he met on the beach was Hazel Plankton. Hazel lived on Seastack Drive, just a block from Old Mermaid Way, and just two blocks from the wooden steps that went down from Tide Street to the beach. She liked to go beachcombing most mornings and the morning she met the stranger was no exception.

Hazel had seen her share of naked men in her life, but seeing a tall well-muscled one on the beach at Seagull Cove, well, that was not something she thought she could get used to.

He saw her first, walking toward him, and when he did, he stopped with his hands fisted and resting on his hips so he looked like a tall tea kettle.

"Ahoy, there," said Hazel. She had her bag, full of shells and pieces of drift wood, slung over her shoulder, the same bag she had taken to the beach for the last twenty years. She wore rubber boots and a yellow hat, the brim flopping down over her eyes.

"Hello," said the man.

Hazel determined, on the spot, that Fred was no threat to her. She prided herself on her good instincts in such cases. If she sensed a threat from the man, she would have turned right around and gone back home. But she didn't.

He had a kind face and non-threatening mannerisms. He did not try to cover himself, which she found interesting, but not alarming. The man was obviously comfortable in his own skin and wasn't ashamed to let others see it. All of it.

"You lost, friend?" she asked him as she got close enough for normal easy conversation.

"Maybe."

"You got a name."

"Pretty sure it's Fred."

"Well, hello Fred," said Hazel.

"Hello," said Fred.

"I'm Hazel."

"Okay," said Fred.

"You're not from here, are you?"

Fred shook his head.

"Our customs require clothing, as a rule. You have any to wear?"

Fred shook his head. "We don't have clothes where I come from."

"And where is that?" asked Hazel.

Fred hooked a thumb behind him, indicating the waves crashing on Lincoln Rock and sending foamy white water around it, like ol' Abe was wearing a furry collar.

"Your boat capsize or something?" she asked.

"What's a boat?" asked Fred.

"Ah. Huh." said Hazel. She took off her jacket and handed it to Fred, who took it, but without any enthusiasm.

He held it between thumb and forefinger, as though it were a rotten piece of meat.

"It's too small for you, obviously," said Hazel. "But I want you to wrap it around yourself so I can get you home without attracting too much attention."

"Home?" said Fred. He looked at Hazel with an expression of bewilderment.

"Yes, home. My home. I'm going to help you out, if you're okay with that."

Fred looked like he was not able to take in everything Hazel was saying. He looked like he was trying to parse it in his head, trying to make some sense of it.

"Oh never mind," said Hazel, and took the jacket back and went behind Fred.

He started to turn around. She touched his shoulder. Slightly, but enough for him to get the message. He wasn't to move. He stopped. She draped the torso of the jacket in front of him and tied the sleeves behind him so the knot rode above his buttocks.

"It isn't ideal," she said, "but it'll have to do for the moment. Now follow me."

She trudged back toward the bottom of the steps. Fred didn't follow right at first. She turned around and motioned him to come on. He still didn't get it.

"Look," she said, "I can see you understand English. You going to come with me or not? You can stay here and take your chances with the other locals. Some of them aren't going to take kindly to your ways. Fair warning."

She put her hand up to her forehead, shading her eyes from the sun.

Fred began to think he might have made a mistake. The jacket around his waist already felt like a restraint he had to get rid of at all costs. But as he thought of returning to the water, he shivered, half from the cold, but also, half from the fear. He didn't think he could live for long in that darkness anymore.

He pressed one foot into the sand and stepped forward with the other.

Fred liked the feel of the dry sand grains under his soles. They were so different from the wet ocean bottom he was used to. And the air around him. It was so thin. He could move through it with ease. He thought he was going to like it here on the shore.

"Good going," said Hazel. "I'll have you warmed up in no time. Then you can tell me your story."

"Story?"

"Of your life," said Hazel. "It's got to be a doozy."

It was mid morning, which Hazel thought was fortunate. It meant most everyone was at work or school, which meant no one saw them walking down the street. They must have been a sight. Hazel leading a tall man with his backside exposed to the world.

Back at her house, Hazel opened her front door and motioned Fred inside. He hesitated, then seemed to remember what that reverse waving of the hand indicated, and he stepped through the doorway.

"Just wait there," she said.

As she went into the back room, she picked up her television remote and turned on her set. CNN bloomed onto the screen with a report of the Mars probe that had dug deep into the Martian soil and uncovered fossil bones. So far, they appeared to be fish fossils. Some grainy pictures of them appeared on the screen.

The reporters covering the story were breathless with wonderment. Here was proof—finally!—of life on another planet. It was millions of years old, but still. It meant something. They were going to bring on a few experts on life and astronomy and space flight to explain it to their viewers.

Hazel registered their wonderment in the back of her mind as she went to Earl's side of the closet and pulled out a shirt and a pair of pants. She had never gotten rid of his clothes, even now, ten years after his death. She always thought, irrationally, there would be a purpose for them. And now there was.

She grabbed a pair of socks and some boxer shorts from his dresser drawer and brought the whole pile out to Fred and handed them to him.

He took them, his left hand supporting the pile, and his right hand resting on top. He stood, waiting.

"Well go on," said Hazel. "Put them on."

Fred looked at the clothes, an expression of bewilderment on his face.

"Oh, you want privacy," said Hazel. "I get it." She took his hand and led him to the guest bedroom, then closed the door behind him.

Then she went to the kitchen and put on a big pot of water and turned her attention back to the television.

A professor of geology was explaining that Mars must have had a deep ocean at one point in the past. Maybe in the recent past, although for the professor recent meant "only" a hundred million years ago.

"What kind of ocean would it have been?" asked the CNN host. "Water?"

"Yes," said the professor. "Water."

"That's so exciting," said the host.

"Yes it is," said the professor.

The kettle began whistling and Hazel turned from the screen and took the kettle off the burner. She got tea bags from the cupboard and put them into a teapot and poured water into it. "Hope the freak likes tea," she said to the air.

She let the tea steep for a while, then went to the guest room door and tapped on it lightly. "How you doing in there?" she asked.

A muffled and indecipherable few words from the other side.

"Need some help? Can I come in?"

Silence.

"I guarantee you don't have anything I haven't seen before. Besides, I've already seen it today."

The door opened and Fred stood in the frame like an awkward imitation of a man. He had socks on his hands, and his pants were on backwards. The boxer shorts were on the floor behind him. The shirt, however, was on and buttoned the way it should be.

"Hmmm," said Hazel. "A good effort, I think, but a few corrections are in order."

She demonstrated how the boxers should go on, and tried to mime how the pants should be turned around and put back on. He seemed to understand.

She closed the door and let him be for a few moments, then returned to the tea.

A few seconds later he emerged looking like a normal person.

He reminded Hazel of Earl. Not his build or looks, just the clothes. She remembered buying that shirt. She remembered when Earl first wore those pants.

Fred stood on the edge of the kitchen, afraid to go any further.

"Earl," she said, forgetting who she was talking to, "what are you waiting for?"

"I think my name is Fred," he said.

Hazel, momentarily lost for words, nodded. Then: "Sorry. I made tea. You like tea?"

"What is it?"

"It'll warm you up. Come on. Sit down." She pulled out a chair for him. He eased himself onto it, apparently taking his cue from how Hazel sat at hers.

"We don't have chairs where I come from."

"Okay," said Hazel. "Must be a strange place. How do people sit down?"

"We do a lot of swimming. Not much sitting down."

Hazel took a sip of her tea, and motioned with her other hand that Fred should do the same.

He gingerly took up the cup and put it to his lips and tilted it very slightly.

"Bitter," he said.

"It's got something to it, though, don't you think?"

"Something," said Fred.

The professor on CNN had been replaced by someone who purported to have written a history of the Martian civilization. The story of the Martian ocean came to him in a dream and he wrote it all down. The CNN reporter was way more kind to him than Hazel would have been.

"Who's Earl?" asked Fred.

"My husband," said Hazel. "We were married a long time. Not as long as that fish fossil has been on Mars, but long enough."

"Where is he?"

"Wherever heart attacks take people. I've often imagined some kind of hospital ward in the sky, where they all congregate and talk about their illnesses, like old people do. It's comforting, in a way."

"It doesn't sound comforting," said Fred.

"You didn't come from the ocean," said Hazel. "You know that, right?"

"Yes I did," said Fred.

"Nope," said Hazel. "If you did, how did you learn English?"

This stopped Fred. He held his cup mid way between the table and his lips and blinked several times.

"You just let that sink in," said Hazel. "I'll be right back. Have to go to the bathroom. You will too, after you've had that cup of tea. Ha!" She slapped Fred on the back as she went by.

When she returned from the bathroom, she found Fred had turned up the volume on the television and was staring at it in rapt attention.

The nut job with the dream diary was gone and now they were talking to an astronaut who very much wanted to go to Mars.

"Now we have a reason," she said. "A real reason."

"And we didn't before?" asked the CNN reporter.

"Well," said the astronaut, "I wouldn't say that, but now it's more urgent."

"These fossils are millions of years old," said the reporter. "It can't be all that urgent."

Fred turned from the screen and grinned at Hazel. "I want to go," he said.

"You have to pee?" she asked.

He shook his head. "No, no. To Mars. I want to go to Mars. It's light there. The ocean isn't dark."

"The ocean is gone," said Hazel. "And anyway, you can't go to Mars. You don't even know who you are."

"I know my name is Fred."

"What else? Where you from? Where's your family?"

He looked up at the ceiling, then back to the screen. "I would do well on Mars," he said. "Mars would be my new home."

But interplanetary travel would have to wait. Later that afternoon, Hazel had Fred do some work in the yard. She showed him how to mow the grass with her lawn mower. He took to the task with enthusiasm, running the machine back and forth quickly.

Hazel looked up from weeding her garden every now and then and watched him with a mixture of admiration and pride. She would have to find out where he was from. *He* needed to know where he was from.

Didn't he?

Fred stopped the mower and bent down on one knee and looked at the grass.

"What's wrong?" she called to him. She hoped he hadn't run over a snake or a frog. She hated when that happened.

Fred laid his palm flat on the grass and pressed down. Hazel watched him for a few seconds, then was startled by his next action. He dug his fingers into the turf and closed his grip and pulled up a big hunk of dirt and grass and tossed it aside.

"What's going on, Fred?" she asked him.

"Something there," he said, and reached back inside and pulled up more dirt.

"I'm not so sure that's a good idea," she said. She got up from her weeding and walked over to him. By the time she was next to him, he had a good pile of dirt going next to a hole approximately two feet deep. He was strong, and he worked fast.

"Looking for something?" she asked.

"Yes," said Fred. He reached down into the hole and grimaced as he worked his hand down there in the depths and the muscles in his arm flexed and tightened. "Found it," he said.

He pulled out a rock about the size of a cantaloupe, and tossed it onto the grass.

"That's it?" said Hazel. "You put a hole in my lawn for a rock?"

"It doesn't belong," said Fred. "It's from Mars."

The rock was covered with black dirt, some of it caked on. It had a smooth surface, like it had been polished.

"Most likely it's from the meteor," said Hazel. "But the meteor didn't come from Mars."

"Had to," said Fred. "It's not from here."

"I heard that," said Hazel, now irritated with him. "But I told you. A million years ago—give or take—a meteor crashed onto the coast here and created the bay. It's down by the marina. When it crashed, it disintegrated and sent pieces of itself all over the region. People are always finding little hunks of the meteorite. You can tell because they don't have sharp edges. That's what you have there. But it *wasn't* from Mars. *Isn't* from Mars."

Fred picked up the rock and cradled it in his hands, like he was holding a crystal ball and wanted to see the future in it.

"You going to fill that hole back in?" she asked.

He didn't answer her, but presently he pushed the dirt back into the hole he had made. She stepped on the dirt to try to tamp it down, but it still left a bulge.

Fred then went down on his knees and leaned over the rock and studied it.

Hazel regarded him with a mixture of irritation and pity. What was going on with him?

"You from another world?" she asked.

"I don't remember," said Fred.

"How did you know about that rock?"

"Felt the field," he said. "Felt its power. Like heat." He held out his hand over the grass. His fingers trembled slightly.

"Maybe we've had enough yard work for one day," she said.

"Maybe."

"Let's figure out how to get you to Mars," she said.

"Good idea," said Fred. "That's a real good idea."

Hazel found the application form on the NASA website and offered to help Fred fill it in.

"It's long," she said. "You sure you want to do this?"

"Is this how people get to Mars?" he asked.

"Well, they're taking applications for the next pool of astronauts. You have as good a chance as anyone."

Fred sat with Hazel's tablet on his lap. NASA's logo glowed on the screen and sent a strange blue shadow over his face.

"Let's do it," he said.

"Okay," she said. "Name first."

"Fred."

She indicated the appropriate spot on the screen. "Go ahead," she said. "Type it in."

He looked at her.

"You can't type?"

He shook his head.

"Can you spell?"

He raised his shoulders up to his ears.

She sighed and took the tablet from him and typed in F R E D. "Last name?" she asked.

"We can come to that later," said Fred.

"That one's pretty important," said Hazel.

"Later."

"You have to have a last name," she said.

"Fred."

"That's your first name."

"And my last one. I won't have any more names. It's the last one I'll ever get."

"That's not what last name means," she said. "What's your family name?"

"Ocean creatures are my family."

Hazel hesitated, then typed in O C E A N.

"Next they want to know your birthdate."

Fred laughed. "Who can remember when they were born?"

"You don't have to remember your birth to know your birth *date*."

Fred was still laughing. "Oh, Hazel," he said. "You are so *funny*."

Hazel didn't see the humor. What was she going to put in that blank?

She typed in a date from thirty years ago. It was the date of her tenth anniversary with Earl. She remembered it because they had taken a trip over to Ashland to see some plays at the Shakespeare festival and spend a few days in the valley.

They hiked some trails, ate in some fancy restaurants, and stayed in a charming little motor court inn. It was one of the best times she had ever had with Earl.

Fred noticed the date. "You remember my birthday?" he asked.

"No," she said. Her voice was a little unsteady and her eyes felt heavy with tears. "Just a guess."

"Guessing is good," said Fred.

"Now your address," said Hazel.

"Can I use yours?"

"You don't live here," said Hazel. "Where do you come from?" she asked. "Where is your home, Fred Ocean? You came to town with nothing. Literally. But everyone has a place they call home, even if they live on the streets."

Fred looked like he wanted to see what was on the other side of the wall in front of him. He stared and stared until Hazel typed in her address.

"There," she said.

"Thank you," said Fred.

"Don't mention it."

They continued filling out the online from, making a lot of guesses, especially the parts about education, former employment, and qualifications. When they were finished she had Fred press the send button.

The tablet whooshed and a message appeared on the screen thanking them for their interest.

"What happens now?" said Fred.

"We wait for their answer."

"It's going to be yes," said Fred. "I know it."

"There are a lot of applicants," said Hazel. "The last time they had an open call for astronaut candidates, they got something like 30,000 of them. Now, with the fossil find, I'm sure it'll be even more."

"Okay," said Fred, "but none of them are going to be like me."

His grin made Hazel laugh.

"I'm sure you're right about that," she said.

Later that evening, once the excitement of applying for a chance to go to Mars wore off, Hazel and Fred sat on the couch and watched some television.

Hazel dozed off in the middle of an episode of *NCIS*, and woke up several hours later with a blanket over her, which Fred must have put there.

She looked around and didn't see him. Disoriented, she wondered if that meant he wasn't there. Or had he gone.

"Earl?" she called.

No answer. She pulled the blanket off and went down the hall and heard snoring from the guest room. She pushed the door open slightly and saw Fred on the bed. He was on his belly, naked, over the covers, as though he didn't want to disturb the sheets.

She wanted to wake him. She was afraid that in the morning he was going to remember his life and decide he didn't need to be here anymore.

Hazel stood in the doorway for a minute or so, then went into the room and pulled the comforter off the other side of the bed and folded it over so it covered Fred. He stirred in his sleep but did not wake.

She was going to leave him, but her own bed was going to be cold and empty. Why not stay here?

She got under the sheets and snuggled down into the warmth that Fred leaked into the room.

She wanted to put her hand on Fred, but decided not to. The man was in a strange mental state. No need to frighten him.

She fell asleep listening to his snores, which were not unlike Earl's snoring. He used to shake the house sometimes. It used to irritate her. Now it filled her heart up.

She woke up hoping Earl was going to be lying next to her. She often woke up with that feeling. She would see Earl everywhere. Around a corner, at the kitchen table, on the couch. He would only be there for a second or two, then disappear.

But of course Earl was not there, and his absence made her heart break just a little each time.

Even worse, Fred was not there either.

Gradually a buzzing sound came from somewhere outside. She got up and looked through the bedroom window and saw Fred pushing the lawn mower over the grass, finishing the job he had started the day before. Thankfully, he was fully clothed.

She opened the window and called his name. He looked up and waved at her.

She waved back, ridiculously happy to see him. She felt like a silly school girl with a crush on a boy.

"I'll make us breakfast," she said.

He smiled and raised his thumb at her, then kept pushing the lawnmower over the grass.

Hazel went into the kitchen and pulled out eggs and bacon from the fridge. She cut up some potatoes and dropped them into a saucepan with some water and got that going.

It was nice to cook for someone besides herself. Even if it was just a simple breakfast.

She cracked some eggs into a bowl and whisked them until they got fluffy.

The potatoes began to boil and she turned the heat down on them, then put several bacon strips into a pan and put the pan on the stove.

The front door opened and closed. She felt herself go electric with anticipation. She remembered how Earl used to come into the house, stamp his feet to shake off any dirt, and then walk over to wherever she was and put his arm around her.

"Hazel," said Fred.

His voice was different. It didn't have that faraway subtext he seemed to carry with him the day before, like he had some forgotten past. Which, Hazel supposed, was just the truth.

She didn't turn around.

"Yes?"

"I remember," he said.

Hazel felt her world tilt. Not a lot, but enough for her knees to weaken just a bit. Fred saw it and came over to her and put his hands on her hips. "You okay?" he asked.

"Fine," she said, and slapped at his hand. He stepped away.

"Sorry," he said.

"You were saying?"

"You don't want to look at me?" he asked.

She took in a deep breath and turned around to face him. He looked completely different. He was in his body and seemed much more relaxed, like he belonged in the world. This world.

"What did you remember?" she asked.

He didn't answer right away. "I thought I'd finish doing the grass. Before I went."

"Where are you going?"

"I live up the coast," he said. "On Vancouver Island."

"How did you get here?"

"I was taking a cruise. I fell overboard."

Hazel nodded. "It seemed like a fishy story that you lived in the sea."

He smiled, slightly. "Yeah. Thank you for your help. I've called my family. I used your phone. Hope you don't mind."

"Family?"

"I have a wife. And two kids. They were worried sick about me."

"I can imagine. What about Mars?"

"I heard it's very cold there," he said.

She nodded.

"Breakfast will be ready in a few. Go wash up."

"I thought I was going to die," said Fred.

"I can imagine."

"It was like the sea was swallowing me up."

"Like the fossil on Mars," said Hazel. "That fish was swallowed up by the sea, and then by Mars itself."

"Or like the rock I found."

Hazel nodded. "That rock lived underground. How did you find it, really?"

"I came to a rise in the lawn," he said. "It seemed strange. Wrong. I knew something was there."

Strange and wrong. Just like he was, yesterday. Now he was different.

Hazel stirred the bacon around in the pan. It was just about ready. She slid the strips out onto plates, then put the pan back on the stove and poured the eggs into the remaining bacon grease.

"Thank you for your help," he said. "Thank you for your kindness."

The eggs took only a few seconds before they were done. They were such a bright yellow. It was like the sun had taken off a piece of itself and dropped it into her pan, right here in her kitchen, next to the man who, only yesterday, wanted nothing better than to go to Mars and leave her all alone in Seagull Cove.

Snow

Snow fell all morning and afternoon, sucking the noise out of the world. Liana, framed like a painting in our living room window, was captured by the storm. She had barely moved for almost an hour. "Mike?" she said.

"Hmmm?"

"What keeps us together?"

I grunted incoherently, an action designed to acknowledge her question without initiating a conversation, and continued reading my newspaper. Liana stared out the window, spellbound, as though she had never seen a good long snowfall before.

"What do you think it is?" she said. "What's the glue that holds people together?"

"I suppose it depends on the people," I said.

Liana ran a finger down the window pane, leaving a long greasy trail. "You're right, of course," she said. "With me it's music, I think. If I didn't have music I would die." She began to hum a tune to herself. The sound of it filled the house and made me feel comfortable and warm. Liana could do that with her voice. She could make my world complete.

I looked through the window. The scene outside was like the aftermath of a pillow fight: white feather clumps fell slowly to the ground, which was itself covered to ankle depth with fluffy flakes. I dropped my newspaper, rose from my chair, and stood beside Liana. I put my hand on her back and looked out the window with her. Her body felt warm and solid. She moved closer to me and I smelled her hair, her skin.

"I thought you meant what keeps *us* together," I said. "You and me."

She laughed. "Of course that's what you thought. You think the world revolves around us."

"Well doesn't it?"

"I'm serious. What keeps you from falling apart? What brings you peace? Gives your life shape?"

"You do."

She rolled her eyes. "You're hopeless, you know that?"

I hugged her close to me. She relaxed in my arms and I felt secure and free. I looked out the window again. The snow continued to fall. "I don't think we'll be able to go to work tomorrow," I said.

"Yes, isn't it wonderful?"

I didn't think it was so wonderful. There was the meeting with the board in the morning and the presentation to give later in the day. I didn't want to have to reschedule either one, but looking at the snow, it seemed inevitable.

"I'll turn on the news," I said. "See if there are going to be any closures tomorrow."

Liana nodded but didn't move from the window. I turned on the TV. A jumble of static and whirling colors filled each channel.

"Snow inside and out," said Liana.

"The storm must have disrupted the feed," I said and turned off the set. The quiet in the room seemed too much to bear.

"Let's go outside," I said.

Liana jumped up and grabbed her coat from the closet. I pulled my own jacket on as she stuffed her hands into a pair of mittens. "Maybe we'll make snow angels," she said.

"Why not?" I said as I retrieved her hat from the top shelf of the closet and handed it to her.

"Think it's that cold?" she said.

"Better safe than sorry."

She shrugged and pulled on the stretchy knitted cap. I touched the top of her head and ran my fingers down her hair. She took my hand and kissed my fingers. "Let's go," she said.

There is no quiet like the soft silence of a windless snowstorm. As we walked, all we could hear were the muffled bumps of our footsteps and the rustling of our clothes. Steam billowed quietly from our mouths: the breath of winter. All background noise had disappeared: no cars, no wind through trees, no *hum*. The white noise of the world was gone. There remained only a clean, pure nothingness and we stopped occasionally to revel in it. The flakes fell around us like silent static. It accumulated on our shoulders, heads, and boots like confetti. I felt as though we were renewing ourselves and this pretty snowfall was in celebration of us.

Liana started singing. It seemed to fill the world on that quiet afternoon. Her voice wrapped itself around each descending snowflake.

She stopped singing and I smiled at her. "That was nice," I said. The sound of my own words boomed in the quiet like great vibrating drums: loud, imposing. But in the next instant the noise was gone, snatched by the greedy white void around us, under us, even in us, for I could see flakes fall on Liana's tongue as she sang, her mouth open to the bleached insulation of the world.

"Sometimes," she said, "I think all I am are my songs, the music. If I didn't have that, I don't know if I would even exist."

These were strange words for Liana to say. I had never heard such a statement from her lips. I laughed uncomfortably.

"It's true," she said. "You don't believe me, but it is true." Then she opened her mouth again and she sang a song that seemed to hold that moment in its grasp forever. My perception of time was warped in the few minutes it took for her to finish the song. I was aware that she did not seem to notice anything around her. She closed her eyes, spread her hands, stretched out her arms, lifted her head to the trees. An inch-thick layer of snow had accumulated on her hat. It looked like lamb's wool cradling her head. The notes from her throat rang true and pure, more lovely than I had ever heard before. I felt an urge to pull her close to me and hug her. I wanted her body to warm me. I wanted her power to flow into my soul.

But I did not move a muscle. I simply stood in front of her, letting the music fill the air, letting her have her moment with the snow. It was the most luminously beautiful sight I have ever seen.

When she stopped she let her arms fall to her sides. I put my hands out to her but she did not fall into them as I had expected and wanted. Instead she crossed her arms and grasped her shoulders and stood shaking with her teeth chattering. "I'm about ready to go back," she said.

"We just started walking," I said.

"Please. I'm getting cold."

"Okay," I said. We walked back to the house, stamped our feet on the front step, and went inside where we heated up water and made hot chocolate from pouches full of sweet brown powder. We sat on the couch together, as we had often done in the past, but this time it was different. Her touch was not the familiar touch I had come to know over the years. Her skin was peculiarly alien to me. She must have felt it too, for after a few minutes she pulled away from me and curled up at the far end of the couch. She sipped her hot chocolate, made a face, and put it down.

"What's wrong?" I said. "Too cold?"

"Too hot," she answered and picked up a magazine and began leafing though it.

I tasted my own cup. It was lukewarm, barely above body temperature. "That's funny," I said. "Mine isn't hot at all."

She looked up from her magazine for a moment. "Well mine is. I'll just let it cool down for a bit."

I nodded. An uncomfortable quiet filled the room. I felt as though Liana wanted me to remain silent. Outside the snow kept rising. It covered the little hills and dips of the lawn and rounded out the curb along the street. It made the world smooth, like cream in a bowl, erasing its character, making it faceless. I looked at Liana. Her face seemed smoother too, the familiar creases and wrinkles somehow removed or covered over.

"Sing for me again," I said. I knew I sounded pitiful, like a child asking for candy from a parent who has forbidden it.

"Here?" said Liana. "You want me to sing now?"

"Like outside. Can't you sing like you just sang outside?"

"Outside was different. There I had an audience."

"You have the same audience here," I said.

She smiled at me.

I could see it was no use and did not pursue it any further. She went back to her magazine. We spent the rest of the day reading, dozing, eating. Towards the end of the evening Liana came to me and unbuttoned my shirt and pressed her hand against my chest. Her palm was cold as an ice cube. Her fingers were like icicles. My skin flinched, but my soul held steady and true. She pulled me to her. Her arms were as cold as her hands. She stepped back to slip off her shirt and pants. We embraced and her entire body was cold now, burning cold where she touched me.

"It will never be like this again," she said softly, her breath in my ear, chilling my cheek, raising bumps of freezing anticipation over my body. I dropped to the floor. She followed and we made love slowly, shivering in the cold flowing from her body. I clung to her like a child. She soothed me, caressed me.

Afterwards we lay on the carpet and I pulled a blanket from the couch to cover us. We slept. Overnight the storm played itself out and in the morning I woke to see a clear blue sky overlooking a world of dazzling white. Snow covered everything to a depth of at least three feet.

Liana had kicked off the blanket in the night. She was still asleep and I covered her with the blanket again. I rose, pulled on my clothes, and began making breakfast. I saw through the kitchen window that the sun was strong and hot. As I watched I could almost see the snow level begin to drop. The wonderland of white would be gone soon and we would have to return to our mundane activities. I heard Liana stir on the living room floor. I took her a cup of coffee and kneeled beside her and smiled as her eyes fluttered open and she stared at me almost unknowingly. "Here's some coffee," I said and put her cup on the floor beside her elbow. I touched her cheek with the back of my hand.

I stopped. Around us the clutter of the world seemed to stop too. My throat tightened and I began to feel a sense of events going out of control. Liana was still cold, but here was something else: my hand had sunk into her cheek and I felt the jostle of hundreds of swirling particles there. It was as though I had put my hand into a chaos of tumbling balls.

I pulled my hand back. Liana sat up. The blanket fell from her and I saw her breasts and belly had turned blue and granular, swirling like the snow on TV.

"Liana, what's happening?"

She pushed the coffee cup away, spilling warm brown liquid onto the carpet. She spoke slowly and the words were garbled, syllables tumbling against each other. "I need a glass of water," she said. "Cold water."

It took me a moment to understand her request. I swallowed hard, unable to assimilate what was happening. Liana was a different being.

"I think you need to be warm," I said. I tried to pull the blanket up to her chin. She pushed it away.

"Water," she said. "Ice water."

I looked at her eyes. I knew her expressions well enough to understand pleading. That much had not changed. I rose and returned with a glass of ice cold water.

She drank it down quickly. "More," she said.

I brought back a pitcher filled with ice and water, that chattered as I carried it. She took it gratefully and drank straight from it, without benefit of a glass. "Thank you," she said.

I nodded.

"I think it's going to be warm today," I said.

"Yes," she said. "The sun's hot. It'll do its work. I told you I was my music, didn't I?"

I nodded. I could find nothing to say, nothing to make her see that I wanted her to stay. We both seemed to know it would not happen.

"It took me," she said. "The snow. It took my song, my music. My soul, I guess. Oh, Mike, I don't know what to say, don't have the words to hold

you here with me, to hold me here. You look strange to me. My eyes—
they're breaking up, can you see it?"

I did not look at her eyes, afraid of what I might see. The glass slipped
from her fingers. Water stained the carpet like blood. I looked at her face
and it was as though I could see her individual molecules now, bumping
against one another, vibrating and humming, making a sad song to the
world, to me.

"Hold me," she said. "Just one more time."

I put my hands out to her. She reached for me and it was like a fog
covered my hand, a fog of Liana's body. I felt only a sad ache that seemed
to weaken my body.

The sun beat down. The house grew warmer. The snow outside was
melting, flattening, diminishing.

"I'm going," said Liana. "Following the song, the words, myself. It's my
own fault, isn't it? I asked the question. Now I have my answer."

I wiped tears from my cheeks. I tried to hold her. My hand pushed
right through her. Liana's words were going too. All of her was going and
there was nothing I could do to keep her. Could a person be so fragile,
so easy to take apart? I watched as she dimmed from a bustle of vibrating
molecules, to a swirl of feathery particles, to a cloud of wispy nothingness.

And then she was gone.

I sat on the floor for ages, unable and unwilling to move. My chest held
a terrible ache that did not diminish as the hours ticked by.

Eventually I rose from the floor and went outside. I stood in the sun
and listened to the gentle crackles of the melting snow falling upon itself
layer by layer. Liana was trapped in those layers. I relaxed and closed my
eyes. I fell back with my arms outstretched, gathering in the world. A great
loud whoosh accompanied my fall and my contact with the snow: a terrific
thump of noise, punctuating the air like an exclamation point. I moved
my outstretched arms and legs spasmodically, pushing wet slushy snow
aside like a snow plow. The cold soaked through my clothes and touched
my skin. It penetrated my body and seemed to freeze my bones. My teeth
started chattering. The sound of them filled my head.

After a few minutes my arms and legs stopped moving. I shivered in my white cradle. From where I lay I saw only blue sky encircled by the snow banks I had created around me. I raised my hand and looked at my palm. It had turned blue and grainy. I thought of Liana.

I rolled onto my stomach and tunneled under the snow. It covered me completely and I began to feel comfortable again. The ache eased. I didn't have Liana but I had a familiar security again.

The snow continued to melt.

I settled into my cold, protective cocoon, and waited for the moment when my body would begin to dissolve with the snow.

Riders

Alone with her thoughts, he sipped his coffee in the quiet lunch room of Carrier's Inc.

—*Martin? Are you there? Are you ready?*

—In a second, Angie.

—*Come on. It's almost time.*

—I just got here. Give me some time to become civil.

—*Okay. Don't be long.*

He could almost feel her pout.

—I won't.

—*And don't drink so much coffee. It's bad for you.*

—Mind your own business, you little brat.

Martin heard her happy laugh in his head, then she broke the connection. He looked around the room. There were three or four other carriers, none of them speaking or moving. They were preparing themselves for their assignments.

"Was that a rider?"

He turned his head to see Kate.

"It's Angie," he said. "I'm due to pick her up in a few minutes."

Scowling, Kate put her tray down, sat across from Martin, and breathed out heavily, obviously tired. Her tray bore two steaming cups of coffee, a large danish wrapped in cellophane, and a couple of candy bars. She brought the danish to her mouth with both hands and broke the package open with her teeth.

"Angie again, huh?" she said.

Martin nodded.

"Doesn't she ever stop?"

"Sure, Angie's all right. Just a little over-anxious."

"What's wrong with her?" she asked, working a bite of danish around, in her mouth. "God, this is *stale*," she said. "Hard as a rock. See?" She thumped what remained of the pastry against her tray.

"I don't know what's wrong with her," said Martin. "Something about her leg. I think."

"It isn't amputated, is it? I had an amputee once. Hated it. Gave me the creeps."

"I really don't know, Kate. I don't think that kind of thing's important."

"Well when does her subscription run out? It's the end of the month you know."

He shrugged and sipped more of his coffee. Kate always wanted to know about the personal lives of her riders. Martin considered this a distasteful and damaging curiosity, a kind of voyeurism of pain. A carrier's job was to take a rider to places and experiences she couldn't manage to get to on her own. Period.

"You know, Martin," said Kate, "you're pretty new at this so you don't know as much as you think you do." She gulped some coffee and peeled the wrapper off one of her candy bars. "I can tell, just by how they feel when they're inside me exactly what's wrong with them. Some of them are sick or crippled, granted, but many are just lazy. Too lazy to get off their fat asses and get outside once in a while. Don't you ever *feel* that?"

"I carry mostly kids, so I haven't really noticed anything like that."

"Oh, I see. Kids aren't lazy, right? Kids don't manipulate. Kids are innocent and pure. You know, you have this unhealthy idealistic picture of childhood."

Martin didn't say anything.

"Anyway," said Kate, "how do you know you carry mostly kids?"

He smiled. "The same way you know what's wrong with them by the way they feel inside you."

"No one can tell about *all* their riders. There are always some that fool you."

He ran a finger around the rim of his cup. "What does it matter, anyway?" he asked. "Knowing too much can make you a bad carrier."

She stopped chewing and looked up. "Do you mean me?"

"Well, you've often said you don't like many of your riders."

"So?"

"So why don't you quit?"

She tilted her head. "It's a fun way to make money, that's why." She paused. "You're different though, aren't you?"

"Maybe." He studied his watch.

"You're looking for something more. After the fun's over and they're gone, you always feel bad, don't you?"

He wanted Angie's voice in his head now, but she wasn't there. He looked away from Kate, across the room.

"Why did you get into the business so late?" she asked. "You're— what—thirty-two?"

"Four," he said quietly. "I'm thirty-four."

"And only your fifth month of carrying. This is a young person's game. People discover their talent in their teens, and then it's all they can do to keep from using it. Right? How old were you when you first knew what your friend was about to say just before he said it? Or the first time you felt someone else's pain, or joy. I mean *really* felt it, in your bones? How old were you? Thirteen, fourteen? What's your story, Martin?"

He did not answer. He felt as though she were examining him for defects.

"I know you sneer at me, Martin. You think I'm dirty and degenerate because I take people to the cesspools of this city, show them the darker side of life—the excitement there. But what of it? I *enjoy* it. I've been up all night with a rider and I'm ready for more. What about you? The only assignments you want are children. If I'm a degenerate, what does that make you?"

Martin's head became hotter. His lips tightened.

Kate raised her eyebrows. "Hit a nerve, hmmm?"

"I carry kids because—" Martin stopped.

Kate leaned forward. "Why? Because why?"

"Because they need me."

Kate laughed. "Bullshit. You need them, we all need them. Makes us feel alive."

Martin's knees were locked in place. He wanted to get up from his chair, walk away from Kate and her questions, her probing.

"You know what I think?" said Kate. "I don't think you're a born telepath. I've heard of them, people who get the ability late in life, usually after some kind of big emotional crisis."

Martin drained his cup and stood up. "I've gotta go now."

Kate leaned back in her chair. "Sure. Six o'clock at my car. Don't be late."

"I wasn't late yesterday," he said.

"Wha—?" She looked up at him with a puzzled expression, then slapped her forehead with the heel of her hand. "Is *that* what's eating you? Look, I'm sorry. I was in a situation with this rider, I couldn't just leave him, you know? He was desperate, he *needed* me. It just slipped my mind your car was in the shop. But it won't happen again. I promise."

He nodded. "Sure," he said. "It's okay."

He started to walk past her. She grabbed his arm. Her voice became soft, losing its harshness. "You're setting yourself up for a fall," she said. "Don't think too highly of them. They're just people, that's all. And they're different from us. We have our minds. They have reality. We live in separate worlds, remember that."

"I've gotta go," he said again, and walked out the door. The air felt fresh and cool on his face.

—Martin, are you ready now?

Angie's voice filled him like water poured from a pitcher into his skull. She felt closer than his own skin.

—You know I am Kid. Where do you want to go today?

—*I don't know. You decide.*

—Angie, you know there's only one place I want to go.

—*Okay, let's go swimming.*

—But we went swimming yesterday. How about the zoo or the science museum? This is supposed to be for you, not me.

—*I know. I like swimming too, though. And besides—Hey! Why haven't you stopped yet? I can't fill you while you're moving.*

He felt her probing at the bottom of his brain. He skipped down the street, dodging people in his path, and called to her to catch up to him.

—*Martin! Hold still. Stop! I'm going to lose you if you don't stop it. Martin!*

—I'm skipping. Don't you know how to skip?

—*I can't even see where you are yet. Come on, hold still.*

—Nope. You have to follow me. I'm captain here, you're only a passenger.

He remembered playing this game with his daughter, only it wasn't through a telepathic link. She would be the passenger riding on his shoulders, and he would be the captain, steering them both down the river of the sidewalk. When he ran he would feel her bumping up and down against his head, and now, as he ran, he felt Angie's voice rattling in his skull. It made him comfortable and secure, like everything was right with the world.

He stopped at an intersection where the light had turned red.

—Okay mate. We haven't much time. Climb aboard before we have to shove off.

Giggling, she paused to find her bearings. Martin stood at attention, breathing heavily, but otherwise completely still. His fingers were extended, his eyes looked straight ahead. He began to feel threads of Angie extend down from his head into his body. The first thing she found were his eyes and he let her move them a little. She looked down, momentarily uncertain of herself, then up. She followed the pathways of his brain and nervous system and found the rest of him that she could reach: both his legs and one arm, most of the motor functions.

When she was completely settled in, she allowed Martin to become used to her. He closed his eyes and concentrated on the new presence within him. He had to find the balance between surrender and control that allowed two people to inhabit the same body. For each rider he carried, this balance was different. With Angie he could surrender control to the point where she could take over and completely direct his actions. She had an enormous will and presence, which seemed to be true of most children, and one reason he liked to carry them best of all.

—Okay Angie, think you can pilot this vessel?

He nudged his left leg slightly. She took the hint and began taking them across the street, hesitantly at first, then with growing confidence. She lost her balance momentarily when she took the leg off the curb, but with Martin's help she pulled the other leg along to catch herself. By the time they crossed the intersection she was moving smoothly, combining visual information through Martin's eyes with the solid feeling of the pavement below her.

—*How's that, Cap'n?*

—Not bad, matie, though I thought you almost lost 'er for a second back there as we shoved off.

—*I always forget about the curb, you should warn me.* They had a couple of blocks to go to the swimming pool. Martin decided to have some fun on the way. He closed his eyes for brief intervals and pretended to bump into people and lampposts and signs, scolding Angie for not watching where she was going.

—Look here mate, I'll have to ask you to leave the bridge if you can't steer a steady course. There are lives depending on the safe passage of this vessel.

She ignored him, and he imagined her gritting her teeth with determination, bent on holding control despite the disruptive signals. Sometimes he would force her off the eyeballs completely, relishing the feel of her draining out of them like water from a punctured can.

—*Hey! What're you doing?*

—Oh, are you still here? You were so quiet I thought you were gone.

—*I will be gone if you don't smarten up.*

And she began to pull herself out, leaving a void where she had occupied his limbs, but he quickly gave in, allowing her the use of his sight again.

—Pardon me, I didn't know you were so touchy.

She did not answer, and he imagined her with lips pressed tightly together and arms crossed, sulking over his antics. When his daughter used to do that it would amuse him and break his heart at the same time.

—Okay, I'll behave myself.

—*Promise?*

—Promise.

They continued walking and chatting until they reached the swimming pool building.

He changed quickly and walked into the pool room. There were few people there, so they would have most of the pool for themselves. That was good. The more freedom they had, the better he liked it.

—*Walk around for a few minutes, I need to get adjusted.*

He circled the pool, feeling the damp, cool floor and the slightly chilled air.

—*What are you thinking about?*

—Nothing.

—*You know, I don't know anything about you.*

He laughed.

—You've been living inside my head everyday for a month. You must know something about me by now.

—*Yes. Some things . . .*

—I hear a but.

—*Well, we still seem like strangers to each other. For instance, do you have a family?*

—No.

—*No one at all?*

—Nope. Come on, are you ready?

—*That's another thing. Why do you like swimming so much?*

—Don't you know?

—*No! That's what I'm trying to tell you.*

—I don't know how to swim. Without a rider I'm helpless in the water.

—That's scary.

—All in the line of duty, my dear. Are you ready now?

—Um.

He did not give her a chance to answer before he lowered them into the water.

She bent their knees slowly, letting him get completely wet all over. He closed his eyes and dunked his head, then pulled it out quickly.

—I feel your chills. It's cold today, isn't it?

—Yeah. Let's go.

She crouched low against the side of the pool, and he brought his right hand to meet his left above his head. Pointing his torso, she pushed forward.

Martin let Angie have complete control of his legs. He felt them kicking furiously behind him, propelling him forward. The only stroke they knew was the crawl. She moved his left hand with a confidence that he tried to match with his right. The effect was similar to what he imagined it would be like if he had artificial legs and an artificial arm. He toyed with the effect, allowing himself to feel his Angie-propelled functions, then allowing them to work independently of himself.

This was easy to do because Angie had to communicate a lot of signals to keep up the steady churning required for swimming. He let these signals flood his mind and filter down through his body, making believe they really were her doing.

When he reached the far end she executed a competent underwater turn and began swimming back. Martin worked hard to maintain the illusion for Angie. He fought the compulsion to take back control of his own body, knowing it could lead to panic and danger if Angie removed herself and her will.

—Martin?

—Yeah?

—I'm getting better.

—I know. That was a very good turn.

—No. I mean, I'm really getting better. I think I'm ready to be on my own again.

They reached their starting point and hung onto the edge of the pool, floating, with the water lapping at his chin.

—*Today's my last day.*

—That's great, Angie. Really.

—*You don't feel bad?*

—No.

—*I wanted to tell you before this, but you never let me. You never even asked me what was wrong with me.*

—I never ask that.

—*Why not?*

—It's bad enough we have to stop. I don't want it hanging over me like a deadline.

—*You make it sound awful.*

He didn't answer.

—*It's not, you know.*

Still no answer.

—*Martin, don't. You're scaring me.*

—I'm sorry Angie. I didn't mean to. You're right. It's not awful. It's wonderful that you're getting better.

—*Really? Do you really believe that?*

—Of course.

—*You don't sound excited.*

—With all this talk we aren't getting much swimming done. Come on. He pushed off but they found he was distracted.

—*Come on Martin, what is it? Tell me.*

—Nothing.

—*Tell me. You're hiding something.*

—No, nothing.

—*I don't want to swim anymore. Let's go outside for a walk.*

Later they sat in the park, tossing sunflower seeds to pigeons.

—*What's it like?*

—Huh?

—*Being telepathic. What does it feel like?*

—It doesn't feel like anything. Why? Do you think I'm weird or something?

—*No, no. It's not that. I just wondered is all.*

He looked at the sky. She waited for him, then, slowly, the words came.

—I didn't know I even had the ability until a year or so ago. After my daughter died my life was a mess. I would have done anything to get her back, but of course there was nothing I could do. She died in an accident. We were on a friend's sailboat, enjoying the day, then, suddenly, she fell overboard. It was so quiet. She had on her life jacket and everything, but she just drowned there, quietly. I still remember that silence, still think about it. One minute she was laughing with me, the next was just quiet.

He could feel Angie there in his mind, collecting his thoughts. He rolled a sunflower seed between his thumb and finger. It felt smooth and hard, dense as a life. He tossed it to one of the pigeons and watched him snatch it off the ground. The words still wanted to come.

—I quit my job and began trying to reach my daughter through mediums.. I spent all of my time at seances and I read everything I could about the occult, looking for some possible method by which I could get a message to her, or she could contact me. All I wanted was to know she was all right, somewhere, in some world, that she was at peace. I became obsessed. My wife couldn't take it after a few months and to save her sanity she left me. I hardly noticed. All of my energy was focused on my daughter, my dead little girl. It was the most important thing in the world that I tell her, one last time, how much I loved her. Those months are mostly a blank now, but I do remember one session, where the medium hypnotized me. He wanted to blank out my mind and allow my daughter to enter it from the spirit world—that's what he called it, the spirit world. Of course it was nonsense. I was an easy mark for all of these people and they took me for all they could, but one good thing came of it. During the hypnosis, while I was under, I could catch a lot of the thoughts the medium was having. It was amazing. That's when I knew he was a fake. And that's when I gave up my psychic efforts to bring back my daughter. I trained as a carrier and I've been at it for about half a year now. At first telepathy *did* feel weird. I didn't like it much because it was more of a bother than anything else. Then I got into being a carrier and everything changed. Now I like it a lot. I look forward to carrying. It makes me feel good. It makes me feel young, alive.

—*How old was she when she died?*

—About the same age as you. It was just before her

twelfth birthday.

—*Martin. Where did you get that idea? I'm not twelve. I'm not a little girl.*

Martin laughed.

—I know you're bright for your age, Angie. I like that. I like precocious kids. You're a challenge.

—*Martin, you aren't hearing me. Listen to what I'm saying.*

Martin laughed again.

—Sure Angie, I'm listening.

—*Dammit, Martin, quit laughing and pay attention.*

There was a harshness he had never felt from her before.

—Angie?

—*Martin, I'm going to give you my address.*

—No Angie, that's not allowed. The rules—

—*Yes. I know all about the rules, but this is more important.*

—Angie, do not, under any circumstances, give me your address.

—*I know you want to see me, Martin.*

—That's not the point. We're not allowed—

—*Fourteen fifty Howey Drive.*

—Oh Angie.

—*There. It's done. You must come and see me Martin.*

—I can't Angie. Don't you understand? I just can't.

—*I'll be here, and I will be expecting you soon.*

—No Angie.

—*Good bye, Martin.*

And she was gone. He probed for her. Nothing. He felt tired, weighed down by his own movements. The lightness he craved seemed to have slipped away forever. He rose from the bench slowly and tried to decide what to do next.

The house was a simple, one story building set back from the street. The yard was well-manicured and the entire effect was very pleasant to

Martin. He would have liked to have lived with his family in just such a house as this one.

He knocked on the front door and was surprised to see it opened by a young woman in a nurse's uniform.

"Yes?" she asked.

From the back of the house, a familiar voice seemed to snake through the halls and rooms like a mist: "Who is it, Marie?"

His heart began to beat terribly fast. The voice was Angie's, he was sure of it, but it was different: scratchy, slow.

"I'm here to see Angela," he said. "I'm her carrier."

"Wait here," said Marie.

She went away and Martin stood in the doorway.

When she returned she had a stern look on her face. "Mrs. Zorich will see you now," she said. "But I can only allow a few minutes. She is very tired, and needs her rest." She led the way to the back of the house and Martin followed.

Mrs. Zorich?

Marie stood by the door and indicated the way in with her hand. "Remember," she said as Martin walked by, "five minutes."

Martin moved slowly into the darkened room. A musty, unpleasant odor made his nose wrinkle involuntarily. An old woman, frail and wrinkled, but with a broad smile on her tiny face, was lying in the bed in the center of the room. On her bedside table was a booster device that allowed her to communicate with a carrier.

"So, you decided to come."

"Angie?" said Martin.

"Of course."

"But I thought—"

"You thought just what you wanted to think. You heard in your head just what you wanted to hear. But now you see what is real."

Her body hardly seemed to make a dent in the bed. He guessed she must have weighed less than ninety pounds.

"I'm sorry," said Martin. "I just never dreamed—"

"Don't be sorry," said Angela Zorich. "Come here and sit beside me."

He took a chair from against the wall and put it beside the bed. He sat in it slowly, as though afraid to disturb the very air in the room. Everything here seemed delicate, breakable.

"You have given me a lot," she said. "You have shown me a lot, but we are different. I am going to die soon, but you, you must not let yourself die."

"What do you mean?"

"Your daughter's death has made you an old man because you want to be young. You want to bring your daughter back and so you save me in the water everyday. You do for me what you could not do for your daughter."

He nodded.

"Yes, it is true. It is killing you, Martin. It is turning you rotten inside. I have been inside your mind, I know what's there. You must leave the past in the past. You must live your life *now*, in your own body, before it is too late and the best you can do is ride in someone else's brain."

Her face was hard now. Her mouth was tight and her eyes glared at him. He remembered the Angie he used to know, the one who climbed into his brain this afternoon, the Angie he imagined as a little girl, scowling at his antics.

Angela Zorich relaxed. Her face became soft again. "I have nothing left," she said. "Even my memories are dim and broken. But I was a little girl for one last time, and for that I am grateful to you, Martin."

He nodded, took her hand and pressed it softly to his lips. "It was my pleasure," he said.

After a few seconds he became aware of Marie standing behind him. "Mrs. Zorich needs to sleep," she said.

Martin stood up.

Angie's eyes were already closed.

When he arrived at Kate's car, she was leaning against the door, looking at her watch.

"You're late," she said. "Where were you?"

"I was in a situation," he said. "I couldn't just leave it."

"You were in a *what?*"

He laughed. "You think you're the only one who can goof off?"

She narrowed her eyes. "Martin, you okay?"

"Never better."

"I felt kind of bad about this morning. I didn't mean to get on your case or anything. It's just that I don't know you. We can't live just in our heads. We have to spend time in this world too."

He nodded. "I know."

"How did it go today?"

"Tell you about it in the car," he said and walked around to the other side. Stones scrapped against the soles of his shoes. The dirt on the door handle felt gritty as he climbed into the car, put his body against the cool, smooth vinyl, and waited for Kate to get into the driver's seat.

The Death of Me

First of all, someone like me, I should never have had a kid. Kids are about life and I'm pretty much the opposite. Also, with my work load, a kid is the last thing I should ever have even thought about. But I was young, (well, youn*ger*) she was the most beautiful woman that ever existed, (I mean, she was *Mother Nature*, for crying out loud) and one thing led to another. You know how these things happen.

My fault, my responsibility, I get that. I made a mistake, but I think I can be forgiven for it. We came to an arrangement, Mother Nature and I. She had a career of her own and didn't want to be raising a kid—so the product of our passion became my responsibility. Fair enough. Esimed, our son, turned out okay even if I couldn't give him all the attention he needed.

Still, for the two of us—Esimed and me—to participate in Take Your Child to Work Day, well, that was maybe not such a great brainstorm. No one should forgive me for that one. The idea was that I was going to show him what I did. How I killed things. And then, maybe, he would find the power in himself. Or something like that. It sounds kind of nutty, to tell you the truth, but there it is.

It started out all right.

"Esimed," I said to my son in the morning, "go fetch my scythe, please."

He went. Obedient young man. I liked that about him. Sweet. That was his mother in him.

"Here it is, Dad," he said a moment later, brandishing the thing with a kind of reverence I had not expected. He held it in both hands and presented it to me like it was his favorite video game. He seemed genuinely proud of his old man. How could I not adore the boy?

I put the bones of my hand on his head. "Thanks, son," I said. Then I snatched my hand away. Had to be careful there.

He grinned up at me. "We're going to have a fun day, Dad," he said. Those trusting eyes. Like I could actually teach him anything. Like he would listen to me. He had way too much of his mother in him. So cheerful and happy.

I put on my robe, adjusted it on my shoulders so it looked menacing draping my skeletal frame, cracked my knuckles, (a good luck superstition I never tired of), took the scythe from Esimed's hands, said "right you are, son," and banged the end of the scythe handle on the floor.

Esimed jumped.

"Sorry," I said. "Didn't mean to startle. Let's get going."

"Are we going to see Mom today?" he asked.

"I don't think so," I said.

"Oh," he said. Such disappointment in his voice. "Why not?"

"Your mother's busy," I said. "Haven't I told you that a million times?"

We stepped out of the house and into the world. Happened to be a forest in Oregon. Lots of trees and greenery. The whole *environment* thick and heavy. "Wow," said Esimed. "Everything's so bright."

I'm sure it looked that way to him. I saw lots of creatures with the glow about them as well. But not all, not by any means. First thing I noticed: a bird, tired. Not interested in eating or flying. It perched with its head drooped down to its chest, barely breathing and obviously near the end. It had had a full bird's life, but now it was done. Happens to every living thing. It was my job to ease its pain. I'm the great humanitarian, don't you know.

The glow was dim around the bird. Poor thing needed release. I reached up to its head and touched it with the end of my white finger bone. The contact lasted for maybe half a second, then I withdrew my finger. The remainder of the bird's glow, dim as it was, grew dimmer still, until, a few seconds later, it winked out completely and the bird lay there, dull and emaciated.

Esimed watched me.

Studied me, my face. It was a little unnerving, his attention, like I was under a microscope and he was paying attention to my every move.

"Is that what you were telling me about last night?" he asked. "How you bring comfort to creatures?"

"Yes, son," I said. "That's exactly it. The poor bird was in pain. It needed my help."

Esimed nodded. "If I ever get in pain, will you comfort me the same way?"

I coughed, surprised by the question. "Well, uh, not exactly," I said. "If you had issues in that direction, I'd be more inclined to have you see a healer. That is, if I couldn't help you myself. Which I'm sure I would be able to. In all probability. But if I needed a, you know, kind of *back-up*, then I'd get a healer. Just to be sure about the whole thing."

"Oh," said Esimed. He looked a little puzzled. If I had a face, I'm sure it would have turned red. I felt like an idiot. He watched the bird as it began to fade away, slipping into the hidden void.

"Okay," I said. "That one's done. Let's move on."

"Why didn't you take the bird to a healer?" he said.

"Um," I said. "Different situation completely. Let's get going. We can't be lingering over one bird. There's lots more to do today."

I took his hand and tried to pull him along with me, but he was fixated on that bird, watching the spot where it had been.

I was on the hunt for other tired creatures. There were lots of them. There always were. I pulled Esimed along until his feet began dragging on the rotting leaves on the ground. I barely noticed. Absent-minded of me, yes, but I was *working*. I didn't have time for his issues.

He tried to pull out of my grip. He put his other hand over my wrist and strained to pull it off him. I gripped harder and tried to yank him next to me, but he wasn't about to accept my insistence and he pushed even harder until his hand slipped out of mine.

I heard his footsteps running and turned around to see him kneeling next to the branch where the bird had been. I sighed and walked back next to him.

His face, well, I had never seen an expression like that on any being not about to receive my touch. Horror, I guess you'd call it.

"You *killed* it," he said. He looked up at me with the kind of eyes that needed no words to convey a meaning, that meaning being: You rat bastard, how could you do this kind of thing and still be my father and how will I ever look at you the same way ever again, and did I mention that you're the worst rat bastard who ever lived?

I'd like to report that I took his silent recriminations in stride, that I told him the truth right then and there, that I explained to him the workings of the universe, that everything had be in balance, and that he understood and accepted and we had a father/son bonding moment. But it wasn't exactly like that.

"What did you think I did?" I said. "Make them chicken soup and rub their feet?"

If he had been looking at me with horror before my, uh, ill-phrased attempt at comfort, what transpired next took my breath away. Or would have, if I had had any breath.

He turned away from me and reached into the void just above the branch. Before my startled eyes, my confounded senses, and my contorted sense of right and wrong, the bird popped back into existence, cradled in my son's hands.

He held the creature tenderly, and stroked its feathers, which were black. Completely. I felt uneasy about what he was doing. I think I might have looked around, with a sense of guilt, hoping no one was watching. When I looked back, the subtlest glow had wrapped itself around the bird. I was fascinated, despite myself. My own son had this power? How could I not have known this? He must have gotten it from his mother.

Esimed cradled the bird for a few minutes. With each passing second the glow around it increased. The feathers took on color. He put the bird up to his mouth and breathed into its beak. Suddenly the creature flapped its wings and opened its beak to let out a cry. Esimed raised his hand so the bird perched against the sky.

It hopped once on his palm, twice, then flew away.

We both watched it soar above the trees until it was a dot against a cloud.

My son and I endured a few seconds of awkward silence.

"Well," I said. "That's a handy skill to have, that, uh, resurrecting thing you've got going there."

He crossed his arms over his chest. "Go ahead," he said.

"Go ahead what?"

"Kill something else." He narrowed his eyes at me. "I'll bring it back to life."

What? My own son was telling me he was going to undo my life's work? My own son, fruit of my loins, product of my youthful passion, was calling me out?

"Esimed," I said, "you don't want to get into this. I've wrestled with these questions and I've come to the only reasonable conclusion. I dispatch them so they don't suffer. If it wasn't for me, their deaths would last much much longer. That bird you think you saved, you only postponed the inevitable. It'll die. They all die. I just make it quicker and easier."

He still had his arms crossed. He still glared at me.

"You know death is necessary, right?" I said. "New creatures are born all the time. If some didn't die to make room for the babies, we'd be hip deep in life in no time. It's like a yin yang thing. Balance."

No response from my kid. Still with the glare and the crossed arms.

"So you're going to stay like that all day?" I said.

No answer.

"Fine," I said, and turned around and walked north until I found a polar bear lying on the tundra, breathing in shallow breaths. Its glow was dim. It was a big bear. Too much for my hand. I tapped its head with my scythe's blade. It immediately relaxed. I saw its face soften. It dimmed and began to shrink into the void.

Then Esimed, yes, my very own blessed and wretched *son*, strode right past me, put both his hands on the flank of the bear and leaned against it, pushing with all his might and kind of kneading the scrawny flesh of the thing. The bear suddenly perked up. Her eyes shone—blazed, actually—and she glowed brighter than a full moon. She got up on all fours and headed off in the direction of some food.

Oh, and Esimed was so proud of himself. He turned to me and put his thumb on his nose and waved his fingers at me.

I ignored him and stepped over to Scotland. A dog. I put it down. Esimed resurrected it. I waded into the Pacific and eased a whale towards its death. Esimed fished it back from the brink. We went on for a while like this. Me doing what needed to be done. Esimed indulging his adolescent fantasies of saving the world. Or fixing Dad's screw-ups. Or whatever was going on in his head.

Finally I stopped.

I scanned the horizon of my world, looking for a particular *type* of creature when—ah ha! I saw what I needed. I sauntered over to New York City and several dozen starving rats. Seems they happened to have stumbled into a neighborhood with a particularly effective rat abatement program. The bunch of them were squirming and writhing in the dimming glow of their once luminescent fur. I strode over to them. Esimed followed, but I noticed his stride did not quite match mine. He was holding back. I approached one of the rats and extended my finger to it.

Now don't get me wrong. I have nothing against rats. They are creatures like any other, and they occupy a useful niche by eating human garbage, but let's face it, they aren't cute. They've got these nasty chewing mouths, with yellow teeth and beady eyes. Not to mention those ropey tales and the waddling walk and the way they are always into garbage. I was counting on these facts to help me help Esimed see the light. So to speak.

I held my finger above one of the rats. It was squirming. Writhing. It was all I could do to keep from executing my duty, but I waited until Esimed stood beside me.

"Why aren't you helping it?" said Esimed.

"If I help it," I said, "will you bring it back?"

He looked at the rat. His face scrunched up. The boy, seriously, did not like this rat. "No," he said.

I withdrew my finger. "Why not?"

"Because it's *gross*," he said. "Disgusting. It deserves to die."

I nodded. "I can see why you would think so. Why don't you do the honors?"

He looked up at me, the innocence back in his eyes. Maybe his old man wasn't quite the monster he had thought I was a few minutes ago. "Me?" he said.

"Sure. You've got a lot of your Mom in you, but half of you is from me. I'm sure you can handle it."

He still hesitated. I took his hand and moved toward the rat. He bit his lip and touched the rat's head. His finger was shaking. The rat relaxed.

Esimed blinked. He had an expression of pure astonishment. The rat stopped squirming. It relaxed, dimmed, and disappeared.

Esimed gasped.

Then grinned.

His first taste of real power. Now there was a big moment.

I let him sit with it, the moment, silently congratulating myself for not stepping on it and ruining it. He looked up at me. Wonder in his eyes.

"How did that feel?" I said.

He licked his lips, unsure how to answer.

"I bet it felt pretty good," I said.

He looked over at another rat. It was as emaciated and pathetic as the first. Esimed put his hand on the rat's head. The rat went into the void. Esimed hopped from rat to rat, killing each one in turn with the merest touch of his finger. Before long the entire herd of them had been moved into the void.

"That was *fun*," he said.

"Told you," I said.

"Let's kill some more."

"Easy there," I said. "You need a little more guidance if you're going to do this."

"What guidance, Dad? I put my finger on something and it dies. What's the big deal? I'm helping them. Easing their pain."

He ran off and began killing creatures with wild abandon. Kangaroos in Australia. Elephants in India. Humans in Europe. Antelope in Africa. And on and on. He worked with frightening speed. I called to him, but he didn't come back.

All of this would have been okay, I suppose, if he was just doing what I would have done anyway, that is, dispatching the dim ones. But that wasn't what he was doing. He was killing everything in his path, even the ones that were bright and healthy.

No, no, this couldn't go on.

"Esimed," I called. "Stop that. Come back here."

He stopped for a second, waved at me from the Antarctic with penguins piled around him, a giant grin on his face, and then went back to his serial killing.

I ran after Esimed. I had to stop the dim-witted little snot.

Er, that is, I needed to offer my son some fatherly advice and the wisdom of my experience to help him develop into a fully rounded being.

"Esimed. Get over here."

But he didn't listen to me. He was having too much fun. He thought I was part of the game and he ran away from me, skipping around the cosmos, if you want to know the truth, laughing and killing like a crazy man. Crazy kid. Jesus. This whole day was turning into a big mistake.

"Esimed. I'm not playing. Get over here. You've got to stop that." I ran after him as best I could, but he was younger than me. By several bazillion years. He had all the energy. I had my clanking skeleton and my stupid scythe, not to mention the damned robes, dragging on me like tired muscles.

I felt a presence next to me. Startled, I turned around.

Mother Nature stood beside me. Amazingly beautiful, as always, what with her hair all wild and free and those white flowing garments, and her lovely face. Did I mention she's beautiful?

"So, how's my son doing?" she said.

"We're having a together day," I said.

She looked at Esimed, far in the distance, romping through the Brazilian rainforest, killing everything in his path.

"Doesn't look too together to me."

Her usual entourage of animals trailed along behind her. Birds and flying insects hovered over her head, making a pleasant sound, like a white noise cocoon. Butterflies flittered in her aura. She always made things better, wherever she went. Truth is, I kind of envied her fame and power. People *liked* her.

"He discovered the power of death," I said.

"I see," she said. "I thought that was your department."

Of course she was right. She left me Esimed because she said I would always protect him. What better protector, after all, than me, who could kill any menace with a simple touch? That was our deal.

"Well," I said, "I'm trying to teach him what his old man does for a living."

"Ah."

I didn't like the sound of that "ah."

"There's this thing, this take your kid to work day, supposed to teach them about life." I shrugged.

"And death?" she said.

"Yeah. And death." I shrugged again. My shoulder blades rattled against my ribs. It didn't sound menacing right at that moment, the way bones are supposed to sound. It sounded pathetic.

"I think he's learning more about death than about life."

I felt miserable. How could she make me feel so small so easily? I was death, dammit, the ultimate. Everyone meets me eventually. I should have the upper hand. But then I saw the life all around her, the way she lit up everything, and I knew.

"I can't get him to listen to me," I said.

"Looks to me like he listened pretty good. Picked up his father's skills in no time."

"I mean now," I said. "I can't get him to come back. Can't make him listen to me."

"You need to entertain them at this age."

"Oh."

"Have you taught him to dance yet?"

"Dance?"

"That's what I saw in you, way back then."

The birds swirling around above her head, which initially had seemed so charming, were beginning to get on my nerves. I remembered some of the issues that broke us up. She had all these living *things* around her *all* the time. It was annoying as hell. I had to consciously make myself not reach over her long silky hair and crush the life out of the incessant chirpers. I managed, but barely. They were so cheerful I wanted to strangle them. And myself.

"Oh," I said. "Dancing. Okay."

"Give it a try," she said. "He's half me. He should like dancing."

"Okay," I said.

She began drifting away. "Bye," she said.

"Hey," I said. "Where you going?"

"I have my work," she said. "Just like you."

"Yeah, but can't you stay for a little while? I haven't seen you in ages. We should catch up."

"I felt a bit of trouble," she said. "But things haven't changed. I don't have time for a child. I have too much life to give to everything else. Nothing to spare."

That old story. Like *I* wasn't busy?

But I saw her point. I *could* protect him better. She was right, she was right. She was always right.

She drifted away. "When will I see you again?" I said.

"Next time you need a little nudge," she said.

Okay.

Then she was gone.

Esimed was still on his happy rampage.

Dancing. Could it possibly be that simple?

I remember how I used to dance. We all danced in those days. I hadn't done it in a long time. But I used to have the moves, it was true.

I grabbed my scythe and tapped it on the ground a few times, then kept going, finding a good beat, a nice rhythm. I made myself look bigger. More somber. I put my hood over my head, hiding my skull in shadow. Always a nice effect. Ominous. I hefted my scythe and went looking for a partner.

I found one nearby, in a small ranch house in a suburb of Tucson. An old woman, not exactly near the end, but not exactly all there either, watching television.

She sensed me nearby and looked around, as though expecting a friend.

I extended my hand. She didn't move at first; then she reached for my bony finger. From her point of view I was at the end of a long white tunnel.

We didn't touch, not quite, but we were close enough to feel each other's presence.

Somehow she knew the steps. Music swelled up from somewhere. A steady drumming like a heart beat. We moved across the ground. For a moment it seemed like we were the only two beings in existence. We had respect for each other. She moved in close, and then pulled away. I wrapped my arm around her, then let her go. We never touched, that was part of the dance, but we were close. We saw each other for what we were.

The dance lasted for I don't know how long. In the steps, a subtle language made itself clear: she wasn't ready. Wasn't ready for me.

I accepted that.

I could wait.

She bowed. I bowed. We separated, for now.

I was glad for my scythe. It supported my weight. Dancing was hard work. I could use a rest. I leaned against the scythe and thought about maybe sitting down somewhere and taking a breather.

"What was that?" Esimed's voice. Wonder in it, which made me happy. It felt like a relief. He stood behind me.

"That, son," I said, "is called the dance of death."

"You didn't touch her." He walked up next to me. His shoulder brushed against my robe.

"No," I said. "She wasn't ready."

He seemed to think about that. Didn't quite know what to make of it.

"How do you know when they're ready?"

How did I know? What a question. Who could answer it? Not me. Too many factors involved. Even with a dim glow, creatures can come back. You have to see the subtle things, the attitude and the energy level. How they see their own world. How tired they are. How much they have in reserve.

"It's hard to say," I told my son. "Practice."

He looked very thoughtful for a few seconds. Mulling something over. "I probably shouldn't have killed all those beings," he said.

"Probably not," I said. "But it's my fault for showing you things you weren't ready for. See, it's all about balance. You have to balance life and death. It's not all one or the other."

"That dancing looked pretty cool."

"Yeah, you think so?" I felt absurdly proud of myself.

"I could do that."

"I'm sure you could."

I showed him the steps. He took to them with no trouble at all. He was good. My son was a good dancer.

After he learned a few steps, really got them under his belt, I told him we had to go back and undo some of his kills. "I never should have let you run loose like that," I said. "A lot of those lives weren't ready to be snuffed out."

He saw the wisdom of what I was saying and agreed. Such a good kid. I couldn't be annoyed with him for long.

As we retraced his wave of destruction—and he pulled some of the deceased back from the void, essentially creating a string of little miracles that were going to confound theologians and scientists for a couple of centuries at the very least—I told him he was a good kid and I loved him. I don't think he knew how to take that.

"Dad?" he said.

"Yeah?"

"How come my Mom never comes around?"

Oh boy. What a question.

"Well," I said, "She's a very busy woman. She doesn't really have time for you. She's too busy creating life."

"You told me that a million times," he said, sounding more lost than a kitten in a rainstorm.

Right there, I wanted to put the scythe blade to my own head. Could I have said anything designed to cut him down any more decisively than that? I don't think so.

"Besides," I said, scrambling to recover, "you've got so many of her best qualities, it's like she's here with us anyway."

"Really?" he said.

Really? Of course not really. It made no sense. It was just something I said to make him feel better about himself. It's what I do. Humanitarian, didn't I say? My way of trying to be a good father and make his way in the world just a little easier.

"Yeah," I said. "Really."

Broken Wings

Charlie read an article about how we are doomed as a species because we are too smart. And squeamish. He told me about it as he got ready for his day of imparting wisdom to undergraduates while *I* fantasized about the two of us in bed, screwing, something that had not happened in a long time.

"Look at rats," he said. "Not real brilliant, but they are persistent, they live on garbage, and they have thrived on every continent on the planet. Same thing with cockroaches. Anything dumb enough to consume waste is smart enough to live forever."

I shook the image of his bare chest from my head. He always tried to be the teacher. "Why don't you start eating garbage, then," I said, "if it's so beneficial?"

"It benefits the *species*, Linda," he said. "I'm not so sure it's a good idea for any individual animal."

Charlie loved to talk about evolutionary issues. Which was odd, since he was an English professor. He talked while he went around the house and emptied all the trash baskets into a large plastic garbage bag. His feathers, arrayed in a delicate line above his eyebrows, around his temples, and over his ears in a pretty arc, rustled audibly as he worked. A lovely sound, silky like flowing water.

While he hauled the garbage to the curb for pick up, I thought about the problem with evolution, namely, that change had to do with the species as a whole. For natural selection to work, the community was always more important than the individual. For individuals like me, carrying around my luggage full of self awareness and desire, natural selection left me feeling short changed. Sure, the species survived, but I had needs that didn't seem to be met by evolution.

I remembered a bird from when I was very young. It had a broken wing and spun on the grass trying to get airborne for a long time while I watched, horrified and fascinated. I felt deep pity for the bird, a foreign and awful feeling for me then. Much more comfortable was the urge that accompanied it: the wish to stomp on the creature and end its existence, which, I surmised, would probably end soon anyway, on a cat's claws and teeth, perhaps, or slowly by starvation. I was conscious of a power to end misery but not to give life. Not to heal. I grew dizzy thinking of what to do. I sensed I should act swiftly, but what act to commit?

"I know rats and seagulls and such live at the dump," I said when Charlie returned from the curb. "Is that what you're saying? That creatures who live on garbage thrive because we provide them with what they need?"

"We do produce a lot of it," said Charlie, "in case you didn't notice. We're part of the evolutionary process."

I considered this. "Our part in evolution is to support vermin?"

Charlie laughed, a sound I liked hearing. "You've got it, dear. That's the purpose of this big brain we have evolved: to support all the creatures dumb enough to eat shit."

"What a horrible thought."

"Maybe," said Charlie.

"No, really," I said. "Shouldn't we be about more than that? What about language and communication? What about art?" I wanted to ask him why I did not seem to arouse him anymore, but could not. It seemed too big for the morning, the post-question discussion stretching to infinity. We were a culmination of the evolutionary process, but neither of us had any idea of how to face truth. Even simple truth.

"I don't know if any of us knows what we're really all about," said Charlie. "Anyway, it's just a little article I read in the paper." He put the newspaper on top of the recycle pile. "And now I've got to get to work," he said.

I leaned over and kissed his cheek. "Have a good day," I said.

"Maybe you didn't hear me. I said I was going to work."

I didn't even pretend to laugh.

"Old joke, getting older, huh?"

"It's not that," I said. "My 'have a good day' isn't particularly original either."

"No one is expected to come up with original niceties."

"I suppose not," I said.

"Evolution has selected for the ultimate niceties. They survive because they work."

"And we just use them because they're there? Like our brains? We wake up one day, and there they are? Is that it?"

He looked puzzled, as though I had said something paradoxical. "Do you have lessons today?" he said.

"Afraid not. Everyone canceled. No one wants to learn the piano anymore." I had been making a pretty good living for many years by teaching piano. Lately it was getting tough to bring people to keyboards made of ivory. They much preferred the kind that came attached to a computer.

"So you going to do anything?"

"I'll spend the day in town. Window shop, maybe. Or catch a movie."

"Sounds good," he said. "Wish I could ditch my day and go with you."

I looked at him. "Really?"

He seemed sightly annoyed. "Yes, really."

"You could, you know. Call in sick."

His resolve withered more quickly than it rose. "Probably not such a good idea," he said.

I sighed. "I suppose not." I looked up at him. "Did you comb your feathers?"

He put his hand to his head and ran his palm along the plumage near his ear. "It's not combing," he said. "it's smoothing, remember? The feather installer said never use a comb or a brush. Smoooooth it out with gentle pressure." He raised his eyes at me.

"Is that an invitation, sir?"

He leaned his head closer to me. I was horrified when Charlie first told me he wanted to have feathers installed. I tried to dissuade him from it but he was adamant and there was not much I could say. When he came home with them, I thought I detected a certain disappointment in his eyes, like he had made a big mistake. I did not want to make him feel worse, so I told him how marvelous they were, how the feathers caught the light and really showed off his eyes. I was half making it up, but as I looked at him with the feathers lining his temple in a quite fetching way, I discovered I actually believed what I was saying. It seemed to make him feel good. He grew his hair longer so it drooped down and touched his feathers, almost blended with them. He loved that look. He beamed and strutted around the house like a proud father.

"Any vermin nestled in there?" I said.

"Maybe, maybe not. If there are, I'm just fulfilling my evolutionary purpose."

I pushed him away from me. "Go," I said. "Get out of here and fulfill your evolutionary purpose by making us some money."

He rose, feigning hurt in his features. "And can I expect you to be here when I get home from pretending to teach freshmen brats how to read literature?"

"Let's just say I'll be waiting for you and I'll be horny."

He smiled, about half a second too late.

The guy at the mall who spent his days installing horns on people's skulls could not have been more bored by the procedure. He showed me different models. Long pointy ones, short stubby ones, curved ones, straight ones. There were many choices. Lots of colors. Textures. I got dizzy looking at all of them. Then the guy explained the best placement options. Temple or forehead, close together or farther apart. And so on. Sure, I could see why he was jaded, but to me it was a wild experience. He could have at least faked some interest.

After letting me look at the pictures in his book for about five minutes, he said, "So, are we ready to make a decision?"

The "we" was a little irritating.

"How long have you been doing this?"

He groaned. He actually groaned.

"What?" I said.

"When people ask about me, it usually means they have doubts about getting the horns and that means I've wasted my time with them. With you. Is that what's going on? You getting cold feet?"

"I just want to know a little something about the guy who's going to stick anchors in my head and screw some horns on them."

"You know," he said, "I never ask people why they do this. Why they get horns stuck into their skull bone. I don't need to know about them."

"Gosh, it's obvious you really love your work."

He looked at me. "I'm guessing your husband doesn't give you the attention he used to," he said. "And you think this is a way to get him back. Am I close?"

I didn't say anything.

He shrugged. "Actually, with your hair line and bone structure, I have just the set for you." He flipped the pages and stopped at a picture of a pair of short black nubs, maybe a quarter of an inch high. "Just above the ends of your eyebrows. The blonde in your hair would set them off nicely."

I was prepared to hate the idea, but as I considered it, I found I really liked it. Charlie would get a kick out of seeing a darker side of me. I hoped. "Okay," I said. "Let's do it."

And so we did.

That night Charlie was late. Some faculty meeting. Or so he said. I waited for him at the piano, playing slow songs, slower than they needed to be. I was no composer, but I played around with some primitive melodies; notes that rose higher in pitch until they floated off into the air, like birds flying out of sight.

Sometimes it seemed like I was always waiting for Charlie. There were times when I didn't want to wait for him anymore. The house was dark. The take out I had brought home was cold on the table.

I was startled when he burst into the house. No. Not burst, exactly. More like sneak. He sneaked into the house. This surprised me, and I got this bristling feeling in the back of my head, like something stabbed me with a million tiny needles all at once. They prodded me with comprehension I didn't want to acknowledge.

"Oh," he said. "You're still up."

I rose and went to him. Took one of his hands and put it on my forehead. His hand moved. His finger tips rippled over my horns and brushed the base where the blood had clotted into a bumpy ring, but had not yet formed a scab. The sensation of his fingertips there was oddly pleasant, especially the way he hesitated, obviously not sure what to make of what I had done. The bottom of his wrist was at my nose level. I smelled something that shouldn't have been there.

"What do you think?" I asked.

"Linda. I had no idea. When did you—?"

"While you were out. Does she always wear that perfume? Or was it a special occasion tonight? Was this an anniversary or something?"

His hand froze. "What?"

I liked it there. His hand on my forehead. It was the end of an era in our lives and simultaneously the beginning as well.

"The woman you've been fucking. Does she do special things for you? Do you wish I wore this perfume?"

"Linda—"

"It kind of reminds me of something. Fruit. A mango, maybe. A mango that has been left out too long so it turns black. An odd scent, don't you think? Kind of like rotting garbage. The kind vermin thrives on."

Now he let his hand drop. It dangled at the end of his arm.

"Evolution only cares about species, not individuals, right? That's why you behave in a manner that will impregnate her and extend the species, but make me feel like shit. Am I right?"

"Linda."

The door behind him remained excruciatingly open, as though it needed to close but neither of us had the energy to move to swing it shut. There was also the question of what side of the door Charlie should be on when it was closed. I think we were both working that one out in our minds. We remained standing and silent for many minutes. Or maybe just a few seconds. It's hard to tell for sure now.

And oh yes. Those damned feathers. They rustled in the silence. I think of them now as trembling, and not very quietly.

"What does she think of your feathers?"

He hesitated. "She likes feathers," he said. Resigned.

"How nice for you both," I said. "Well, come on. Let's get you packed and out of here." I started up the stairs. He was weeping behind me. I turned and went back down and slapped his face as hard as I could.

"There'll be no more of that," I said.

He looked stunned, but stopped crying. One of his feathers dislodged and floated down. I caught it in my hand. I made a fist but it would not stay collapsed. It sprang back to its original shape as soon as I relaxed my hand. Cheap plastic crap. Just like him.

"Now get upstairs," I said.

He was trying to keep his back from me. This seemed odd. He edged up the stairs sideways, but could not completely hide the bumps under his shirt on his shoulder blades.

"What the hell?" I said. I grabbed his shirt collar and yanked at it.

"Hey," he said. "What are you doing?"

"What's on your back?"

"Nothing."

"Liar." I yanked on his shirt again, so some of his buttons popped. Then I grabbed his arm and spun him around so his back was to me. I pulled his shirt down.

I didn't expect to see wings there, but he had two of them, one on each shoulder blade. I reached up and touched them. They were made of mylar, or something like that. They were brightly colored with reds and greens and yellows, like an exotic parrot. They folded up nicely, snug and neat against his back. They looked like he had been born with them. Despite myself, I was intrigued.

"Do they work?" I said.

"You mean can I fly?"

"No, nitwit," I said. "I mean do they work? Do they spread out or do they just hang there?"

"They don't do anything now, but when I've trained my muscles to use them, they will open up. It'll take a while."

"Too bad I won't see that."

He had the decency to look sad. "Yeah, too bad."

"When I got the horns today, I saw feathers in the shop. And wings were available too. They're quite a fad now, yes?"

He shrugged. "I guess. That's not why I got them. I've never been stylish. It's just that the species is moving to something else."

"Spare me," I said.

"No, really. If I lived on Mars, I would be able to fly with these. Eventually."

"Do you have feathers for brains?" I said. "If you lived on Mars you'd freeze to death or suffocate."

"You know what I mean. The Earth is getting old. It may be time for us all to move on."

"Exactly my point. Time for you to move on. Let's go."

I pushed him up the stairs. His wing feathers tickled my nose. I regretted getting the horns for Charlie, but realized I did not regret *having* them. I could hook a new life on my horns. If I was lucky.

In the bedroom I pulled out a large suitcase and started putting some of his shirts and underwear in them.

"This will just be temporary," I said. "You need something for the next few days because you can't come around here. I'd probably kill you."

"Linda."

"Maybe not kill. But I'd hurt you bad, for sure. After a week or so, though, I'm sure I'll be fine. Then you can come back for the rest of it. Fair enough?"

"Maybe I should be doing this," he said.

"Nonsense. What else are wives for? By serving our trashy men we serve the species, right? We help you guys out when you need it so you can go on doing the work of keeping evolution going. Is she pregnant yet?"

"Linda, please. I'm sorry about it all."

I raised my hand again. "What did I say?"

He looked confused. "About what?"

"Crying."

"I'm not crying."

He was right, he wasn't. But he should have been. My mouth tried to move into position for laughter but I stopped it. Then my eyes began welling up. No. Not now. After he's gone, but not now. Not in front of him.

I put my hand on his shoulder and eased him around. Then I took a hold of his left wing and gripped it as strongly as I could. "I so much want to yank this off," I said.

He did not move. He knew such action was not part of my usual operating system. Which fact infuriated me. I tightened my grip. Felt my face turn hot.

"Does she have wings, too?" I asked.

"Linda, don't do this."

"*Does she?*"

"Yes."

"And she wanted you to get a set of your own?"

"Yes. She didn't say that, but it was clear."

"Tell me she's not a student. At least not that. Not one of your students."

"Linda! Please. She's a professor."

"Assistant?"

"Full."

"Tenured?"

"No. But I'm not either."

"Oh. Well. Good, then." Sweat began to dampen my hand where it touched his wing. "The feathers you installed before the wings," I said. "They were a trial run, I suppose? Just to see how you liked it?"

He waited a long time to answer. I was no longer impatient for a reply. I didn't need to know that minute, but I needed to know at some point. So I waited. He cleared his throat.

"Actually, more to see how she liked it."

I slapped him again. Between the shoulder blades. So hard he must have lost some of his breath.

I thought of that dying bird from when I was kid. I remember feeling cursed by an impulse to benign action, an inheritance from generations of ancestors who lived long enough to create more people who lived long enough to create more people and on and on until this time here, culminating in me, wanting to hurt Charlie, hovering here in front of me.

I didn't want to create anything with him. I just wanted to hurt him. The thought gave me a sick feeling in my belly. At least we never had children. That was an odd comfort.

Back then, I knew only one thing. I ran from that dying bird, that spinning life draining. Turned my back and only heard one small chirp. I ran to my mother. We went back to the bird together. But it was gone by the time we returned. Miraculously healed? Or just eaten? Who knew. My mother held me and I asked why things had to die.

"Charlie," I said. "I know this won't matter because you can replace them, but I need to do this."

I strengthened my grip. He moved, but not quickly enough. I yanked down hard and fast. The wing popped from his back like cork coming out of a wine bottle. Blood trickled down his back. I dropped the wing to the floor. I reached for the other one but he slid away and turned to me.

His face was red, his eyes blazed. His hair, pulled back, exposed his forehead. And there, above his brows, just at the edge of his hair line, a pair of pointed golden nubs sparkled in the light as he raised his arm, not to strike me, but to reach for something higher, something beyond both of us.

The Eyes Come From China

"Where did the eyes come from?" Gary asked Dr. Hanes.

She didn't want to answer, Gary could tell. His acoustic viewer, hooked into his brain and capable of detecting the most subtle of facial changes, registered hesitation, the kind he had grown to recognize. It happened often when people first met him and didn't know how to react to or deal with a blind man. This rustling of the signals was exactly like that, even thought Dr. Hanes was not new to his blindness.

"Why do you want to know that?" asked Dr. Hanes.

"Is it something I'm not allowed to know?"

"The donor asked to remain anonymous."

"Ahhh," said Gary. The examining room was cold. The door was open. He felt a bit of cool air coming from that direction. Dr. Hanes wore a stiff lab coat. Gary heard it's crusty scratching at the air. It sent small shivers over his skin, raising bumps on his arms.

"Just general terms, then," said Gary. "Age. Gender. How they died."

"They don't tell me that."

"Come on, Doc. Maybe not officially, but people in places like hospitals, they hear things. You know what's up."

"Listen," said Dr. Hanes, "none of that matters. You should think of the eyes as just something that came from a manufacturer. Some factory in China, say. It's easier that way."

"But they came from a *person*," said Gary.

Dr. Hanes moved some instruments around on a table. "Lean closer, please," she said.

Gary pushed his face closer to whatever instrument Dr. Hanes had put in his path. A cold metal barrier caught him at the forehead and another supported him at the chin. He felt her relief. She liked when she was doing something doctorly and he was being a compliant patient.

"Probably a car accident, I bet," said Gary.

"I don't know," said Dr. Hanes quietly.

"I heard you transplant docs are going to be in trouble when the self driving cars take off. It'll all but eliminate car accident deaths, which means you won't have nice fresh organs from young people to put into geezers like me."

Dr. Hanes's breath was warm and moist on his face. She was close to him. He thought he could almost hear her heartbeat.

"You talk a lot," she said.

"You state the obvious," said Gary.

They sat in silence while Dr. Hanes carried on her examination, their breaths mingling in the air like the tongues of dragon lovers.

"Everything looks fine," she said after a minute or so. "Are you ready for this? Are you ready to have eyes that will actually see?"

She pushed away from him. The rollers on the chair bumped on the floor. There was excessive dust there, which made the roll less than smooth. Gary heard the bumps like static. They probably needed to clean up in the room. It bothered Gary that they weren't on top of the cleaning as much as they should be.

"I'm ready," said Gary.

"Good."

"But my wife isn't."

After the surgery, which was a marathon session lasting ten hours, Gary was groggy in the recovery room. The nurse comforted him with soothing words as he came out of the anesthesia.

Gary still couldn't see anything. His eyes were covered. Dr. Hanes told him it would be this way at first, but it was still startling.

What was worse, he couldn't use his acoustic apparatus. They had taken that away. Dr. Hanes had warned him about that, too.

He was more blind than he had been in many years. He could still use acoustic ranging, done manually, but it was not as good as his former computer aided device had been. He tried to discern where he was. It was different from the examining room. There were curtains, for one thing, he could feel how they rustled the air. Also, there was a window. It was open, a crack. The air from it swirled around the air in the room, just a few degrees cooler, but enough that it felt like ropes of different fiber snaking through the space above and around him.

"Where's Linda?" he asked.

"Your wife?" asked the nurse.

Gary nodded.

"She's on her way."

Gary blinked. "You mean she hasn't been here, waiting for me to come out of it?"

The nurse patted his hand. He pulled it away. "Don't do that," he said before he could stop himself.

"Sorry," said the nurse. "Didn't mean to offend."

"I can't see you," said Gary. "I don't know what you're doing."

"I know. I shouldn't have touched you."

"The doctor said it would take a few days, right?"

"Could be sooner. I've had people pass the vision test on their second day."

"My wife thinks this is a mistake," said Gary.

The nurse said nothing.

"No one wants to talk about that," said Gary.

"Your wife, I'm sure, is thrilled that you're going to get your sight back."

"That's what you think," said Gary.

Linda never did appear that day.

The next day the nurse removed the covering over his new eyes. The air hurt. Gary blinked and blinked, producing lots of tears that the nurse wiped away.

Gary tried to adjust to being flooded by sensations that he was told was light. Strange thing, light. It was big and thick. It was everywhere, like it wanted to fill up the world. There were great blobs of it all around him. They were like oversized balloons that threatened to break and loose their contents onto everything, soaking light into every crack and opening and hole and nook and cranny.

He dropped his eyelids over his eyes to block out the bounty. How did people deal with all this sensory overload?

He kept his eyelids closed for a long time, then gingerly opened the again. The nurse was a strange shaped hunk of light, all white and pink and a patch of darkly lit hair at the top of her head.

"Where's Linda?" he asked.

"How are you feeling?" asked the nurse, smoothly glossing over his question, making it seem like he hadn't even asked the question.

"I'm getting a serious headache," said Gary. "Light is not an easy thing to deal with."

"It'll get better when it's all in focus."

"Focus?"

"At first, your brain doesn't know what to do with the input. It's all fuzzy and soft, right?"

Gary nodded.

"Well, that's normal. In a few days what you see will get sharper."

"It still hurts," he said.

"I'll dim the lights for you," she said.

She went to the wall where the switch was and turned the dial down. Gary felt like a blanket had been put over him. The blobs got dimmer and less threatening. It was as though the room had been injected with ink. The darkness flowed down and wrapped itself around objects.

The shadows were fascinating. They were these bulbous things trailing behind objects. Almost as though they were holding things up with their thickness. His acoustic apparatus never told him about shadows, but there they were, big as life.

"My wife," said Gary. "Where is she?"

Again, the silence from the nurse. It was unnerving. He wanted something—anything—to fill the space around him. It needed illumination that only came with sound. Words. Human speech.

"If you keep quiet like that for much longer," said Gary, "I think you're going to have to give me a sedative, because I'm just going to scream like a crazy man."

"I don't know where your wife is," said the nurse.

"Call her. Let me call her."

"We *have* called her. Do you have any other family?"

"What do you mean? Are you telling me something about Linda? What happened to her?"

"Nothing's happened to her. That we know of. Kids? Do you have kids?"

"No," said Gary.

"Parents? Friends? Anyone?"

"Stop asking me who can help me, and just help me. Tell me where my wife is."

"Look," said the nurse. "These things—these operations—they can be traumatizing on people. Your wife needs some time to adjust."

"Bullshit," said Gary. "Something happened to her but you're not telling me. Where's Dr. Hanes? She'll tell me what's going on. Get Dr. Hanes."

The nurse went to pat his hand, but stopped before she made contact. "Doctor is gone home," she said.

"When will she be back?"

"In the morning."

He looked up at the wall. There was a blob of light with murky dark patches thrown on it like someone had splashed ink. "That a clock?" he asked.

"Yes," said the nurse.

"It looks strange. I didn't expect a clock to look like that."

"I expect you're in for a lot of surprises," said the nurse.

The next morning, after a deep sleep aided by pills from the nurse, Gary stood up and tried to walk around the room without closing his eyes.

He managed pretty well. He went to the window and opened it wider, so he could see outside.

The hospital grounds were covered in grass. He expected to see color, but he wasn't sure he was. He knew grass was green, people had told him, but he didn't know if what he was perceiving was green. Maybe he was seeing texture rather than color. What was color, anyway? He grasped for some understanding of the concept, then decided it was something people brain's imposed on the outside world. Color didn't exist. It was an invention.

"Enjoying the view?" asked Dr. Hanes as she strode into the room behind Gary.

Gary turned around. The doctor was a shape before him. He saw her mouth wide, bared to show teeth. The teeth were strange things: tiny but strong. They were all lined up, as though someone had put them next to each other on purpose.

"I'm not sure I'm enjoying any of this," said Gary.

She stepped forward and Gary endured her touch. She leaned close and examined his eyes, pulling away the skin at the bottom and top of his eyes for a better look.

"Some redness," she said. "That's to be expected. Look up?"

Gary wasn't sure how to do that.

Dr. Hanes waited for a few seconds, then suggested he contract the muscles above his eyeballs.

Gary understood that. He did as instructed and was rewarded with a view of the ceiling.

"Now contract your lower muscles."

Gary looked down at the floor. It was without color. He knew that was usually called white. He matched that color to the lab coat Dr. Hanes was wearing. A small wonderment took hold of him. The coat was the same color as the floor. Huh.

"We heard from your wife," said Dr. Hanes.

"She's here?" asked Gary, full of urgency. "Why didn't you let her in?"

"She's not here," said Dr. Hanes. "She's not coming."

"What?"

"How well do you know your wife?" asked the doctor.

"We've been married 26 years."

"A long time, to be sure, but how well do you know her?"

"What are you getting at?"

"Did she ever tell you what she looks like?"

"She probably looks like you," said Gary. "Like everyone. You're all balloon heads with things stuck on you like noses and ears and hair. Light blobs on light blobs, like fleshy fractals."

Dr. Hanes frowned, then forced a laugh. "Yes, well, that's true as far as it goes, but there's more."

"More?"

"Some people are more—well—attractive than others. More pleasing to the eye."

"Doc," said Gary, "I've been blind since birth, but that doesn't mean I'm stupid. I know about attractiveness."

"But it never figured in your relationship with your wife because you never saw her."

Gary felt a strange pressure on his heart. His tear ducts opened up even more than they had been and his nose began to run. He fumbled for some tissue. Hanes handed a box to him. Gary took some of the sheets and blew his nose.

"You're telling me my wife is—what?"

"She doesn't think she's attractive," said Dr. Hanes.

"Ridiculous."

"She's afraid you'll see her and think she's ugly."

"She told you this?"

"Yes."

"No one is ugly," said Gary. "Not to a blind man."

"You're not blind anymore," said Dr. Hanes.

"Now I wish I still was," said Gary.

The next day Linda still didn't come to see him. Don, an acquaintance of his, an artist who lived a few blocks away, did come.

"Hey, Gary," he said as he walked in.

Gary turned to him. "Hi Don. What are you doing here?"

"Heard you were getting your sight back. Wanted to see how you were doing."

"They're letting me out tomorrow."

"Good news," said Don.

Gary shrugged. "Have you seen Linda?"

Don shimmered in the air in front of Gary. He shook his head, which made his whole balloon body jiggle and tremble. Gary was not sure he was ever going to get used to the movements that bodies made. It gave him a little bit of a headache, actually, and he wanted to close his eyes.

"I don't know where she is," said Gary.

"I'm sure she's fine."

"She thinks she's ugly."

"What?"

"That's what the doctor said."

Don didn't answer.

"You don't think she's ugly, do you? You'd paint her portrait, wouldn't you?"

"Of course," said Don.

"You don't sound convincing."

"Linda is a beautiful person," said Don.

"It's not like I care," said Gary. "Doesn't she know that?"

"Have you talked to her?"

"No! That's what I'm trying to tell you. I don't know where she is."

"She goes off sometimes. On her own. You know that."

"But she *tells* me. Not this time. She just—took off."

"Look, I don't know what's been going on between you two," said Don.

"What's that supposed to mean?"

"Married couples. Sometimes they—get into fights and stuff."

"This wisdom from a lifelong bachelor."

"Yeah, well."

Gary looked away from Don. He let his gaze wander to the wall next to him. "I asked the doctor to reverse the procedure. She though I was crazy."

"It is crazy," said Don.

"I can see your paintings, now. I just thought of that. Before this, all I could do was feel how the paint sat on the canvas."

"That's true," said Don.

"You know you're supposed to bring stuff to someone in the hospital. You know, like chocolate or flowers. Something."

"Figured you wouldn't want any of that," said Don.

"You figured wrong. Go buy me something. I'll wait."

Don laughed.

Gary asked him what was so funny.

"Oh," said Don. "You're serious." He stood up, slightly confused, then patted his pants pocket. "I have some money," he said. "There's a gift shop on the first floor."

"Perfect," said Gary.

"What do you want?" asked Don.

"Surprise me."

"Okay. Though it seems you've had enough surprises for now."

"You could be right," said Gary.

On the last day of his stay in the hospital, Gary spent some time looking through old issues of *People Weekly*. It was difficult to connect the patches of ink on the pages to the actual people they were supposed to represent. Did the readers of these magazines really believe they were seeing the true images of real people?

Don arrived in the early afternoon.

"I'm here to take you home," he said.

"I should learn to drive, now," said Gary. "I guess."

"You should," said Don.

"Things were easier when I was blind."

"That's hard to believe."

"The world was simpler. Now it's way too complicated."

Gary put on his jacket. It was blue. He was pretty sure of that. He walked slowly with Don down the hall to the parking lot. Along the way Gary saw people passing by. They were so wondrous, the look of them. It was as though they had descended from some ethereal realm. They were luminous and they floated on the air, only touching the floor with their feet, just to give them a little bit of a bounce.

"Easy there," said Don, yanking his arm and keeping him from walking into a cart that had been parked against the wall.

Gary didn't like the yank. It hurt his arm. He retaliated by swinging his other arm around and forming a fist mid-arc and connecting with the side of Don's head.

Don stumbled away from Gary, probably more surprised than hurt, but he ended up slumped on the floor against the opposite wall.

Nurses came running to his aid.

Gary dropped to his knees. "I'm sorry," he said. "I'm sorry, Don. I didn't mean to hit you."

Don waved his hand at him. "It's okay," he said.

The world was suddenly sharply in focus. Gary saw the blobs of light all around him as actual people, not indistinct patches. This was somewhat shocking.

The facial features of the nurses were no longer incongruous. They looked like they belonged.

He had an instinct to back away from them all, but chose not to. Instead he watched them help Don to his feet. Don looked at him. His features contorted into what Gary had come to realize was called an expression. What that expression conveyed, he was not sure of.

"You got some swing there," he said.

"I didn't mean to knock you down."

"He doesn't usually do that sort of thing," came a voice from behind. A familiar voice. Gary turned around.

"Linda?"

"The one and only," said a woman with a round face and a full cheeks. She walked toward Gary, but stopped a distance away from him.

"Can you really see?" she asked.

Gary nodded. "Where were you?"

"Camped out in the parking lot. I couldn't come in."

"For days?" asked Gary.

She nodded. "For days."

"I didn't know you were there," said Don.

"No one knew. I told the doctor I was out of town."

"Why?" asked Gary.

She lifted her hands above her head and dropped them down the sides of her body with a flourish. "Because of this," she said.

The nurses all went silent. Kind of an ominous silence. The sort of silence that should lead to something else. Some kind of epiphany or revelation. Gary listened for it, hoping it would come out of the air and hit him in the face.

But nothing was there. It was just the two of them at that moment. Looking at each other.

Linda's face had turned a shade darker, like the blood had invaded her face. Gary knew what that was. Embarrassment. Shame.

He kept his eyes wide open, blinking away salt water as best he could. It was hard to tell if the tears were from his eyes still adjusting or from the pain of seeing Linda in distress.

"I don't know what beauty is," said Gary.

"That's good," said Linda.

"But I know you're beautiful."

"Liar."

"How can you say that?"

"I'm overweight. My hair is scraggly. My nose is too big. My eyes are drab. I've got a double chin. And I *feel* completely unattractive."

The silence around them was like bubbles of meaning floating here and there. No one wanted to contradict Linda, but no one wanted to reassure her, either. It seemed like they sensed her devotion to her belief.

Gary shook his head. "You're wrong," he said.

"I'm not."

"You're beautiful."

"You're just saying that because you're married to me. No one else believes it."

"Is that why you married me?" he asked. "Because you figured a blind guy wouldn't see the real you?"

"Something like that," she said.

The nurses swirled around him. They wanted to protect him, it seemed, but from what?

Linda got lost in the motions. Where was she? He couldn't tell. He couldn't *see*.

"Linda," he said, as he reached for her.

"I'm here," she said, but not very convincingly. The voice was definitely her, he had not doubt of that. But the rest of her. The blobs of light. Where did they go?

The nurses stopped.

They had never been moving, not like he had imagined. He saw them for what they were: people trying to help him.

"You've got some anger issues going on," one of them said.

"You need to get that taken care of. Transplant recipients have a lot of emotional stuff to deal with."

Gary didn't care about any of that.

"Where's Linda?" he asked.

"Linda Linda Linda," said Don. "That's all you think about."

"I want my wife," said Gary.

"You never *had* a wife," said Don.

Gary blinked. The world disappeared for an instant, then returned. He wanted to argue with Don, but he could not. He knew Don was right.

"I made her up?" said Gary.

Don nodded.

Gary looked around his immediate surroundings. There was nothing anywhere to indicate he was anything but a normal man standing in a hall with other people surrounding him. There was nothing to indicate he had made up a life companion for himself. There was also nothing to indicate to anyone that hie eyes were anything but his own.

Dr. Hanes emerged from a room down the hall. She advanced toward Gary.

"You lied to me," said Gary. "You said you talked to my wife."

Don put his hand on Gary's shoulder. "It's for your own good, man. They were trying to help."

Dr. Hanes got close and closer. She was sharply in focus. All her features were as crisp and cutting as her lab coat. Gary longed for the hours when everything was soft and blobby. That was the way he wanted everything to be. That was the way he knew things should be.

But they weren't. Dr. Hanes smiled and smiled, her teeth shining like rows of lights, and she extended her hand and just kept walking toward Gary.

The Half Life Of Sympathy is Not Much More Than About Two Days

Everyone pretty much had it wrong about ghosts, but I didn't find out the truth until I *was* one. My death was not, all things considered, a particularly unpleasant turn of events, but it did have its element of surprise.

To begin with, I shouldn't have died at all. I was way too young. I'm sure many dead people feel the same way, and while I was no kid, it still seems as though 42 is a teensy bit early, especially for a late bloomer who was just beginning to find out what he wanted to do with his life.

Then there was the revelation that the circumstances of one's death apparently determines how you spend the afterlife. I don't mean whether you were a good person or not. I mean the actual nitty gritty of *how* you die matters a lot because you end up existing in that spot for quite a while.

My expiration date came up this way: I was in my car tooling along Washington State's Highway 14 on the Columbia River, passing through a little town called Stevenson. My destination was Portland, Oregon, where I had an appointment with a recruiter for a high tech firm who was going to interview me for a job in their public relations department. Not exactly a higher calling, I suppose, but I needed the money and I knew I could do the work.

Imagine my shock when out of nowhere a semi truck pulled out in front of me, expecting, I can only assume, that I would slow down and allow it safe passage. Alas, as much as I too would have been happy to see that happen, the laws of physics apparently would not allow it. I applied my brakes and had to steer my vehicle into the other lane, which, unhappily, put me in the path of an oncoming vehicle. The driver of *that* vehicle registered surprise. I veered again and she veered. We nevertheless collided, me spinning off towards a lamppost and a realty building. My last living memories are of blurred colors bleeding past my field of vision. I hit the post, which, somehow, seemed to *increase* my kinetic energy, and I spun even more rapidly into the side of the realty establishment. My head hit the side windshield of my car, cracking open my skull and just like that, wham bam, I was a dead duck, my life fading away while my car creaked and squeaked and settled down around me.

I remember some voices asking if he (meaning me) was okay, but that didn't last long. Very soon all was quiet, warm, and soft. It felt good to be dead. This worried me at first, until I realized that I was going to spend most of my existence in this state, so why *not* let it be pleasant?

Now here's where the unexpected stuff really started to kick in. First off, I couldn't see anything. All was white. And not like a bright light leading me on to the other side. No, just white. Blank. Also, I couldn't hear or smell. All my senses were on hold. Very disconcerting, and what I was mostly thinking then, before I knew the full extent of my predicament, was that maybe I wasn't really dead. I was on an operating table somewhere and doctors were trying to revive me. I cheered them on. Go docs! I'm pulling for you. But soon I decided that wasn't what was going on at all. I really was dead and this is what was left for me: endless nothing. It was a chilling thought and I fervently hoped it wasn't so. I also thought that if nothing registered anymore, then my subconscious (whatever that had become) would begin filling in stuff for me, just to keep me occupied. Which would make me a dead insane person. Ah, the beauty of existence.

Then the voice.

—*Who you?*

I heard it, but it didn't really want to register it, still hoping I could make myself hallucination proof.

—*Do you believe in ghosts?*

This time I took notice. It seemed an odd question for my subconscious to be asking me.

—*If you want to see, you have to believe. Do you believe?*

Well, I never really believed any of that new age, positive thinking junk. Things didn't happen just because you believed them. Life didn't work that way.

Oh. But maybe death did?

—*I don't have much time. Other dead people await me. Do you believe?*

What could I say?

—Yeah, I believe.

—*Liar.*

Then laughter. What was this? God having a good old joke on me?

—*I ask again, for the last time. Do you believe?*

—Do I believe in what?

—*Good answer. I want to know if you are ready to accept what has happened to you.*

Now I was starting to understand.

—You mean that I'm dead?

—*Dead. Yes yes.*

—I think so.

—*And that you're not gone. You still exist. You are a ghost.*

Should I believe the voice? How do I know if I'm really a ghost or not?

—Show me proof.

—*Oops. Wrong answer. Bye bye.*

Silence again. The voice disappeared and I was alone. After a while things weren't so warm anymore. Cold began seeping into me from my feet and hands, moving toward my torso. I found that I could move my extremities around, or it felt like I could. I didn't know what my extremities were anymore.

It felt like centuries passed. Time was like a heavy smothering pillow and I was going crazy trying to keep from losing my mind. But nothing changed. Nothing. Then the voice again.

—*Some think that ghosts are shadows of elementary particles. When you die, you leave behind a residue, an imprint of the stuff you were made of. Like the junk given off when bigger particles collide. You are now the result of a collision of your atoms with the fabric of reality. When you died, your mind created this copy of yourself as a way of self-preservation, the only preservation a mind has: thoughts as an accumulation of quantum particles. Ghosts are nothing but the dreams of dead people.*

There was a pause from the voice. I didn't know if I was expected to comment on it's comments but I did not hesitate for long.

—Yes, yes, that is the way it is. I believe you. I believe that.

Laughter from the voice.

—*That is the explanation we reserve for simpletons who cannot understand any other way of existing.*

—Okay.

—*Then you are a simpleton?*

—If that's what it takes to be a part of something again.

—*You should be getting some sensory input soon. Good luck.*

Gone again. And I was alone again. But this time it was different because over the course of a few days, a scene deepened around me. I saw the corner where I died. I saw traffic going by me on Highway 14. I was suspended over the sidewalk, in a sitting position, with my head flopped over to one side, which is how they found me. Which is how I died, and now I saw the truth: my imprint remained exactly where I died. I had not moved, though my wrecked car was gone, and the glass had been swept up. My body was also not here. Just me. A ghost stuck like a bug in amber.

A woman passed through me. A brother and sister, walking their dog, also moved right through my body. Or the image of my body. Or whatever I was. I didn't like this.

—Hey! Someone get me out of this.

From over my shoulder, in the distance, I heard a voice. Not like the one I had heard before. This one was female.

—*It's no use. We're not going anywhere and no one can help us.*

—Who are you?

—*The one you smashed into.*

I groaned.

—You died too?

—*Thanks to your inept driving.*

—It wasn't my fault!

—If you had just slid into that semi, I'd still be alive. So I think it is *your fault.*

—But then I'd be dead.

—Just as you are now.

She had a point.

—People like you are what was wrong with the world. Selfish. Never thinking about other people.

I didn't know what to say to this, so I said nothing.

Down towards the river I saw a riverboat coming in to dock at the pier. As it came closer a crowd of people pressed against the railing. I believed. I believed I was a ghost and I was going to haunt some of these people.

They approached me and kept going over and through me. One of them, an older man with white hair and a silly beard stopped just in front of me. He had three people with him: An older man and two other younger people in their twenties, evidently the older man's children, as they referred to him as Dad. They were overwhelmingly sad looking.

"I'm getting some readings over here," said Silly Beard.

He held his hands to his forehead and looked in my direction. In fact, directly *at* me. I was unnerved by his gaze. He seemed to *know.*

But the father motioned to him. "No," he said. "Linda died over here."

Silly Beard seemed to leave the place in front of me reluctantly.

—This is my family.

—I guessed.

—See what you did? I had a family. I had a life. That's my husband, Ralph, and my children Stacey and Albert.

She sounded more resigned than sad.

—They're here to look for me. I told them, if I ever died, to look for me. I would find a way to let them know. I would.

I thought that they must have been an odd little family, but didn't say anything to Linda.

—I never left any instructions like that.

She didn't answer.

Ralph stood respectfully by Silly Beard as he repeated the actions he had taken before: hands on the side of his head, piercing look in the direction of

Linda. Linda seemed to understand something important was transpiring and I felt like an intruder on their private moments, their private life.

Linda's children clung to Ralph's arm.

"What can you tell me?" said Ralph.

"Her spirit is strong," said Silly Beard. "She definitely wants you all to know she is well and is thinking of you."

—*Tell them I love them.*

"She says she loves you very very much."

—*Tell them I will wait for them.*

"She says she is looking forward to seeing you after a long long time."

—How does he know that?

—*Well, what else would people say? What else can you say?*

—How about telling them that when they die, make sure they are somewhere where they have a terrific view of the ocean, or the mountains, or a big beautiful valley, because they are going to be looking at it for a long long time.

She shrugged.

—*Not that long.*

Ralph and Stacey and Albert hugged each other and cried. Linda did not look at them. I got the feeling she couldn't look at them because it was too hard for her. Silly Beard came over to me again. I ignored him.

—What do you mean, not that long?

—*Haven't you noticed?*

—What?

—*We're falling.*

I looked down. Linda was right. I was closer to the pavement than before. A lot closer. In fact, my foot was about to contact the road.

—Whoa, I didn't expect this.

—*Shut up.*

—What? What did I say?

—*I really hate you for putting me here. I was supposed to have another good forty or fifty years. Maybe more. Do you see what you've done? Do you?*

I was getting tired of her accusations. I was trying to *save* people when

I died. It wasn't my fault that some asshole truck driver cut in front of me. It wasn't my fault. It wasn't.

Now Silly Beard was sniffing around me. He leaned into my face and I looked at him again. Really tried to penetrate his eyes, and he stopped and tilted his head and his eyes seemed to focus on me, but just for a briefest instant. Then it was gone, our connection. I wondered, was he the real thing? Could he tell that I was here?

He stood up and scratched his cheek and seemed to be thinking. Ralph came over to him, pumped his hand, and said "Thank you" about six times.

Linda was sobbing.

—I'm sorry you lost your family.

She cried some more, then stopped.

—*Thank you.*

—Don't mention it.

I looked down at my foot again. It had contacted the pavement and was partly submerged in it. So this was to be my fate. I was going to fall into the earth. Like getting into a hot tub. Only this hot tub would take me, where?

—Why can't we move?

—*Because we're not really here?*

—No, that's not right. We are here. Silly Beard can sense us.

She seemed to consider this.

—*I thought you weren't sure about him.*

I wiggled my toe and felt some resistance. That was intriguing.

—I can feel the ground.

—*No you can't. That's impossible.*

I looked at Linda. She had not yet contacted the earth.

—Just wait. When you get close enough, you'll feel it too.

She looked at me and at the spot of ground beneath her.

—*We're falling, you know. We have mass, that's the kicker. There isn't much to us, but what there is is influenced by gravity.*

—Apparently.

Silly Beard remained on the scene. Ralph and Stacey and Albert headed down the hill toward the river boat. I guess they got what they wanted. Or needed. But what of Silly Beard? He stood and listened and fretted and scratched his head and fretted some more. Poor guy. He probably never actually was near a newly dead person like this. I bet most psychics don't get called in to look for something until much later, sometimes years after death. If Linda and I were any indication, that would be years too late to actually find anything.

—*Hey, I'm feeling it too. The pavement is like sandpaper going through me.*

—Yeah, that's it. Me too.

—*This is crazy.*

—You noticed.

Silly Beard still wanted something. He still needed to see, I suppose, or understand. My foot was fully in the ground now and I could push against the soil. I felt enough resistance to try something. I braced myself and waited until Silly Beard came close again. Then I pushed off with my leg. I moved. Slowly, but I moved. It was like swimming in molasses or getting caught in a vat of whipped cream.

I slow motioned my way over to Silly Beard and reached my hand around and grabbed him by the elbow. He trembled. My hand went through his elbow but I felt some drag there. If I continued, I thought I could maybe get a hold of him again. I could push off the ground and jump into him. Silly Beard, to give him some credit, did not flinch or pull away. He had committed himself to investigating this sort of thing, and now that it was really and truly happening to him, he was going to overcome his natural inclination to run like hell. He stayed right where he was.

Silly Beard, apparently, was to be my first haunting.

—*Hey! What are you doing to him?*

—Don't bother me now. I'm beginning to see how this works. If you don't want to fall into the center of the Earth and live out your death cheek by jowl with the rest of the dead people, then you better find someone too.

I pushed my arm into his torso and there was a satisfying sense of solidity to it. My arm still came out, but not as quickly. I needed to get more of my mass in there. I pushed off with my foot again. My body contacted his body and then I was there. I reached around him with my arms and bear hugged myself into him. I was looking out the back of his head, but that didn't matter. I had a body. I was doing my first haunting. It felt good.

—Get out of there.

—Linda, mind your own business.

—He's scared. He's going to have a heart attack.

—You're not going to stop me from doing this. This is our only way to have any semblance of a life.

—You asshole, you're dead. *You don't* have *a life. Not anymore.*

Silly Beard's head abruptly pulled away from mine and that lack of solidity immediately alarmed me. I spun around inside him and then his torso left mine and I was only in his legs. Passersby had stopped in concern.

"Are you okay, sir?"

"Someone call 9-1-1. This man is hurting."

Eventually I was left standing in his feet and Silly Beard, poor man, was sprawled out on the sidewalk, clutching his chest and crying, gasping. I wanted to help him, but what could I do? I reached into his chest and felt his heart. It was weak, hardly pumping at all. I tried to make him feel better by petting his heart, but that felt ridiculous. Where was the ambulance? Where was someone to help him?

—Here, let me.

Linda was beside me. She had pushed her away along the ground, step by step, and she was tired. But she knew. She put both her hands into his chest. I felt them going through mine like a breeze blowing through my dreams. It was that slight, and that real.

—Pull away.

That last comment in a whisper in my head.

I pulled away and she pumped his heart. Massaged it there in his rib cage, blood pumping through it, his face still contorted and scared, so scared, but not as white now. There was color in his face and I felt enormously relieved.

—You're doing it.

—I'm a doctor. Or I was *one.*

—What kind of doctor?

—My specialty was dermatology. I had an uncanny ability to diagnose rashes.

She continued massaging while people milled around the man. Someone put a blanket on him. "We should keep him warm," she said. "I read a book once, where you should keep people warm when they're hurt."

The paramedics arrived and put Silly Beard on a stretcher, and whisked him away. I wished him the best. Hoped he lived many more years.

Linda looked up at me, still standing in the pavement, buried all the way up to my mid calves.

—Will he be all right?

—I think so. I had seen patients like him when I was alive. That fear. Now I guess I know what it was. The people had seen something of the other side and they didn't like it.

—I'm sorry I did that to him.

—You should be.

I looked at the rising level of the sidewalk. It was already up to my knees.

—You're not going to latch onto anyone, are you?

—After seeing what you did here? I don't think so.

—Then the end for us is the center of the planet. Down instead of up. A kind of hell? I never expected that.

Linda laughed.

—There's a lot they don't tell us about back there when we were still alive. It could be that it isn't hell. Maybe it's a kind of heaven.

I put out my hand, hoping she would put hers in mine.

She did.

We fell a long long time and grew to appreciate, if not exactly love, the taste of Earth in our insubstantial bodies.

But just before we slipped under the surface for good, and began our long life of darkness, Silly Beard returned. It was later that evening. The only illumination was a few streetlights. Silly Beard stood in a steady rain, his face and hair dripping wet. He had a little meter thing in his hand and he waved it over the pavement. He looked at the display and blinked several times.

—*What's he doing back here?*

—I don't know. Maybe he just wants to be sure.

Then Silly Beard shivered. He put the meter down on the pavement and stomped on it, smashing it to bits. And then I knew. We both knew, the doctor and me, that it was over for us. There's just so long that anyone can care for anyone else before it all gets to be too much.

It was comforting to know that, in an odd way. Life continues, even in death.

The Oak's Tale

Evita and I got married at midnight.

It was a trendy thing to do, sure, but we were both interested in trendy things back then. It meant the marriage would last until noon.

That was a magical time. Midday. It did seem like an awfully long time, a marriage taking up a full 12 hours, but the upside was that after the divorce we would still have a good amount of daylight left and a chance to spend time with friends, sort through who was going to be loyal to who, and come to terms with all that residue of a shattered life together before the next cycle of darkness.

We chose a park on the outskirts of town. The air was damp and cool and redolent of blossoms weary with the task of scenting the air, but still awfully good at it.

The stars shone bright. A full moon hung above us. That was a nice touch.

Our guests arrived wearing the costumes we had specified in the invitations. Which meant we were surrounded by giant animals: coyotes, bears, raccoons, and tigers. Evita and I—well, we were overwhelmed that our friends were so into the animal costume aspect of the ceremony.

Evita was resplendent in a white swan costume. Her wings had the grace of evolution's long flight to perfection.

I wore a penguin's outfit, smart with a tuxedo look, as though I had just stepped out of a formal reception at a research station in the Antarctic.

We both knew we held the world spellbound, but we were not boastful about it. After all, most marrying couples mesmerize the world.

Around us, we heard the sounds of night. Distant owls hooting. Some vague scratchings and growlings punctuating the milky darkness. We stood in front of a big oak, the kind with branches that take crooked lightning paths from the trunk to the sky.

The oak asked us if we loved and adored each other.

We answered that of course we did. What did the oak think? That this was all some kind of joke?

Then we both hugged the oak, on opposite sides. It was big around, but not too big that our hands did not touch. We had made sure our costumes did not cover our hands.

As we stood there for a few seconds, with our bodies forming a protective circle around the oak, I knew that we had made the right decision.

Then we released our grasp and I pulled a short length of vine off the oak and wound it around Evita's ring finger. She did the same for me.

We held up our hands and our guests cheered.

Later, during the reception, our guests offered best wishes in the voices of animals. It was amusing, awe-inspiring, and ridiculous all at the same time. I mentioned to Evita that our reception was like life.

She nodded, but I was not sure she understood my meaning. No matter. We would have hours to get to know each other before the inevitable decline.

Once the guests had all left, some with winking nods in our direction, apparently with thoughts of our honeymoon in mind, we were alone in the woods. We sat at one of the benches with a view of a copse of large trees, and held hands and looked into each others costume eyes.

A young man in black clothes and a tight woolen cap, obviously on his way to rob a house, passed by our bench. He waved at us.

We waved back.

"Find a better way to make a living," I called to him.

"Okay grandpa," he said.

That hurt me, a little. Was I already so boring and mainstream that young people saw me as old and stodgy?

"Your mother wouldn't want you to be breaking into houses," said Evita.

"Society doesn't let me do anything else," he called back as he disappeared into the darkness.

I murmured to Evita that it was a good thing we had decided not to have children. Our kid probably would have ended up like that thief. Completely without empathy or remorse.

"About that," said Evita, in a voice with very little dreaminess in it and a lot of urgency snaking through it. My heart sank. I felt a terrible emptiness in my core, like some animal, a tiger, perhaps, had ripped me open.

I had hoped for at least a couple of hours of marital bliss, but it appeared cracks in our relationship had already appeared.

"Yes," I said.

"I'm not so sure I don't want kids anymore."

I stiffened. She pulled away from me.

"But we talked about this," I said.

"I know," she said, "but now that we're married, things are different. We've been solid for almost an hour. I feel like we have the foundation to provide for a child."

I stood and removed the penguin head from my own head. The cool night air wrapped itself immediately around my ears and nose and neck and hair, draping me in cool caresses. It felt like an enormous relief to be out of the costume, at least partly.

Evita also stood and removed the top of her costume. Now she looked like a strange bird with a human head. So disconcerting. Who was she? Were we really married? It hardly seemed possible.

Evita looked lost. How did *that* happen? Hadn't I been a good and loyal husband?

"I only know how I feel," she said.

"And I only know how I feel," I said. "I was very clear about children."

"You were clear that children scared you," she said. "It doesn't have to be that way now."

I did not want to have this conversation. Not again. It was futile, in its way. I still had my thoughts on the subject, and though Evita had changed her mind, that did not mean I would or should change mine.

Mosquitoes swarmed around us. I batted them away. The wedding ceremony, which had seemed magical and awesome, like we had taken a bit of heaven and wrapped ourselves in it, was now only a sour memory, something I would recall with infinite bitterness as a symbol of what might have been, but would never come to fruition.

We entered a phase of our marriage that was difficult, to say the least. I moved away from Evita and sat on the end of the bench.

She did not try to come closer. She sat on her end of the bench, and we waited for the sun to come up. Perhaps the light of day would bring its wisdom to our hearts, make us into something other than a tiresome quarreling couple.

It was still very dark.

I got up and went to the table of food and loaded up a plate, aware that I was about to stress eat, but not caring. I grabbed pieces of chicken, a mound of potato salad, a cut of prime rib, some salmon soaked in a ginger-lime marinade, and chips and salsa, not to mention a slice of lemon meringue pie and a piece of chocolate cake. We spent a lot on catering and I was pleased to get to eat a good portion of it.

I went back to the bench and commenced consuming my plate's bounty. Evita's revulsion for my chewing noises was apparent. I felt her steaming displeasure and resentment and disapproval waft into the air along with the mosquitoes that still wanted my blood.

As I ate from my plate, the wind picked up. This was a blessing. It cleared the air, a little.

Evita rose while I was eating and extended her swan wings. Such a beautiful sight. I wanted to hold the vision of her forever, even though we were not getting along.

She stepped lightly around the park grounds. It was as though she were performing a dance. Milky moonlight filled all the shadow places around us. There was no music, save what might be unspooling in Evita's head. It would be some melody the rest of the universe shared with her.

At that moment, I felt disgust for myself. I tossed the plate, still laden with half the food I had put on it, into the trash.

It made a rattling sound, but she didn't notice. She had discovered some intricate steps in the night. They floated down from the tops of the trees and entered her feet and her arms, and there a kind of ethereal grace upended her mundane existence, and she appeared to float on the air. It was as though the world was lifting her up on its own dreams.

I wanted to call her name, but stifled the urge. I recognized this was not good. I was becoming estranged from my bride.

I wasted some more precious time, considering my options. The cosmic clock ticked away. I imagined giant gears grinding away above my head. The stars and moon moving, the earth tilting.

"All right," I said.

She kept dancing.

I cleared my throat, so that the world would hear me, not just Evita.

"Let's have children."

She stopped dancing. Her wings were still extended. She floated toward me. She was a vision all wrapped in moonlight and carrying the wonder of the world with her.

Nature determined the course of the next half hour or so. We shared our ecstasy. Felt the power of life coursing through us and not only consummated our marriage, but began a new life.

My original reason for not wanting children still had validity. I thought it irresponsible of any couple that would be together for only 12 hours, half a day, to doom a child to a broken home.

There were many who agreed with me. They saw the wisdom of a childless marriage for those, like Evita and me, who did not believe in a life long commitment. We believed the beauty of an experience did not have to last a lifetime to be beautiful.

But then, my love for her changed everything. She changed her mind, and I could not deny her.

Evita had an easy pregnancy.

Our daughter was born as the sky was lightening and the moon was setting. We called her Dawn.

The next couple of hours were spent feeding Dawn, watching her take her first steps, seeing her through illnesses which lasted as long as thirty seconds at times. Those were terrible trials for me. More than once I thought our daughter would not make it.

But she did. Evita said all couples are extra vigilant about their first baby. The next ones don't inspire quite so much in the way of overt protectiveness.

Next ones?

"I'm not sure I want another child," I said.

"Of course we do," she said. "We don't want Dawn to be lonely."

By this time we had moved into our house. We lived in a nice neighborhood. People looked after each other. I noticed that we had only about five hours left of our marriage.

"I don't think so," I said to Evita. "I don't think we should bring *another* child into the world."

Evita heard what I said, but I don't think she took it in, not completely. She only hummed a tune, as though music would take care of us, all three of us.

I had to admit that Dawn was a blessing in my life. My relationship with Evita had settled into benign tolerance. We saw each other as mere shadows of who we once were and that was sad, but we were functional and I do believe we provided a good home for Dawn.

I gathered the courage, some time around 7:23, to ask her how she felt about our marriage.

Dawn was immediately philosophic. "It's not what I expected," she said, "but few things in life are. Look at Dawn. You thought she would be a burden, but she isn't. She is now your purpose in life. She gives your life meaning. Isn't that so?"

I told her it was so, but I wanted to know about her. About us. Our marriage was over half gone. What did it mean to her? What was she going to take away from it?

She extended her hand and tapped me, lightly, on the nose, as though it was something she had done for years and years, as though it was a private *thing* between us, only it wasn't, so it felt—odd. I pulled away from her. She noticed, but did not comment.

"Silly man," she said. "Why do you want to know about my inner thoughts, now? You never wanted to know before. You only thing you wanted to know was that I adored you."

I remembered our wedding, how she lit up the night. It was a fond memory. Would I hold it forever? I hoped so. But there was no illumination now. Only a sense of the world winding down.

Dawn crawled off my wife's lap and came over to me and grabbed my hand and wanted me to play with her. She adored stacking blocks and loved it when I stacked blocks with her.

I felt tears begin to well up in my eyes.

Children grow up so fast. If you blink, you could miss it all.

I could have waited until after the divorce. It would have been so easy. So decent.

But I did not.

I left Evita and Dawn some time before 8:00 and walked a short distance down the block and around a corner. There I found the house of Isabelle, one of our wedding guests. She was the giraffe. She was a friend of Dawn's, but I knew, on some deep level where words don't count, that she was attracted to me and I to her.

I knocked on her door and she let me in. She felt the same urgency I did and we betrayed my wife, together, each of us wanting some kind of connection, but each of us, also, filled with shame as we coupled.

After we did what we shouldn't have done, she wanted me to leave. I wanted to stay, at least for a few moments, to help me get myself to a place where I could face Evita.

But Isabelle had no patience for that. "Out," she said. "Get out. I have to get ready for work."

I left.

The morning was already warm. The sun hung in the sky like a scolding parent raining down shame upon me. The walk back home was the most miserable few minutes I had spent, probably ever.

Our house looked odd in the bright sunlight, as though the sun had bleached it to a shining white cipher of a house. It made me think of a tooth among teeth, about to be rotted away.

I pushed the front door open. Dawn was doing her homework. We had decided to homeschool her. She was up to calculus already, and preparing to master relativistic physics.

"Where have you been?" asked Evita.

"I needed a walk."

"You missed a big chunk of Dawn's early development," she said.

"I know," I said. "I regret that."

Evita wanted to ask me more questions, I could see that. But she shook her head at me. I felt another load of shame pour over me. I knew I exuded misery.

I looked at Dawn, bent over her pages, intent on her lessons. She glanced up at me, briefly, but did not greet or acknowledge me. I felt I deserved no better, and went into the kitchen to see about preparing breakfast.

I worked alone. Evita and Dawn had their own world, one that I was now mostly barred from.

I made stacks of pancakes and cooked sausage and put them on plates and set the plates on the kitchen table with a plate of butter and a bottle of maple syrup and called them into the dining room.

They came, though you could tell they weren't that interested. It was an obligation to be in the same room with me.

I clasped my hands and bent my head.

"What's this?" asked Evita.

"I'm saying grace."

"Why? Do you feel guilty? Prayer has not been part of our lives up to now."

My face reddened. I did feel guilty, but also didn't think I could tell Evita why.

A long silence wormed its way into the space between us.

Dawn noticed it. She got very quiet. The sounds of silverware against dinnerware as she cut her pancakes and sausage with knife and fork were distant relatives of the cracking and popping sounds of a forest fire burning in the night and sending up embers that glowed along long arcs, than faded to nothing.

I looked at Evita. She looked back at me and she knew, immediately. "Isabelle?" she asked.

I was overwhelmed with shame and guilt. I had nothing to say. I only nodded.

"Is it over?"

I nodded again.

She studied me. "I suppose these kinds of things can happen," she said. "We'll stay together for the sake of Dawn. But once she's grown, that's the end. You couldn't wait? Not even until noon?"

"I'm sorry," I said.

We finished breakfast. Dawn and Evita went outside to help provide Dawn with some experience of nature.

In the meantime I did the dishes and put the kitchen in order. I appreciated the opportunity to make something look and feel good. When I was finished, the counters gleamed and everything was in its proper place.

Dawn and Evita returned and sat in the living room with me. Dawn was so grown up already. I felt like I had missed her life. It passed by while I was involved with other things.

"We need to prepare for the end," said Evita.

I nodded. "Should we invite the people who were at the wedding?"

"That would be a nice touch," said Evita.

"I can help," said Dawn.

"You shouldn't help your parents break up," I said.

"It's okay, Dad," said my only daughter. "I knew this was coming."

Dawn and Evita got the invitations out. They texted and emailed. It took them a long hour. I did not have the energy to assist. I had mixed feeling about the impending divorce ceremony. I knew it was customary to finish the union with a ritual. It was meant to mirror the bonding ritual.

But I also felt like our marriage had been a fraud in many ways. After all, our prenuptial agreement had flown out the window. We had a child I had not planned on. I strayed from the marriage when I was sure I would not.

The marriage was a shambles. Why commemorate it with a ritual? I asked Evita if it would be okay if we just both simply shook hands and walked away.

"No," she said. "I want the ritual."

I did not argue with her. After all, she had put up with me for long enough. The least I could do was go along with her wishes.

Many of our invited guests said they could not attend the dissolution ceremony. I had expected this. Evita had not. "Why would they desert us now?" she asked.

"They have jobs," I said. "Commitments. Many will be on a short lunch hour around noon."

She nodded. "Should have thought of that," she said.

"Can't think of everything," I said.

I absentmindedly reached for her hand. The vine around my ring finer had wilted some, but was still green and springy.

Evita's vined finger trembled along with her hand. I thought, for one insane second, that she would place her hand over mine and we might have some small healing, but it didn't happen.

Instead, she turned from me and helped Dawn prepare for the ceremony.

We arrived at the oak, a bedraggled party consisting of me, Evita, Dawn, and four or five guests.

We stood in front of the oak, as we had done half a day previously, and listened to the woods around us. So different now. The sounds were much more abundant, a swirl of bird songs and rustling leaves and flying things.

None of us bothered with costumes.

The oak asked us if we wanted to dissolve our union.

We answered that we did, for the good of all.

We extended our hands, but did not touch.

Dawn removed the vines from our ring fingers and tossed them to the air so they went high up.

Our few guests clapped and then Evita and I clapped as well. It was a freeing moment, a beautiful recognition that our lives would go on. We would, perhaps, find beauty in the world again, and feel the power of life all around us.

Dawn grinned up at both of us. Evita and I each put a hand on her shoulder. We had already worked out custody and Evita was to have Dawn for the first week.

They turned from me, arm in arm, and walked out of the park.

The guests offered their condolences and best wishes for a happy life.

I couldn't see it, not then. My heart was like a lump of lead in my chest, and as I stood beneath the oak, unable to move, I went over the marriage in my mind, playing over the missteps and the betrayals as though they were a bad movie unspooling with nauseating certainty to a horrible conclusion.

I nursed the feeling for a few minutes, shed a tear or two, then raised my chin to the sun, felt its cleansing warmth on my skin, and determined that next time I would do better, even if it meant I would have to change who I was.

I put my hand on the oak. It felt like it was breathing. Its bark bit into my skin. I pressed as hard as I could, so hard that my fingers trembled.

When I pulled away, I looked at my palm. It held a landscape of hills and valleys, the negative of the oak's façade.

I stared at my palm for many minutes while the indentations gradually smoothed out and disappeared.

The Wedding Journey

On her wedding day Leesa rose before the sun and prepared for her journey to the oasis twenty miles distant where her ceremony would take place. She knew nothing of her future husband, only that her parents had chosen wisely. She was certain she would grow to love him, whoever he was, and if not, then he would at least be a tolerable person of high moral standing who would be a good father to her children.

She put on traveling robes and buckled on a good sturdy pair of walking boots. Both were gifts from her father. As she folded up her bedding and stored them in her closet for the last time, her mother entered her bedroom with a piece of cake. It had bits of fruit and nuts embedded in it and bore a thick slab of white frosting.

"This is a piece of your grandparents' wedding cake," said her mother. "Take it with you. It will sustain you on your journey and remind you of your family. Be careful not to share it with anyone unworthy."

Leesa wrapped the cake in a cloth and put it in her pocket. "I will be careful," she said. "I wish you were coming with me." She embraced her mother.

"I made the wedding journey on my own," said her mother. "You must do so as well. We will be there waiting for you."

Leesa did not eat breakfast. She stepped out of her childhood home and began walking along the road in front of her house. She turned around at the first curve and waved at her mother and father. They stood at the front door and waved back.

Leesa was not used to waking so early. It was still dark, although the sky was lightening a little from the sun not yet over the horizon. The woods around her rang wild with sounds and movements. She felt hunger pangs before she had gone a mile and stopped to take a bite from the cake.

It was dry and crumbling, but tasted wonderful. The frosting was hard as glass. She broke off a piece and placed it on her tongue where it melted and filled her head with dizziness. She dropped to the ground. So much sweetness at once. She thought of her grandparents, dead for several years. They had been married for decades and loved each other very much. That must have been why her mother gave her some of their wedding cake.

Gradually the dizziness subsided. Leesa felt tired. She put her head down on the ground. For only a minute, she told herself. She would rest, then continue her journey.

Leesa fell into a deep sleep. She dreamed of coupling with bears. This disturbed her so much that she cried out, waking herself.

The sun had risen. It peeked over the trees down the road. Sweat covered Leesa's face and chest. She got up off the ground and continued walking.

She tried to scrub her memory clean of the dream. Who would have such dreams? They could not have been her own. She must have somehow received someone else's dream. The forest here was mysterious. All sorts of odd things could happen.

Miles went by. The sun beat down hot and strong. Leesa longed for cloud cover but none came.

After a few hours she saw a man in the distance. He walked toward her. Meeting a man on the road like this could be dangerous. There was no place for her to hide. The forest had thinned out to just a few bushes amidst vast plains of grass on either side of her.

The man got closer and closer. Leesa saw that he was tall and handsome. He smiled at her as he approached.

"Hello," he said. "Are you enjoying the journey to your wedding?"

"How do you know I am going to my wedding?" said Leesa.

"No young woman travels alone on foot for any other reason," he said. He smiled at her. Leesa instantly liked the man. No, it was more than like. She suddenly wanted to pull him close and feel her skin against against his.

"Well, it is none of your business, I'm sure," she said, "but yes, I am going to my wedding."

"I know what you're thinking," said the man. "I know a place we can go to be alone."

Leesa felt her face redden. She said nothing. The man took her hand. She let him.

"Come on," he said. "You will like this place."

They walked off the road along a path which descended to a ravine and a big cave. Leesa and the man went into the cave. It was wonderfully cool. Leesa decided she didn't want to leave the cave, ever. But she did begin to wonder if she was doing the right thing by running off with this stranger.

She stopped. "I cannot go any further with you," she said to the stranger. "I must remain worthy of my future husband."

"Do not fret," said the stranger. "He would want you to eat."

Eat? Leesa wondered what the stranger meant by this.

They continued walking and came to a wide open area. A table set with porcelain plates and glass goblets stood at one edge of the clearing. Two chairs were pushed in on opposite sides of the table. The man pulled out a chair and Leesa, now confused, sat down in it.

"Every young woman needs to have one last meal prepared for her before she becomes a wife," said the man. "Don't you agree?"

Leesa did not disagree. She also began to understand this encounter was not exactly what she had anticipated.

The man disappeared behind a stalagmite and returned with a roast turkey which he placed in the middle of the table. Then he added platters of potatoes, fruit, sliced bread, vegetables, and yogurt. He poured them both glasses of wine. Leesa ate with a gusto she had never known before. She could barely pause long enough to load her fork with food.

The man ate with her and spoke of love. He said there is no greater thing in the world and he wished her only love and happiness in her new life.

Lisa gave the man a piece of her grandparent's wedding cake. The man accepted it with great humility. Then he helped Leesa out of her chair and guided her back to the road. Leesa continued her journey.

The grass thinned even more as Leesa walked. The bushes disappeared. Bits of sand began swirling around in the air. Some pieces of grit lodged in her eyes. She stopped to remove them.

A tinkling sound ahead made her look up. Leesa's vision was bleary with tears, but she had no doubt of what she saw: a skeleton dancing in the road.

The skeleton talked to her. "Go back," it said. "Go back now, before you die." Then the skeleton laughed so hard its jaw clattered and shook loose a couple of teeth. The skeleton retrieved the teeth from the ground and pushed them back into place.

"You don't scare me," said Leesa.

The skeleton raised its bony arms, as if it was about to pounce on Leesa. Leesa did not move back. She planted her feet firmly on the ground and took out the remains of her grandparents' cake. She placed it on her palm and held her hand up high for the skeleton to see the white frosting.

The skeleton retreated two or three steps and dropped its arms. They clattered against its own ribs.

Leesa knew a cake such as this, with its strong sugars, would devour the skeleton in no time and turn it into a heap of decaying bones, like rotten teeth. She stepped forward. The skeleton cowered, turned, and ran.

Leesa put the cake back into her pocket, then threw her head back and laughed as loud as she could. The sun touched her tongue. It snuck into her throat and down to her belly, warming her with hot licks.

Leesa felt hungry again. She wanted to eat the last of the cake but was wary of losing her only real protection.

Hummingbirds came to her. They hovered over her head and dropped water onto her hair. Leesa put her hand to her hair and felt the dampness there, then licked her hand. She realized she was almost as thirsty as she was hungry. She tilted her head up. The hummingbirds filled her mouth with moisture. One after the other flew up and left droplets.

She kept walking.

She saw an oasis in front of her and rejoiced. Her journey would soon be over.

The oasis proved to be a mirage. Leesa felt disappointed, though not defeated. The mountains in the distance looked green and lush. Surely the oasis would be there, if not sooner. She put one foot in front of the other. She kept her eyes on the mountains. They seemed to hold up the sky and this gave her hope. Nature would always provide. It was as her mother had told her: "Trust the future. It is all we have."

She walked another few miles and came to a very old woman standing in the road. She was wrinkled and stooped over.

"May I have my cake, please," said the woman. She held out a thin arm.

"Grandmother?" said Leesa. "Is that you?"

"Of course not," said the old woman. "Your grandmother is dead. I am the baker of that cake. I never tasted it before I delivered it to the wedding. I believe there may be something amiss with it. I need to have it back."

How was this possible? thought Leesa. Her grandparents were married seventy years ago. Surely the baker must now be long dead.

The woman remained completely still, with her hand held palm up in front of Leesa, like a beggar asking for silver coins.

"I wish to offer some of this cake to my husband to be," said Leesa.

"He does not need it," said the woman. "Give it to me." Her eyes looked like oyster shells. Her teeth glowed yellow.

Leesa hesitated.

A flash of color moved behind the old woman. Children, three of them. They wore red and orange robes and ran with energy and purpose. They stopped beside the old woman. They held out their hands. "We want cake too," they said.

"You see?" said the old woman. "You cannot keep that cake to yourself. It is meant to share."

She stepped forward. The children also moved closer.

Suddenly Leesa saw fangs sprout in their mouths. The children grew claws and held them up menacingly.

"Give us what we want," they said.

The old woman smiled and nodded. As her head bent over, Leesa saw horns growing out of the woman's hair. This was no baker but the devil herself! And these children must be her demons.

Leesa broke off a small piece of the frosting and threw it at one of the children, hitting him squarely in the chest. The child vanished. The robe fell to the ground in a heap. The other two children, seeing this, took the old woman by her hands and quickly led her away. They went down the road farther and farther from Leesa until they disappeared from view.

Leesa bent down and retrieved the piece of frosting from the folds of the robe. She put the frosting and the remaining crumbs of the cake back into her pocket. She lifted the child's robe from the ground. She liked the deep red color. She knew it could warn people that whoever wore it was to be feared. She shook the robe to release the grains of sand from it. Then she folded it over several times and wrapped it around her head.

The sun retreated in the sky. Leesa had the sensation of ice around her head.

She saw several more mirages as she walked. They did not distress her. The road had many surprises. It was only natural that some of them would be illusions.

Nevertheless, the journey taxed Leesa's energy. She cursed the tradition that made her walk so far simply to get married. This should not be a day of labor. It should be a day of joy.

And what of her husband to be? He was privileged to spend the day at a comfortable oasis, waiting for her. Drinking with his friends, no doubt. Perhaps cavorting with the women of the oasis for one last time. Huh!

Leesa stared at her boots as she walked and cursed. She hardly noticed that the sand and dirt of the road had given way to cool grass and wildflowers. It was not until bees began to buzz around her that she lifted her eyes and realized she had come to her destination.

Before her, a magnificent lake glistened blue and white. Her parents stood on the shore of the lake. Another couple stood a short distance from them. Palm trees swayed in a cool breeze. Leesa stopped. She unwrapped the robe from her head and let it drop to the ground. She saw that the robe held clumps of hair in its folds. Her hair. She touched her head. She was completely bald.

Leesa bent down and unbuckled her boots and slipped them off and put her feet on the cool grass. Blades tickled the soles of her feet. She wiggled her toes.

Bare on top and on bottom.

She never felt more at home in the world.

She walked to her parents with her head held high. They greeted her with embraces and her father's eyes were wet with tears.

"How was your trip, my dear mother and my dear father?" said Leesa.

"We came by wagon," said her mother. "Our journey was easier than yours. But there was much more at stake for you. Were you careful with your grandmother's wedding cake?"

Leesa still had some of the cake in her pocket. "I did what needed to be done," she said.

"That is good," said her father. "Did you save any for your husband?"

"I did, father," said Leesa. "Where is he? Where is my husband to be?"

"My son has not completed his journey as yet," said the woman of the other couple.

His journey?

"We can do nothing but wait," said Leesa's father.

"He had to journey, just as I did?" said Leesa.

Her mother smiled. "Of course. Did you think you were the only one? Oh child, you are so amusing."

"It is good you arrived first," said her father. "The one who gets to the ceremony first shall be the superior in the marriage."

Leesa was not sure she wanted to be the superior. Would she, a simple country girl, know how to be superior?

"Must we wait here?" she said.

"He shouldn't be long," said her future father-in-law.

"All right," said Leesa. "Then I will wait here."

She looked across the lake. A mountain on the other side gleamed white with snow.

The sun set. The world began to darken.

Leesa was beginning to think of her young man would never arrive. "Is he lost?" she asked. "Should we go find him? He may be hurt. He may need our help."

"Shhh," said her mother.

Darkness covered the oasis. Chattering night creatures filled the air. Leesa stood waiting. Her parents retired for the evening, as did her future in-laws. As they left they instructed Leesa not to move from her spot. "It is important to be here, waiting," said her father. "We will come back tomorrow. You will have a beautiful ceremony, you will see."

By this time Leesa did not care about any ceremony. She wanted only to sleep. She resolved, however, to do as she was told.

The lake was so inviting. Moonlight sparkled on its surface. Reflections of stars danced in the waves. Leesa resisted as long as she could. After an hour she walked down to the shore and removed her robes and stepped into the lake.

The water was cool, but not so cool as to be uncomfortable. She dove into the water and swam across the length of the lake. The water was silky on her skin. She swam for a long time and then returned to the shore and put her traveling robes back on. She walked back up the hill. As she neared her waiting place she saw the figure of a man. He turned to her.

"Hello," he said. "Are you my intended?"

"My name is Leesa. Who are you?"

"Rickard. I am pleased that we are to be married."

Rickard. The name sounded foreign to Leesa. Where did he come from? She could not see his features in the darkness. She did see he had no hair, just like her.

"I offer my apologies for arriving so late," said Rickard. "The journey was arduous." He dropped to his knee. "Will you accept me as your husband?"

She could not see him. She did not know who he was. He came late to the oasis. Did that mean he was weak? Or lazy? Or both?

She took out the last pieces of her grandparent's wedding cake. She handed them to him. He looked up. His eyes shone in the darkness. Faintly, but they did shine.

He took a fragment of the frosting and put it on his tongue.

She placed her hand on his back.

The moon shadowed flying bats above her.

The future lay before her, an unknown land. Was she ready for uncertainty? With this man?

She went down on one knee herself. She took the last corner of the frosting and dropped it on her tongue.

The night swirled around them both.

The ground tilted and bucked.

"Yes," she said, an instant before they kissed.

Lobster Love

In those days the pictures of the dead lobsters were everywhere. Especially in my head. And your head. Everyone's head. Maybe also in your pet cat's head and all the animal's heads, insect heads even, crab heads, slug heads. No one knew for sure if they got into the "lower animals," but there were sure a lot of experiments trying to find out.

No experiments necessary for the likes of me and you. We just had to close our eyes so see them: broken pink shells with purple flesh oozing out of the cracks; crustacean limbs strewn about smoldering ruins; crushed heads ground into dust and completely unrecognizable as once living creatures if we had not had the countering images which showed aliens ambulatory and healthy. Or what we thought was healthy. Who could know the truth of what we were seeing?

There were theories:

The pictures are war atrocities and the brains of humans on Earth have somehow been used as storage devices to preserve the memory of the massacre. This had a romantic war correspondent tinge to it and was very popular for a while. It might even be true.

The people of Earth are suffering from a Jung-like archetypal malady in which repressed images from our collective unconscious are coming back to haunt us. Kind of intriguing in its way, but too intellectual for the masses.

Everyone is going crazy. This at least had the benefit of verisimilitude. Who has not considered the possibility that we are all at least slightly insane?

Hollywood was experimenting with some new technology that allowed direct-to-brain imaging without need for projector and screen, and it had gotten out of hand and we were all seeing previews from the first feature to use the technology. The tabloids really liked this one. It pushed the Bigfoot babies and the celebrity diets right off the front pages for a few weeks at least.

Mostly, after the initial reaction of revulsion, everyone was simply annoyed by the images. Some people figured out the images would go away if you slept. So sleeping became a popular activity. Sales of over the counter sleep aids shot up dramatically. And then, what had begun unexpectedly just as quickly stopped. Overnight, three weeks after it had begun, no more dead or dying alien lobster pictures plagued any human brains. Or at least very few. I knew I still had them, but I was afraid to tell anyone for a long time.

As for the rest of the world, most people felt like they could breathe again. Life returned to normal, which is to say, most everyone got back to plotting their next lay, bickering with one another, and watching television.

Maybe here is a good place to tell you something about me. My name is Eric. My home is a modest house in Newport, a small tourist and fishing town on the Oregon coast. I used to be married until Claire, my wife, realized I was never going to drop Margaret, my girlfriend, (she knew it before I did) and divorced me about 4 years ago after 5 years of (not quite) marital bliss. She found a job with a graphics design firm in Portland. Fortunately, we did not have kids. I moved in with Margaret, thus ruining a perfectly good relationship.

Two years later the lobster images appeared and a month after that Margaret got fed up with me and moved to Portland. I imagine the two of them, Claire and Margaret, commiserating about me over espressos at some downtown coffee shop, even though I know that most likely neither of them ever even thinks about me anymore. But I like to have my illusions.

Nowadays I keep a little job at the local newspaper doing production work and some ad sales. Mostly I walk on the beach. For hours. It's a great way to pass the time. I especially like looking into tide pools. Such alien life there, green blobby anemones, sea stars, and algae. They don't seem to belong on our world.

Lots of my friends have completely forgotten the lobster images. I have never been able to shake them loose. They haunt me still.

Before she got wise and dumped me, Claire shared some of her art interests with me. She was especially fascinated with a particular etching by a 16th century artist named Hendrick Goltzius called *The Dragon Devouring the Companions of Cadmus*. If you've ever seen it you won't forget it. It shows a dragon with its claws raking the torso and thigh of a man. The dragon's jaws are clamped around another man's face. There is blood streaming down this second man's head and he has his hand reaching out, blindly, to the dragon's neck, all of it obviously futile. In the foreground is a raggedly severed head, probably that of the first man's, apparently there to hint at the ultimate fate of the (for now) still living man. You know you are seeing the last moments of the life of this man.

The picture is as alien to me as the lobster images that have plagued my days. Claire said it made her think of how vulnerable we were to the whims of nature. I saw her point, but it made me think how Claire's fascination with the image was not a healthy thing.

Later, when Margaret and I were living together, I hung up the facsimile of it that Claire had left at the house before she moved out. It was there in the kitchen where I could see it every morning, a morbid reminder of my life with Claire. Margaret took it down a couple of times. I put it back up. We may have fought over that picture more than anything else we had together. It may have been that picture that made people want to stay away from our house and that was the end for Margaret.

I told her she was breaking my heart when she left. She didn't believe me. Some people can arrange their lives to work for them, all the pieces in place like completed jigsaw puzzles. Others hang up gruesome pictures of serpents eating people, and then their puzzles fall to pieces.

I found a support group. They had a small ad in a Portland tabloid, *Willamette Week*, nestled in with the hooker ads at the back. These ads, I'm sure, are the main reason for the existence of such publications, despite the in-depth stories about school funding and police corruption that tend to show up on their covers. The ad was very simple: "Still plagued by those lobster visions? Come talk about it." Then it gave a phone number. I called. A woman answered.

"I saw your ad about the visions," I said.

She gave me an address in Portland and the nights that they met, one of which, as it happened, was that very night. I told her I would be there and hung up.

What to wear to the first meeting with one's fellow crazies? I mentally scrolled through my choices. I had lots of beach gear. Sweatshirts, mostly. One or two nice button down shirts. Several pairs of sneakers and one nice pair of shoes. And jeans, lots of jeans. I wondered why I was so concerned about my wardrobe.

In truth I was not sure I was going to go, but went through the motions of getting ready. It was a two hour drive to Portland. I could always start heading that way, then catch a movie if I decided I wanted to avoid listening to others talk about their visions. I had my own. I didn't need to know about theirs. Or maybe I did. I didn't know. Should I go find out?

I dressed in my best casuals, even brushed my hair, something I seldom did. I left as the sun was going down. One hundred and sixteen minutes later I arrived at the house, a modest two bedroom in the northeast district of town. I bounded up the stairs and knocked on the door. Inside I found about a dozen people milling around a table with bowls of chips and dips. Snatches of conversation.

"Is this the lobster group?" I asked.

They all stopped talking and swung around to look at me. No one offered to be my friend. Not yet. That was fine with me. I wasn't all that good with friends anyway.

"Why are you here?" someone asked.

"I've got the lobster images."

The someone nodded. "Yes," she said. "Of course. We all do. But why are you *here*?"

So it was going to be one of those kinds of groups. Motivation was all. "I want to get rid of them."

She didn't say anything, just studied my face. I looked around at some of the others, but they had completely deferred to her. No one spoke, no one wanted to interrupt her for an instant.

"Some people like them," she said. "Some people want to keep them forever. We need to make sure you aren't one of those."

I spread my hands. "I'm not." That seemed simple enough.

"Do you have a gruesome picture to share?"

I felt myself turn red. "Gruesome . . ." I said.

"A photo, a painting, a drawing. We've all got one. You?"

Was this a test? I looked around at everyone a second time. Most looked down at the floor or right through me. As it happened, I did have a small photocopy of the Goltzius engraving. It fit in my wallet. It was a bit worn, but clearly showed what it was. I took it out and handed it to the woman. She looked at it, then smiled, and returned it to me.

"I pass?" I said.

"You pass. Everyone here has something like this." She turned to the group. "Don't we?" she said.

I was surprised to see each of them pull out a picture from their pocket, or purse, or wallet. They held them up so I could see. Each had a violent image of some sort or another. Mutilated war dead photo, snapshot of a hundred year old lynching, drawing of someone killing themselves, and so on. It was a grim gallery, to say the least. "I see," was all I could say.

"People like us, we have all been compelled to become intimately familiar with one such image," said the woman.

"Okay," I said.

"My name is Dottie."

"Eric," I said.

"Hello Eric," they all chorused, like we were at an AA meeting.

I held up my hand and gave a small wave, feeling foolish. "Glad to be here," I said. "I think."

"Don't worry," said Dottie. "We're friendly. Want something to eat?"

I advanced on the table, suddenly feeling famished. I noticed there was no seafood. Just as well. The conversation resumed. I was stuffing my face when a familiar voice sounded in my ear.

"Can't get rid of you for nothing, can I?"

I turned around. "Claire." I said.

"Oh, you remember? How's that bimbo you tossed me for?"

"I thought you tossed me. And she isn't a bimbo. And we split up."

She smiled and nodded with unreserved pleasure. It was the least I deserved. "Chalk another one up for our side," she said.

"What have you been up to?" I asked.

"Working hard. I've been doing a series based on the lobsters."

"Claire," I said. "No."

"Can't be helped. I tried doing other pictures. Nothing worked."

"You aren't still at that graphics place?"

"Old history," she said. "Kind of like you." She pressed a finger on my chest.

"Am I going to get ribbed all night?"

"Maybe. You know we're all crazy here."

"Everyone's crazy. That's how we know we're human."

"I know what they mean," she said.

"What?"

"The pictures. The lobster pictures."

"We all *think* we know. Or thought we did, once. But we all got over it. You should too. For your own sake."

"Okay," she said. "Suit yourself." She shrugged, then turned and walked out the door.

I popped the corn chip in my hand into my mouth and hurried to the door. I looked outside. Claire was already gone from view. The darkness of the street highlighted the lobster images in my brain. They glowed and hovered above the street like preternatural paintings. It was as though I could look through them and see inside these creatures. I saw two of them, immense beasts, grappling weakly with one another. Their blood had spilled out. Gaping holes in their shells revealed expanses of slick flesh. They were frozen in the space, obviously an arrested moment from a long battle they had been engaging in for some time. Their claws (they each had four) grappled and thrust and swung. Their heads almost touched and I noticed a kind of melancholy about them, as though they had been at this for a long time and needed to find something better to do with their lives.

I blinked. The image shifted and blurred. For a moment I saw only the night sky, spangled with stars. Then another image came to me. More of the lobsters. In fact, hundreds of them, small ones. Children, maybe. Babies. Baby lobsters. I couldn't tell for sure, but they were running as fast as they could. It wasn't fast enough. A larger lobster was pursuing them with vengeance, and was training some kind of odd weapon on them. The weapon had discharged a slimy stream of something like acid. The fleeing lobster kids melted as they ran. Their legs turned into pools of grotesque pink fluid where they intersected the path of the slime and they fell into themselves.

I felt a hand on my back.

"Claire," I asked, turning.

"No," said Dottie. "You looked like you were having a difficult time."

"Do you know Claire?"

"Sure. She's been coming here for a long time."

"Will you tell me where she lives?"

"I don't think she likes you," said Dottie.

"I know. If she did we would probably still be married."

Dottie's eyes widened. "She never said anything about being married."

"It was a while ago."

"You're upset by the images," said Dottie. "I can see that. Claire isn't going to help you."

I thought of the times she did help me. Times when I was beyond help, really, wallowing in my own self pity. I used to weep for no reason I could express and Claire was always there, comforting me. Which really made things worse, because then I thought of Margaret and what I shit I was being by carrying on with her. But Claire stuck by me. That was the amazing part.

"I need to help her," I said to Dottie.

Dottie laughed. "Sure," she said, in a tone that made it clear she did not believe I could help anyone.

"What do you do at these meetings?" I said.

"Just talk." She led me back into the house. She patted my hand as I sank into the couch. I recalled one of the lobster pictures I had seen years ago. It showed lobsters splayed open on a large stepped platform, rather similar to the couch I was sitting on. It gave me a strange sense of comfort. I thought about Claire, how it was a mistake for me to have let her go. But what could I have done differently? Not have continued on with Margaret, for starters. That might have helped a little. Sure, but I didn't want Margaret to happen. She just came into my life and then I didn't want to let her go. Could not.

I stopped that train of thought. "I have to find Claire," I said.

Dottie shushed me. "Stop it," she said sharply. I sat down. "I am not going to tell you where Claire is. Now listen to Dale. He was telling us about the images."

I looked over at Dale. He seemed a little disgusted by my presence. "Sorry," I said. "I'm listening now."

"As I was saying," said Dale. "I have this friend who has studied the images for a long time. And he's studied why some people—like us—still see them when everyone else doesn't anymore. It is his contention, and I agree with him, that those such as we, that is, all of us here tonight, must be very careful with our minds. We see things more clearly than others. We can see depths that others cannot and we see truth that others cannot."

I tried to listen. I really did. Dale blathered on about how we have been raised in a warrior culture, and images of death and mutilation are very comfortable to us, so we *crave* the images we're getting. That's why our lobster pictures did not go away. That's why we all seemed to be at least a little obsessed with violent images. Or *one* violent image. It sounded like all the claptrap I had been hearing for too long.

I had a to-do list in my shirt pocket from several days ago. I pulled it out and looked at it:

Go to bank.
Take back library books.
Buy groceries.
Get bicycle tire fixed.
Clean the house.
Cut the grass.
Break the neighbors window.
Harass the cat.

And so on. Each item had a line through it. It was a modest list, but it kept me busy. Very important way to alleviate the stress of seeing all those pictures. No one needs constant violence in their lives, but taken in moderation, a good jolt to the system can be rejuvenating. I think it was that general spirit that made me crumple the list into a tight ball and tossed it in Dale's direction. He saw it coming. Stopped talking in mid word, so that he froze there for a moment with his mouth wide open, and waited for my modest missile to bonk him on the top of the head. A direct hit. It bounced off and fell to the floor.

Well, you would have thought I had shot the man dead. Everyone looked at me. Some with fear in their eyes. Others with disbelief.

"I had an urge," I said.

Dale picked up the ball and threw it back at me. Hard. It actually stung my shoulder where it hit me.

"Are you quite done?" he said.

"Not even close," I answered and threw the paper back at him even harder than he had thrown it at me.

Dottie stood up. "Stop that," she said. "Stop that right now."

Most everyone had a notebook or a pad. They all, except for Dottie, pulled off a sheet or two and began wadding them up into balls. Dottie was speechless. Then we all started throwing them at each other. Some of them kind of hesitantly at first, but before long we all got into the battle with gusto.

This went on for some minutes. We all broke the circle and got behind furniture to protect ourselves from incoming paper balls. It reminded me of a snowball fight, the kind that children like to engage in. Eventually even Dottie got in on the fun. When we were mostly sated and tired out, we all flopped onto the carpet and looked at each other. Some observing. Some laughing.

"What does your friend say about such behavior as this?" I asked Dale.

"I'm not sure where it would fit into his theory," he said.

"Well done, Dale," I said. "You are an honest man. Boring, but honest."

Everyone laughed. Even Dale.

"It's not your fault," I said.

"I know," said Dale. "I just have that kind of voice."

Dottie looked from Dale to me. "Are you really one of us?" she said.

"Sure. I've got the pictures, still. I want them gone." I shrugged. "Something like this can do wonders. Don't you think?"

"Nothing like this has ever happened here. We mostly just—talk."

"Well, I think that's your problem. You have to move, not just talk."

Dottie nodded.

Someone's cell phone rang. Normally this would make a rage rise up in me. I hated that there were people who brought cell phones to other people's houses, allowing them to ring at inopportune moments. Such people really needed to be taken out and shot. Ripped limb from limb, as it were. Maybe even eviscerated and dipped in oil then set afire. People who let their cell phones ring within the hearing of those not interested in their lives or conversations should do the world a favor and remove themselves from the face of the planet.

Such were my normal thoughts about cell phones.

This time, though, it was different. This time it didn't matter.

Dale fumbled in his pocket and pulled out his phone.

"Hello," he said. Then, after a pause, he said "Sure," and handed me the phone. "It's for you."

I took the phone and put it to my ear. Claire's voice. "That's Dale," she said.

"I know."

"He was the first guy I slept with after I left you."

"Okay."

"Thought you might want to know that. Why didn't you follow me?"

"Where are you?" I said.

"Six-twelve Evans."

Then she hung up.

I gave the phone back to Dale. Strangely, I didn't want him to die or suffer. I just wanted to thank him, so I did, though not too effusively.

"What can we learn from this episode?" said Dottie. No one answered her.

"I think we created a group spontaneity," I said.

"Yes," said Dale. "It actually goes along with what my friend was saying about us. Us and the images. They are our communal experience. They bring us together."

"That's fascinating, Dale," I said. "But I think I've had enough for one night."

Dale blinked. Someone else said "Don't go. We're just starting to have fun."

This was true. But Claire awaited me and at that moment nothing was more important. I said good bye and drove downtown. The address Claire had given me turned out to be an art gallery. I went inside. Every inch of the wall space in the gallery was covered with a mural. The mural was huge, bold. It was mutilated lobster after decaying lobster after broken lobster. It was bleeding lobster and chopped up lobster. It was strong and vivid and I knew immediately it had to be Claire's.

She came around a corner from the back. "I thought you'd follow me," she said. She stopped a few yards away from me. I wanted to lean into her warmth but she had a way of letting me know when she wanted me to keep my distance.

"You were too fast for me," I said.

"That's a switch. I could never keep up with your life, and now . . ."

I indicated the expanse of alien art. "And now this."

"How do you like it?"

I was not so much interested in the mural as I was in touching Claire. Why did I see to it that I would make her life with me intolerable?

"You hated having the visions. Why would you live with them like this for so long? This mural must have taken months."

"One and a half years. The gallery stayed open the whole time. People could come and watch me work."

"And did they?"

"Some. Most were put off by the subject matter."

I nodded. "Sure, most of them had the mural, or something like it, in their heads already."

She shook her head slowly. "Eric. You're not seeing the point. Look closely."

"Do I have to?"

She put her hand on top of my head and spun my skull like it was on a swivel so that I had to look up at her work. This work.

I stared for a long time. Claire had tried to teach me how to read a painting. I tried to understand, but it didn't click in my brain. The lines, perspective, the *juxtapositioning*. I had a sense that there was some meaning to this jumble. There was a pattern to it. But so obscure. Like trying to read a language one doesn't know. No, worse that that, trying to read a language in which you know a few words, but not enough to really understand anything more complicated than a name.

"What?" I said. "What am I supposed to be looking for?"

"It's all there," she said. "The truth of it all."

I looked again. There were faces, now. Hidden behind the lobster eyes and mouth parts, lurking like ghosts, recognizable and not so recognizable faces. I felt a chill go through me.

Not *alien war atrocities*.

Now I saw that the lobsters were all related. They were in love with each other. The lobsters had a society of caring for each other. They cared by killing those that had to die.

Not *archetypes*.

The suffering was not inflicted by the tormentors. In fact, there were no tormentors. The suffering was already there and those that dispatched the lobsters were the merciful benefactors in the lobster world.

Not *crazy*.

"Claire," I said. "They look like us. Like you and me."

Not *Hollywood*.

"I know," she said. "This is our future. All of us. The visions are a picture of the future world, of the creatures we will evolve into."

I still wanted to fall into her arms. I still wanted to feel her flesh against mine and cursed myself for my actions which now prevented that from happening.

But also.

In a small place in my interior life that I could barely even recognize as myself, I felt an urge to flex my claws. Open them wide and click them closed with a sure and satisfying firmness. I began to understand the lure of a tough exterior.

Other books by Emen:
Assa's Eggs • The Institute • Thieves

About the author:
Emen is writer of many books. You can find them where books are sold. Emen is loving life of being a writer. Much better than working at cranberry processing plant. That is job Emen had in his life once upon a time ago. Emen had to perform test of chemistry on cranberries to pin the point of how red were the berries. The redder the berries, the more the grower got paid. Get it? Was not most terrible job ever, but was not best one either. Not by long gunshot. Emen leave all behind now that he is writer.